PALM BEACH BLUES

TOM TURNER

COPYRIGHT

CONTENTS

BROKEN HOUSE

THE SAVANNAH MADAM SERIES
SNEAK PEAK

1

Sunny Hedstrom was on her way back from the gym. The gym was her new favorite place—more so than any bar, restaurant, or Worth Avenue clothing or jewelry shop. That was because, as of last Thursday night, her trainer had become her lover. She hadn't seen it heading in that direction during their first workout, a month back, but as a great philosopher once said, *Shit happens.* Anthony had a gentle soul and spoke softly and patiently as he guided her through her forty-five-minute workout. But in bed… *watch out.* The guy was an acrobatic maniac, a Flying Wallenda of the boudoir.

Sunny's only concern was that Wayne had found out about Anthony. Or maybe not found out, but at least suspected.

"I called you for three straight hours," Wayne told her the day before. "Where the hell were you?"

Fortunately, she'd thought up an excuse in advance, knowing how possessive Wayne could be. "Didn't I tell you before? At my nephew's basketball game. I left my phone behind."

"No, you never told me," Wayne said. "How was it?"

"The basketball game?"

"Yeah."

Like he cared. "It was okay. Not that I'm a big basketball fan or anything. My sister and I just yakked a lot."

"Where was it?" Wayne asked.

"Worthington High. The gym there."

Wayne snickered. "Well, yeah, I didn't figure they played in the library."

Another annoying thing about Wayne… he had a lame sense of humor.

"How'd he do? Your nephew?"

"Pretty good."

"Score many points?"

"I think so. I wasn't really keeping track."

"What's his name?"

"Danny."

"Danny who?"

"Harris."

Sunny knew Wayne was asking her about facts he could check. He couldn't have cared less about her nephew or his basketball prowess.

She headed north on South Olive and hit her blinker for her house on Granada Road in the El Cid neighborhood of West Palm Beach. Well, not her house; it was Wayne's. Wayne, she knew, had a number of houses sprinkled around the area. She'd guessed, not inaccurately, that they were for Wayne's gal pals, and for the last ten months, which was as long as she had been living there, he hadn't charged her rent. But, of course, she did pay a price.

As she turned onto Granada, she hit her garage-door opener the way she always did. Her house was the fourth on the left. She was thinking about Anthony and the grueling abductor-muscle exercises he'd put her through as she turned into her driveway.

That was when she saw her beloved Westie puppy, Winston, with his leash around his neck, dangling from the handle of the opened garage door.

2

I t took Sunny a moment to comprehend what she was seeing, that she'd accidentally hanged her own dog.

She quickly hit the button again to close the garage door, and slowly—too slowly—it descended. Like it was in slow motion. Winston was writhing on the cement as she braked, jammed the car into park, and started running.

She heard the hysteria in her own voice as she screamed, "Help!" Then, "Oh my God, Winston…" She reached down and loosened the leash, but she could see it was too late. The little guy was a goner.

WAYNE CRABB DESCRIBED himself as a real estate developer, but others called him a grave dancer. By that they meant someone on the lookout for projects that were either financially shaky or in default. Overleveraged, under-financed, or poorly managed—better yet, all three. He'd swoop in and buy the property at a discount, then nurse it back to good health. His biggest coup was buying a casino in the Bahamas for thirty-seven million dollars, then flipping it two years later for sixty-three million while spending only a few million to renovate it. The profit from that deal had helped pay for a lot of smaller projects, one of which was located in the heart of Palm Beach.

Crabb was in his office with his assistant, Mary Beth Hudson, whom he kept very busy. Unlike most Florida real estate offices, whose walls were decorated with photos and architectural renderings of tall buildings, apartment complexes, or luxurious resorts, Wayne Crabb's office on South County Road was dominated by blown-up posters of surfers cutting through the water, arms extended for balance, mountainous waves behind them. If a visitor looked closely, they would see that the primary surfer in the photos was Wayne himself. Tanned and, if not chiseled, at least in good shape for a sixty-one-year-old. Whenever Wayne took a vacation, often with a woman less than half his age, sometimes two, he would go to places famous for towering waves and exotic beauty. Hawaii, Australia, New Zealand, and Peru had become his favorite destinations.

Palm Beach, while a long way from any of the surf capitals of the world, did have a dedicated group of surfers who rode the waves up on the north end of the island. Crabb surfed there four or five times a week with a revolving cast of twenty- and thirty-somethings—mostly men, but with a few women thrown in. Wayne, known as "the geez" or just plain "geez" to the young surfers, was universally reviled as a wave-hog. That is, he'd paddle after every wave that had potential, often blocking others from having their shots at the rollers. Sometimes he'd ride his board perilously close to another surfer; other times, he'd cut them off altogether. The younger guys got silent satisfaction when Wayne would end up in a body-churning wipeout, and it annoyed them when he'd bob to the surface with a *far out, that was fun!* smile on his face.

Having read through all his emails, Wayne looked up at Mary Beth. "I want you to evict Sunny Hedstrom from the house on Granada."

Mary Beth nodded. "Okay, on what grounds?"

"Since when do I need grounds?"

"I just—"

"That she's ten months late on her rent."

"But she never had a lease."

"Well, back-date one and forge her signature," Wayne said, like that was a normal business practice. "We've got her signature somewhere."

Long ago, Mary Beth had accepted the fact that forging signatures was a normal part of her job. Wayne Crabb, after all, tended to be quite generous with Christmas bonuses. Evictions like this were typical operating procedure for Wayne, who seemed to be subsidizing anywhere between four and seven women at any given time. He expected those women to be on call whenever the spirit moved him, and it moved him a lot. He also expected them to be exclusive to him. That meant no boyfriends, lovers, or even one-night stands.

Mary Beth assumed that Sunny Hedstrom had violated Wayne's code. Her boss was an unforgiving man.

"Process server?" Mary Beth asked.

"Yeah, get that weasel from Collectron on it."

"Chris Carter?"

"Yeah, tell him I want her out by the end of the week."

Mary Beth nodded. "I'm on it," she said. "You want me to do anything on the Sabal House today?"

Wayne thrummed his desktop and emitted a long, slow sigh. "You know what's bothering the hell out of me about that place?"

"What's that?" She had a pretty good guess.

"That Platt's out there tooling around in that shiny new yacht he bought with Sabal House money."

He was referring to Preston Platt, his partner in the now-notorious Sabal House on Royal Palm Way in Palm Beach. They had bought the former hotel together to convert into high-end condominiums. The deal soon went sideways, however, taking down some twenty-odd investors in the process.

"So, what are you going to do?" Mary Beth asked.

"What I always do, sue the bastard," Wayne said with a throaty rumble of a laugh.

"You think that will do any good?"

Crabb sighed and thought for a moment. "Not if I can't track down the money."

They heard footsteps in the reception area, then a shout. "You sadistic son-of-a-bitch!" a woman's voice rang out, and Sunny Hedstrom burst into Wayne's office.

Mary Beth shot from her chair to intercept Sunny as she charged at Wayne.

"You evil, evil pig," Sunny said, jabbing a finger at the seated Wayne. "How could you do such a cruel thing?"

"What are you talking about?" Wayne asked. "I have no idea what—"

"Bullshit. It had to be you. You killed my dog. You're the only one who has the key to the house."

Wayne held up his hands. "Think what you want, but I have no idea what you're talking about." He glanced at Mary Beth standing between him and Sunny. "By the way, I'm afraid you're going to have to vacate the Granada Road house."

Sunny put her hands on her hips. "What? Why?"

"Well, for one thing, this unrestrained outburst of yours accusing me of such a barbaric thing. I can't have someone living in one of my houses calling me a son-of-a-bitch and a pig. And for another, because you haven't paid rent for the past ten months."

"Are you crazy? That was never the deal, paying rent."

"Sorry, Sunny. You're going to have to pack up and go."

Sunny took a step toward Crabb, but Mary Beth blocked her. "You'll have to leave now, Ms. Hedstrom."

Sunny shook her head. "You are the sleaziest, creepiest low-life I've ever met."

Wayne made a shooing motion with one hand. "Good-bye, Sunny," he said. "Have a nice life."

3

With Mary Beth still in his office, Wayne slipped off his khaki pants, revealing long, flowery-patterned swim trunks underneath. Then he shed his white button-down shirt, under which he wore a vintage yellow T-shirt that read *Hobie Surfboards*. He hung up his khakis and the button-down in a closet and slipped into a pair of flip-flops.

"I'll be back later," he told Mary Beth, who was accustomed to her boss interrupting work with his favorite activity. Well, second-favorite actually… his favorite being to drop in on nubile tenants.

THERE WERE four surfers up on the north end—three guys, appropriately blond-streaked and hard-bodied, and a raven-haired woman whom Wayne had never seen before.

Needless to say, he tried to hit on her. The way he looked at it, with Sunny Hedstrom having been cut from the team, he had a vacancy.

The woman acted friendly enough but didn't encourage anything more than a quick conversation. The surfers always shook their heads —half in disbelief, half in grudging admiration—whenever Wayne tried to put his well-worn moves on women forty years younger than he.

A few minutes later, Wayne and one of the young surfers were sitting on their boards on the lookout for a wave.

"Who's the babe, anyway?" Wayne asked, flipping his head in the direction of the woman, board in hand, leaving the beach.

The surfer shook his head. "You're relentless, man. Don't you have a wife or something?"

Wayne nodded. "I do, but she's really old."

The surfer chuckled. "Got news for you, dude. So are you."

Wayne shrugged. "You're as young as you feel," he said, then pointed. "Hey, what's that?"

The surfer looked off into the distance. "I don't know, man, kinda looks like a drone."

A silver-colored drone was flying fifty feet above the ocean and coming toward them.

Wayne huffed. "I thought Palm Beach outlawed those things."

The surfer shrugged. As he watched the drone approach, it suddenly stopped in midair, steadied, and made a loud crackling sound, followed by a sharp groan from Wayne. The surfer turned to see the older man's chest bleeding profusely. Another crackling sound emitted from the drone, and Wayne's forehead became a patch of red. Without a word, he tumbled headfirst into the ocean.

"Holy shit!" said the surfer, leaning low on his board and paddling furiously for shore.

As the other surfers watched from the beach, the silver drone exploded, sending shards of metal in all directions.

As several beachgoers grabbed their cellphones to dial 911, Wayne's body sank beneath the surface of the sea. His surfboard, though, was caught by a big wave and flipped high up in the air, a ribbon of blood near its tip.

The sexagenarian surfer, Wayne Crabb, had ridden his last wave.

4

Palm Beach Police Detectives Charlie Crawford and Mort Ott reached the beach ten minutes after the first 911 call came in. Turned out their vic had died not far from the site of a murder they'd investigated the year before: a man had been left buried in the sand up to his neck and the rising tide, along with a clattering pack of crabs, had done the rest.

"Popular spot for murder," Ott said to his partner as they approached the body.

Crawford looked down the beach. "Yeah, only about a hundred yards apart."

A cluster of onlookeers had gathered around the victim. Mostly young men and women in bathing suits, but a few older beach-strollers, too. Two uniformed cops, Jake Needham and Mel Mennino, had arrived five minutes before Crawford and Ott.

"Hey," Crawford said, nodding to the officers. "Know who he is?"

"Name's Wayne Crabb," Mennino said. "A local businessman. Comes up here to surf couple times a week."

"Oh, yeah," Ott said, nodding. "I know all about the guy."

Crawford knew the name from somewhere but couldn't place it.

He figured Ott would fill him in later. He looked around at the crowd and raised his voice. "So, who saw what happened?"

Three of the surfers raised their hands.

Crawford nodded to one and walked over to him. "Tell us what you saw, please."

Ott took out his old leather pad and got ready to write.

"Well, I was out there with Wayne, waiting for a wave," the surfer said. "All of a sudden I heard this noise and saw this drone off in the distance. Coming at us. Then these pops. Gunshots, I guess. One hits Wayne in the chest, the other—" he pointed down at Crabb's body "—in the forehead."

Crawford nodded.

The surfer next to him stepped forward. "Couple seconds later the drone blew up. Like it had been hit by a missile or something. It was crazy."

"Did you see something actually hit the drone?" Ott asked.

The second guy shook his head. "Nah, it just, like, exploded."

"One of the pieces hit me," said the surfer who had been out with Crabb. He pointed to a cut on his shoulder.

"How long did all this take?" Crawford asked the surfer with the cut.

"No more than, like, fifteen seconds from when I heard the thing 'til it blew up," he said.

"So, did any of you see anyone with a remote control device or anything like that?" Ott asked and pointed away from the beach. "Maybe up at one of those houses or something?"

All of the surfers who had witnessed the attack shook their heads.

"And then what happened, the man's body just washed up on the shore?" Crawford asked.

"Pretty much," said one of the surfers. "At first he sank, but then we saw his body floating a little way out and went and got him."

A few others nodded.

Crawford saw two crime-scene techs in blue jackets walking down to them from North Ocean Boulevard. One was his *special friend,* Dominica McCarthy. The other was Robin Gold.

"All right, thanks," Crawford said. "If you could make way for these women—" he flicked his head toward Dominica and Robin "—they'll need some space to examine the victim."

As the knot of beachgoers backed away from Wayne Crabb's body, Crawford met the arriving techs and explained what had happened.

Robin Gold got down in a crouch to examine the body.

Crawford caught Dominica's eye and he led her away from the others.

"This is a first, huh?" she said. "A drone?"

"Yeah, you believe it?"

Ott walked over to them. They were no longer within earshot of the onlookers.

"What do you think about getting some divers out there?" Dominica flicked her head toward the ocean. "See what wreckage of the drone they can find."

"Yeah, I agree," Crawford said.

"Pretty slick… blowing up the thing after mission-accomplished," said Ott.

"No kidding," Dominica said.

"Do you know who this guy is?" Ott asked Crawford.

"Name's familiar," Crawford said. "Can't quite remember from where."

"Guess you're not a *Glossy* reader," Ott said, referring to the *Palm Beach Daily Reporter*, the local gossip rag. "He's one of the guys who owns the Sabal House on Royal Palm Way. He and his partner scammed a bunch of investors."

"Oh, yeah, I kind of remember now," Crawford said.

Ott nodded. "So what happened was, about two years ago Crabb and this other guy named Platt—I forget his first name—bought the Sabal House Hotel. The plan, as I remember it, was to do like a twenty- or thirty-million-dollar renovation and sell off ultra-high-end condos. About fifty of them, I think. They had a fancy prospectus with projections of what they were going to sell for, along with renderings of what they'd look like."

Dominica nodded. "Yeah, I remember, they were amazing. All glass and high-tech."

"Exactly," Ott said. "Okay, here's the complicated part, so pay close attention, kiddies." He took a long breath. "See, the government's got something called an EB-5 program, which basically gives foreign nationals a chance to become permanent U.S. residents if they invest in projects here that create jobs."

Dominica gave Ott a fist bump on the shoulder. "I'm impressed, Mort. How do you know all this? Harvard Business School?"

"Almost as good. Cuyahoga Community College, econ major. I love reading about shit like this. *The Glossy* did this big exposé on the whole thing," Ott said. "According to one of the articles, these guys defrauded dozens of foreign investors. Mainly from China, Iran, and Turkey, as I remember. One article even mentioned one of the Chinese guys was a suspected member of the Triads. That would be one guy I would *not* want to mess with."

"What do you mean defrauded them? How?" Crawford asked.

"Simple. Took the investors' money and ran. Only spent a million or two on the renovation," Ott said. "You've driven past the place, right?"

"Yeah, a real eyesore," Crawford said. "Big chain-link fence around it, weeds everywhere, looks like it's been abandoned for years."

"Yeah, two years," Ott said. "So next thing that happens is Crabb claims Platt took all the money."

"Didn't I read Platt bought a humongous yacht?" Dominica asked.

"And a big waterfront house somewhere, like Nantucket or Martha's Vineyard."

"Jesus," Crawford said. "How did they think they were going to get away with it?"

"I don't know, that's where it gets a little murky. Meanwhile, there are some very pissed-off investors from all over the world in the middle of a major lawsuit."

"While Platt's living high on the hog with investor money," Dominica said.

"Yeah, but then what happens is Platt claims *Crabb's* got the money, not him. Got it squirreled away in some Cayman Islands account," Ott said.

Crawford shook his head slowly. "Wherever it is, sounds like we got a long list of potential suspects."

Ott nodded. "Sure do, and like I said, from all over the world. Iran, Turkey, China—"

"Speaking of China," Crawford said, "aren't they pretty good at making drones?"

"Yup," said Ott. "Practically invented the damn things."

5

C rawford figured that talking to Preston Platt was the logical place to start, and it wasn't hard to find out where he lived. He just Googled him and found out he lived at 267 Emerald Lane in Palm Beach. With Ott at the wheel, they pulled into the circular driveway on Emerald and parked in front of the imposing two-story Monterey-style home.

Crawford pushed the doorbell and a few moments later a tall, blonde woman came to the door. She looked to be in her late forties and was what is known in some circles as a *hard body*. Or, if she had kids, a *yummy mummy.* Provocative in any case. Crawford guessed she kept to a sensible diet and had a demanding personal trainer.

"Mrs. Platt?"

"Yes," she said, smiling at Crawford. "Let me guess, Jehovah's Witnesses?"

Feeble senses of humor ran rampant in Palm Beach.

"I'm Detective Crawford and this is my partner, Detective Ott. Is your husband here?"

She extended her hand. "No, he's not. He's at work. I'm Gina Platt."

The three shook hands.

"What is this all about?" she asked.

"A case we're working on. We'd like to ask him some questions."

"Are you always so… guarded… in what you say, Detective?"

"Mrs. Platt, Wayne Crabb was just murdered."

Gina Platt's hands moved to her mouth and she gasped.

"That's what we'd like to talk to your husband about."

"Oh, my God, I can't believe it. What—"

"He was shot." Crawford didn't want to go into the whole drone explanation, although he knew word would spread fast.

"That's horrible," she said. "Preston's in his office. At Phillips Point. The west tower."

Crawford nodded. "Thank you very much."

"SHE DIDN'T SEEM ALL that broken up," Ott said as he started the Crown Vic.

"Yeah, that was my take, too."

"Like maybe her hamster died."

A few minutes later, Crawford pointed to a sign at the end of Dunbar Road. It said:

OPEN HOUSE
Rose Clarke

"Hey, pull in. We can pick Rose's brain."

"Good thinking," Ott said, parking the Crown Vic in the driveway.

Rose Clarke was, year after year, the top producer of all real estate agents in Palm Beach. Which was probably the reason her name was on the sign instead of her company's name. The fact was, her name carried a lot more clout than her company's. Rose also knew everybody in Palm Beach. And, because she had a reputation for being discreet, people told her things without fear that she'd quote them later. With Crawford, though, she shared freely, knowing what she told him would stop there.

The front door to the white British Colonial was open and they walked in.

"Hello?" Crawford said, raising his voice.

"Hel-lo," came Rose's voice from the kitchen.

She walked into the living room and saw Crawford and Ott. "What a pleasant surprise," she said. "My two favorite men."

"Thank you, Rose," Ott said. "Honored to be included in that select group."

"Hi, Rose," Crawford said.

"So, what's up? You guys want to buy a house? A mere nine million. For you, eight."

Crawford smiled but cut right to it. "You know a man named Wayne Crabb?"

"Sure. Real estate developer and big-time dirtball."

"Was," Crawford said. "He was murdered about an hour ago."

"Oh, God," she said, shaking her head slowly. "What happened?"

"He was shot," Crawford said, skipping the details again.

"You know, that's not all that surprising," Rose said. "The way I heard it, the man had a ton of enemies."

"So, do you have any ideas who we should talk to?" Crawford asked. "We were on our way to Preston Platt's office when we saw your sign."

"We figured you might be able to shed some light on things," Ott added.

"Here, sit," Rose said, pointing to an arrangement of furniture and sitting in a love seat.

Crawford and Ott sat facing her.

"Preston Platt is the right place to start," Rose said. "Story is, his wife was sleeping with Crabb. Lots of other women were, too."

Crawford shook his head. "Jesus, are there any faithful wives in Palm Beach?"

"There are quite a few, actually. You just don't hear about them.

They don't make the gossip columns," Rose said. "What I heard was Gina Platt was sleeping with him for business reasons."

"Wait? What?" Crawford asked, cocking his head to the side.

"See, Crabb, among other things, is a builder. He built a ten-million-dollar spec house on Emerald—"

"Where we just came from."

Rose nodded. "And Preston Platt, who had just sold his house in Manalapan, wanted to buy it. Platt wasn't that liquid, I heard, so he got Crabb to take back an eighty-percent mortgage if he paid the full asking price."

"So, an eight-million-dollar mortgage?" Crawford said.

Rose chuckled. "Very good, Charlie. That Dartmouth education shining through."

Crawford smiled. "Keep going."

"That's about it," Rose said. "Except, apparently, Platt wasn't making the payments in what they call a 'timely fashion'. So, the story is, Crabb threatened to foreclose unless Gina slept with him."

Ott's mouth hung open wide. "Christ, are you kidding? How messed up is *that?*"

Rose laughed. "I know, even for Palm Beach."

"Who else would you put on the Crabb suspect list?" Crawford asked.

"Jeez, Charlie, I haven't had any time to think about it…" Her eyes drifted away and she looked out the living-room picture window. "But I do remember hearing about this guy… what was it now?" She snapped her fingers. "Oh, yeah, I remember. See, Crabb's MO was to set up young women in apartments or houses he owned and not charge them rent. He also had this female golfer—really young, like twenty-one or so—who he sponsored on the LPGA tour. Meaning, he paid for her golf clubs and clothes and trainers and hotels, in return for…"

"Got it," Crawford said.

"Only problem was, she had—"

"Let me guess. A boyfriend?"

Rose shook her head. "Worse. A husband. Back in Missouri or somewhere."

"So, he found out?" Ott asked.

"So I heard," Rose said. "Jumped on the first plane, came here, and beat the hell out of Wayne."

"This is all pretty sordid," Crawford said.

"I know," Rose said. "Just 'cause I'm telling you about it doesn't mean I think it's the way normal people act."

Crawford slowly shook his head "I mean, it just—"

"I know. Offends your New England sensibilities?"

Crawford smiled.

"Not to mention my puritanical Midwestern ones," Ott added.

Rose laughed. "You're not in Cleveland anymore, Mort."

Ott laughed. "Okay, Dorothy."

"So, back to the golfer and her husband," Crawford said.

"Well, apparently they patched things up, because he went back to Missouri. Next thing you know, Wayne's seeing the golfer again."

"You'd have thought he learned his lesson," Crawford said.

"Apparently not," said Rose

"Christ, this guy deserves to be dead," Ott blurted.

Crawford stifled a chuckle. "Uh, that's not really something you should be quoted as saying."

"Hey, it's Rose," Ott said. "My secrets are safe with her."

6

They spent ten more minutes with Rose, who also recalled that Wayne Crabb had owned a hotel in the Bahamas that there had been some controversy about. She couldn't remember exactly what it was—a dispute with a partner, or maybe with the seller. Mort added it to a page in his leather-bound notebook and they thanked her and left for Preston Platt's office at Phillips Point.

Crawford had Googled the Phillips Point complex once for a case and remembered that it had sold back in 2015 for close to a quarter-billion dollars. It was the preeminent location for banks, and its 500,000 square feet of space included Citibank, Northern Trust, and Morgan Stanley, as well as leading law firms. It also featured spectacular views of the Intracoastal, Palm Beach, and the ocean beyond. And it had a Morton's Steak House on the ground floor, for good measure.

When they arrived, Crawford and Ott found the elevator of the west tower and took it to the ninth floor, where Preston Platt's office was located.

"So, this guy has his wife boff Crabb so Crabb won't foreclose on him," Ott said, shaking his head. "That's a first."

Crawford chuckled. "'Boff'? Jesus, Mort, what century did you grow up in?"

The door opened and their conversation came to a halt.

They walked down the hallway to Suite 919. *Platt Worldwide Properties,* the sign on the door boasted.

They walked into a well-decorated reception area with what looked like an expensive Persian rug and a number of large potted plants. The walls were made of burnished mahogany planks.

But no one was at the reception desk.

Crawford saw a silver bell and rang it. No one came out, so he rang it again.

Finally, a man appeared. He was about sixty and wore khakis and a blue-striped shirt. He had a feral look about him, including a small mouth with teeth that looked like they could rip the flesh off a rhino. His hair rose up in a lumpish mound in front.

"Let me guess," the man said, "detectives from the Palm Beach Police Department?"

Crawford nodded. "I'm Detective Crawford. This is my partner, Detective Ott."

Nobody made a move to shake hands.

"I'm Preston Platt," he said. "My wife said she had the pleasure of meeting you at our house a little while ago. I was sorry to hear about Wayne, but as far as who might have done it, I can't help you."

The man was, in a word, business-like, Crawford thought. "But you don't have a problem with us asking you a few questions, do you?" he asked.

"No. No problem at all. Why don't we sit?" Platt said, sitting in one of the four leather chairs in the reception area.

Crawford turned one of the chairs so it was facing Platt. Ott did the same.

"I'm just going to start with a question that we'll be asking everyone we speak to," Crawford said. "Where were you between eleven and twelve this morning?"

"Right here," Platt said. "Working out the particulars of a real estate deal."

"Was anyone else here in your office?"

"No. Solo."

"And do you have any other employees working here?" Ott asked.

Platt turned to him. "Not at the moment."

"Not an assistant or a receptionist?" Ott asked.

"Nope. At the moment I'm running a lean operation."

Crawford nodded, thinking that it probably hadn't always been that way. "Did you make any calls from here between eleven and twelve?"

Platt thought for a second, then shook his head. "Guess if you're looking for an alibi from me, I don't really have one. I've got a hotel/golf-course deal I'm putting together a prospectus on. That's what I was doing all morning."

Crawford nodded again, wondering exactly how to phrase his question about Platt's wife. "Mr. Platt... I'm just gonna flat-out ask—we heard Wayne Crabb wouldn't foreclose on a delinquent mortgage of yours as long as your wife had, ah, relations with him."

To his surprise, Platt laughed out loud. "Not a question you ask every day, huh, Detective?"

Crawford smiled uneasily.

"First of all, Gina never slept with Wayne," Platt said. "Not even close. I know that's the rumor that was going around. Did Crabb ever proposition her?" Platt nodded. "All day, every day. The guy was relentless. When I was out of town, he'd take her out for lunch, go shopping with her on Worth Avenue, buy her stuff. Hey, look, if he was offering to buy her a new dress at Charlotte Kellogg, she'd let him." Platt shrugged. "Hell, why not?"

"But you're certain nothing ever happened between the two of them?" Crawford asked. "Of a sexual nature?"

"Absolutely certain. Gina can flirt, but that's as far as it ever went.

And, in case you haven't heard yet, Crabb has women parked all over town. Meaning, he's sugar daddy to a hell of a lot of young trim. Or was, anyway."

"Yeah, so I've heard. Do you know any of their names?"

"No, but you can find out from his assistant, Mary Beth. She knows everything there is to know about Wayne's life."

"Do you have the address of his office?" Ott asked.

"Of course." Platt gave them an address on South County Road. "Now, let me ask you a question."

"Okay," Crawford said.

"You asked me for an alibi... why do you think I might have killed Wayne? What would have been my motive?"

Crawford first glanced at Ott, then back at Platt. "I don't mind answering that. First of all, because of what we heard about your wife. But now... now that you've assured us that wasn't true, I guess it rules that out... But another motive might be to not have the pressure of making those mortgage payments."

Platt shook his head and frowned. "Wait a minute, you think just because a guy dies, that's the end of a mortgage?"

"No, 'course not. I'm just saying you're not gonna have Crabb on your back threatening to foreclose. Maybe you buy a little more time."

"Don't kid yourself, my friend. Wayne's lawyer is like a dog with a bone. And I sincerely doubt that Wayne's wife is gonna go, 'Hey, that's okay, take your time, Pres, ol' pal.'"

That was someone they hadn't heard a word about. "His wife?" Crawford said. "What can you tell us about her? I don't even know her name."

"Her name is Betsy and she's a very nice lady. She's been leading a life pretty independent of Wayne for a long time. Plays a lot of tennis, very big in the garden club, and doesn't seem to care much who Wayne sleeps with—" he chuckled "—as long as he doesn't drag 'em home with him."

"So, you're saying it didn't bother her, him sleeping around?" Ott asked.

"I really wouldn't know for sure, but it didn't seem to," Platt said with a shrug. "I heard she maybe has a boy toy somewhere in West Palm."

"Really?"

"Yeah, supposedly."

Ott leaned forward. "Another motive of yours might have had something to do with the whole Sabal House thing."

Platt shook his head pugnaciously. "You don't know what you're talking about. Wayne stashed the Sabal House money in some offshore account."

"That's your story," Ott said.

Platt glared at Ott. "No, that's what *happened*."

It was time for Crawford to weigh in with a line of questioning he and Ott often used with suspects. "Mr. Platt, you obviously knew Wayne Crabb pretty well. Who do *you* think we should be talking to?"

"You mean, who's on his enemies list?"

"Yeah, possible suspects," Crawford said.

"I've been thinking about that ever since my wife called," Platt said. "I got a couple of candidates. There's this guy, supposedly had Mafia connections, who Wayne was going to sell his casino in Nassau to. Name's Singer. Don't remember his first name."

"That doesn't sound like a Mafia name," said Ott

Platt put his hand on his chin. "Does Meyer Lansky?"

"Good point," said Ott.

"Anyway, the way I heard it was Wayne had a handshake to sell the casino to this guy. Then he reneged when another buyer offered him another five million."

"And Singer didn't like that?"

"Didn't like it? I heard he threatened to bury Wayne right next to Jimmy Hoffa."

"So, in the end zone of Giants Stadium, you mean?" Ott asked.

"I heard it was a sausage factory in Detroit."

"Anybody else?" Crawford asked.

"You might want to look into Wayne's son-in-law," Platt said.

"Why? What's the story with him?"

"He's this sort of nebbishy guy who's a dentist up in Jupiter," Platt said. "A nebbishy guy with no patients is what I've heard."

"What do you mean?" Ott asked.

"Well, we just assume all doctors and dentists have patients, right? Like that's just the way it is. What I heard about Arthur—his name's Arthur Doe—is he doesn't have any patients 'cause he's got a shitty bedside manner. No gift of the gab. Plus, he's only a marginal dentist."

"So why would that make him a suspect?"

"Because Wayne was a cheapskate with his daughter, Lauren. And, supposedly, she was always bitching to Arthur about living in the shitty condo of theirs and having to buy her clothes at TJ Maxx. That kind of thing."

Crawford had just bought two nice pairs of Izod pants at TJ Maxx. *He* considered them nice, anyway. Twenty-three bucks each, plus one pair came with a belt.

"So, you're saying his motive might be to kill Crabb to get at his wife's inheritance?"

Platt nodded. "Why not? It happens."

Crawford glanced at Ott, who looked like he needed convincing.

"Anybody else?" Ott asked.

"Not that I can think of."

"Back to Sabal House," Crawford said. "We heard there were a lot of very unhappy investors."

Platt's right foot started tapping as if to an Irish jig. "Yeah, I guess, maybe."

"You 'guess, maybe'… Mr. Platt, isn't there a massive lawsuit alleging you cheated these people out of thirty million dollars?"

"That's wildly inflated."

"Okay, twenty million."

"We heard something about the Triads," Crawford said. "Can you tell us about that?"

Platt shrugged. "I don't even know what that is."

"Sure, you do," Crawford said. "The Chinese mafia."

"So, what we got, Mr. Platt," Ott put in, "are members of the American mafia *and* the Chinese mafia as possible suspects. How 'bout the Iranian mafia? Or the Turkish mafia? 'Cause we heard there were some Iranians and Turks who lost their shirts, too."

"You're gonna have to talk to my lawyers about that," Platt said, clearly uncomfortable with where the conversation had drifted. "Hey, I gotta get back to work here. I've been very cooperative with you fellas."

Crawford nodded. "Yes, you have. We only need one more thing from you."

"What's that?"

"A list of your Sabal House investors."

"And what do you need that for?"

"It should be pretty obvious," Crawford said. "If they all thought Sabal House was one big scam and that Wayne Crabb was part of that scam, then it stands to reason they'd either want to recover their money—hence, the lawsuit—or possibly take more drastic measures."

"Which would be to terminate one of the perpetrators of the scam," Ott said.

"I get it," Platt said with a grim look.

"Just a suggestion, Mr. Platt, but based on what happened to Crabb, you might want to be careful," Crawford said. "You never know."

"I appreciate you being concerned about my welfare, Detective," Platt said.

Crawford nodded. "So, if you would, that list of investors?"

Platt sighed and stood up. "All right, give me a few minutes."

He walked through the office's double doors.

"So, what do you think?" Ott whispered.

"I'm not getting a guilty vibe," Crawford said. "Or him having much of a motive."

"Hard to tell," Ott said.

Crawford nodded back. "Daughter and son-in-law are worth a look."

"Definitely."

"I think we should see Crabb's assistant first, then his wife, then the daughter and son-in-law. That way we'll have some background on the son-in-law before we meet him."

Ott nodded. "Okay, I'll set 'em up."

"We can swing by Crabb's office, see the assistant right after here," Crawford said.

The door opened and Platt walked out.

"That was fast," Crawford said.

"Yeah, well, I knew exactly where it was," Platt said, handing Crawford the list. "That's a copy."

Crawford scanned it. It included not only investors' names, but also their addresses.

Crawford folded the list and put it in the breast pocket of his jacket. "Okay, well, thanks."

Platt nodded. "Hey, I'm all about being cooperative with the law."

That seemed questionable. "By the way," Crawford said, "I was thinking… For your safety, maybe you want a few of our men to protect you? You know, keep an eye on you, at least for a while."

"You mean, like bodyguards?"

"Kind of."

"Nah, but thanks. I'll be okay," Platt said. "By the way, you might want to add Crabb's girlfriends to your list."

"Why do you say that?" Crawford asked, getting to his feet.

Platt shrugged. "I don't know. He was constantly suing 'em, evicting 'em, kicking 'em out of his places on Christmas Eve. You know, after making 'em do kinky shit. So I heard, anyway. Maybe one of 'em decided, 'Enough of this shit.'"

Crawford turned and faced Platt. "Let me ask you one more question," he said. "Did Wayne Crabb have any good qualities?"

Platt put his hand on his chin, thought for a few moments, then shook his head. "Not that I'm aware of."

7

Crawford and Ott's next stop was at Wayne Crabb's office at South County Road. It wasn't far. Before they'd left Platt's office, he'd pointed out Crabb's office from his window, straight across the Intracoastal from Phillips Point.

"Maybe his assistant can come up with something good to say about the guy," Ott said as they parked the car on South County. "'Cause nobody else is."

"We'll see," said Crawford, slamming the door of the Crown Vic.

Wayne Crabb's assistant, Mary Beth Hudson, had heard about her boss's murder from a reporter at the *Palm Beach Post*. The reporter had called, mistakenly believing he was calling Crabb's home number. He had apparently been hoping to get a reaction, and maybe a quote, from Crabb's wife. A tad insensitive, Crawford thought. After all, what was Mrs. Crabb supposed to say? "Good riddance. Never could stand that cheatin' bastard anyway."

Mary Beth Hudson was clearly grief-stricken and seemed close to hysterical. But when her tears cleared, it was apparent to Crawford that her distress was more about being suddenly out-of-work and paycheck-less.

"What am I supposed to do now?" she asked Crawford twice, like he might know someone who was hiring.

Sitting across from her in the conference room, they asked a few questions, but Mary Beth was clearly having a difficult time focusing. She finally worked her way through a recounting of what had happened earlier that morning, though—how a woman named Sunny Hedstrom had stormed into the office and accused Crabb of being responsible for the death of her dog, Winston. And how he had told Mary Beth he wanted Hedstrom evicted. Then, as if nothing of consequence had happened, he'd stripped down to his bathing suit and a T-shirt and left the office to go surfing.

"Ms. Hudson," Crawford asked, "you mentioned you've been working for Mr. Crabb for over thirty years."

The woman, wearing simple clothing and inexpensive jewelry, nodded.

"So, who do you think might have been capable of such an elaborate murder plan?"

"Oh my God, I have no idea," she said with a full-shouldered shrug. "I mean, to be honest Wayne had, well, a few enemies. He was spiteful. He was litigious. He could be ruthless. But for someone to go to the trouble of attacking him and killing him with a drone, I just can't begin to fathom that."

Crawford looked around at the blown-up surfing photos, and his stare returned to Mary Beth. When in doubt, repeat the question. "But, if you had to come up with a list of people capable of killing your boss, who would be on it?"

Ott had his leather notebook out, but so far he hadn't written anything in it.

Mary Beth thought for a few moments. "Well, okay, there was that nasty man from New Jersey..." She stalled out.

"'From New Jersey'... What was his name? What was his connection to your boss?"

"He was in the hotel business. I think he had one in Atlantic City. Maybe other ones up there."

Crawford remembered what Preston Platt had said. "Was his name Singer? The man who was going to buy Crabb's hotel in Nassau?"

"Yes, yes, that's him. Levi Singer. What a nasty piece of work he was. Called here and threatened Wayne. I wouldn't be surprised if he did it. Wayne told me he showed up at his house once and almost got into a fight with him on the front doorstep. Betsy called the cops. That was quite a while ago, though."

"How long?"

"Oh, I'd say twelve to fifteen years."

Ott, finally writing in his notebook, looked up. "Wait, so Singer was in Palm Beach?"

"Oh, yes. Actually, he's got a house here. Up on the north end, as I recall."

"You said he threatened Crabb. Did he ever threaten to kill him?" Crawford asked.

"I wouldn't be surprised if he did."

"But did you ever hear him, or did Crabb ever say he had?"

"No, not that I remember."

"Who else would be on your list?" Ott asked.

She raised her arms. "Oh, jeez, I haven't even had time to think about this."

"We understand," Crawford said. "But any help you can provide might help us find his killer."

Mary Beth nodded. "Well—" She stopped. "I guess I won't be betraying any confidence since Wayne is… deceased, but he had a lot of women friends…" She stalled out again.

"Please, Ms. Hudson, keep going," Crawford said.

"Woman friends who… it ended badly with sometimes."

"Can you spell that out, please?" Ott said, not looking up from his notetaking.

"Well, like Sunny Hedstrom, who I told you about earlier… and her poor dog. Then there was this one, Erica was her name, who Wayne just evicted from his yacht."

"She was living on his yacht?" Crawford asked.

"Yes, a couple of women have over the years."

"Really?"

Mary Beth nodded.

"And why did he evict her?"

"Well, to tell you the truth, he never filled me in on all the details. But I always had my theories."

"And what was your theory about Erica?"

"That she was, um, having sex with the bosun."

"The bosun, huh?" Ott said, looking up this time.

She nodded.

"And how do you know she was having sex with him?" Ott asked, his head back down as he scribbled.

"I overheard a call Wayne had with her once. He accused her of, like I said, having sex with him. His name was Jake. Wayne fired him. I have no idea how Wayne found out or whether he was just guessing."

"Do you know where she is now? Erica."

"No idea."

"Or what her last name is?"

"That I do know. Erica Janus. J-a-n-u-s."

"Thank you," Crawford said. "What other women… did it end badly with?"

Mary Beth Hudson spent the next five minutes giving Crawford and Ott six first names, for which she remembered three last names, but she claimed she had no idea where the women were now.

After Ott had filled a couple of pages of notes about Crabb's ex-girlfriends, Crawford veered in a different direction. "What can you tell us about Crabb's wife, Betsy, and his children?"

"Well, he only has one child. A daughter, Lauren."

"And is she married?" he asked, even though he knew the answer.

"Yes, to Arthur. Arthur Doe." May Beth chuckled. "Wayne always used to call him, *Arthur who's got no dough.* Meaning—"

"Gotcha," Crawford said.

"He's a dentist up in Jupiter."

"Thank you," said Ott.

"And what about Betsy?" Crawford asked.

"The woman's a saint. She had to be, to put up with Wayne and all his shenanigans."

Crawford could see Mary Beth was loosening up. "How long were they married?" he asked.

"Forever… let's see. Forty-one years, I think. They got married when Wayne had no money. Way I heard it, she basically put him through business school."

And that's how he paid her back, Crawford thought, screwing everything within a fifty-square-mile radius? Ott snuck a peek at him and Crawford could tell he was thinking the same thing.

"Ms. Hudson, it doesn't seem like Crabb went to great lengths to hide his, ah, philandering, so, the question is, how did his wife deal with all of it?"

Mary Beth thought for a moment then smiled. "Simple. By closing her eyes and putting her hands over her ears."

8

Mary Beth Hudson gave them the address of Wayne and Betsy Crabb's house as well as Betsy's cell number. Crawford and Ott walked out the back of Crabb's building and, in a spot marked *Crabb Development*, saw an old, white Camry with a dent on the passenger side. Ott pointed it out to his partner and noted how Mary Beth Hudson probably hadn't had a raise in a while. Crawford called Betsy Crabb's number and got her voicemail. He gave his standard 'sorry about your loss' consolation and said he and his partner were on their way to her house to speak to her.

"Did it occur to you that Mary Beth might have been the only one to know where Crabb was going?" Ott asked.

"Yeah, I was just thinking about that. One of us should get her cell and office call records. See if she called anyone after he left."

"I'll do it."

Ten minutes later they were on Betsy Crabb's porch. Crawford pressed the buzzer.

A few moments later a woman in a light-blue uniform answered the door. Because she was somewhat overweight and plain-looking,

Crawford guessed that Betsy Crabb had probably hired her. So there wouldn't be any possibility of coitus under her roof.

"Hello," Crawford said. "My name's Detective Crawford and this is my partner, Detective Ott." Ott nodded. "Is Mrs. Crabb here?"

"Yes, she is, but—"

"I'm right here, Denise." A white-haired woman appeared, wearing a prim dark-blue dress. She put out her hand. "I just got your message. Detective Crawford?"

Crawford shook her hand. "Yes, ma'am, and my partner, Detective Ott."

Ott nodded and shook her hand.

"Nice to meet you both. Please come in."

"We're both very sorry about your loss, ma'am," Crawford said.

Ott nodded again.

"Thank you," Betsy said.

They followed her into a beautifully furnished living room. As somber as the moment was, the room looked the opposite: it had three large bouquets of brilliantly colored flowers and two white orchids in vases. The couches, love seats, and tufted chairs were upholstered in vibrant primary and pastel colors.

They all sat.

"So, my husband's secretary, Mary Beth, called and told me what happened," Betsy said in a labored tone. "I'm still having trouble comprehending it. A drone? I hardly know what that is."

"They're called UAVs, which stands for 'Unmanned Aerial Vehicles'," Ott said. "This one had a gun attached to it."

Betsy nodded. "I mean, it's just so inconceivable to me. Who would ever…" She was clearly having difficulty wrapping her mind around the whole concept, not uncommon for a spouse in a state of shock.

"That's what we're trying to find out," Crawford said. "Just who might have done it, and why."

She just sat there, slowly shaking her head. She seemed, however, a long way from tears.

Ott moved forward in his chair. "Mrs. Crabb, we've spoken to

Preston Platt and Mary Beth Hudson so far. We really need whatever thoughts you might have as to who could have done this."

She side-glanced Ott with a quizzical look. "It's just all so unbelievable to me," she said again with a sigh. "I mean, I know Wayne had enemies, but my God, not someone who would ever kill him."

"Are you familiar with the Sabal House—" Crawford wasn't quite sure what word to use "—situation?"

"Yes, but that has more to do with Preston Platt, doesn't it?" Betsy Crabb asked. "I heard he, what's the word, *misappropriated* investors' funds. Preston, I'm referring to."

That would be the version she heard.

Crawford nodded. "But they were partners and apparently the investors thought your husband was to blame, too."

"Oh, really?" Betsy said, shrugging. "That doesn't sound like Wayne."

"Is there anyone else you think we should investigate?" Ott asked. "Or who might be worth talking to? Who might have information that would be helpful to us? Anybody at all?"

Betsy glanced out the window and sighed. "I don't know much about this, but maybe there's something here… Do you know what Equestra-World is?"

"I've heard of it," Crawford said. "Isn't it a development out in Wellington for people who like to ride… and play polo?"

"Yes. Among other things, it's also got three golf courses and a bunch of tennis courts. Anyway, Wayne owns it. He bought it in foreclosure about fifteen years ago. After he bought it, he closed down two of the golf courses because, apparently, they were losing money. So, as I understand it anyway, he bought it together with an Indian tribe. Wayne was trying to get the two golf courses re-zoned for a new casino."

"What tribe? Do you remember, Mrs. Crabb?" Crawford prompted her.

"Oh, let me think," she said, tapping a side table next to her. "The Tacat… something. Oh, I remember now, the Tacatacurus."

Crawford had zero idea where this was going but saw Ott scribbling notes.

"So, what I heard," Mrs. Crabb continued, "was Wayne and the chief had an agreement about who was going to get what share of the ownership, and of the profits, too, I guess. Let's see—" She was struggling with the details "—anyway, then they had a big dispute about it. The chief said Wayne promised him such-and-such and Wayne denied it. Wayne showed him the contract but then the chief denied ever signing it. Said the signature on the contract was forged. Next thing I heard was the chief threatened to do harm to Wayne."

"'Do harm to him'?" Crawford said. "Do you mean, kill him?"

Betsy nodded and lowered her voice. "Possibly."

"How do you know that?" Ott asked.

"There were a lot of people present when he said it, apparently," she said. "So, I asked Wayne about it because, naturally, I was concerned about his well-being. He told me he pulled the plug on the whole casino thing. He didn't need a partner who was going around and threatening him."

"What was the chief's name?" Ott asked.

She thought for a moment. "Leroy Mack."

Crawford watched Ott frown. He could see Ott was disappointed with it being such an ordinary name. It didn't have the pizazz of a Sitting Bull, Geronimo or Crazy Horse.

Crawford straightened out in his chair. "How long ago did this take place, Mrs. Crabb?"

She put her hand on her chin. "Not so long ago. Maybe three weeks. I know the chief called Wayne a couple of times since then. But I don't think Wayne spoke to him again."

"Well, we'll certainly look into that. Thank you, that's very helpful," Crawford said. "Anybody else?"

She slowly shook her head.

Ott looked up. "Speaking of casinos, what about a man named Levi Singer? We've heard he and your husband might have had a falling-out over a hotel casino in Nassau."

"I forgot about him," Mrs. Crabb said. "But that was such a long time ago. I haven't heard that name in years."

"So you wouldn't think he'd be a suspect?"

She shrugged. "I don't really know."

"Well," said Crawford, "we appreciate your time and once again sorry about—"

"Thank you," she said, nodding. "I appreciate your kind sentiments, gentlemen."

"You're very welcome. Oh, one last thing, Mrs. Crabb," Ott said, standing. "Can you give us the phone numbers for your daughter and son-in-law?"

"Why do you want—?"

"We just typically speak to all family members," Ott said. "Part of the routine we go through."

"I see." She gave them the numbers as she walked them to the front door.

The woman in the light-blue uniform appeared and opened the door for them.

"Thanks again," Crawford said to Mrs. Crabb, and Ott nodded.

"You're welcome."

Crawford stepped out on the porch, then turned back to Betsy Crabb. "We'll let you know when we have something."

"Please do," Betsy said as the door closed.

Ott lowered his voice. "You believe that whole Indian chief thing?"

"Yeah, pretty crazy."

"And that really dumb name?"

"Tacatacurus? Leroy Mack?"

"No, not that," Ott said. "Equestra-World. Who the hell would ever want to live in a place called Equestra-World?"

9

Crawford and Ott were headed back to the station in their Crown Vic when Crawford's cellphone rang.

He looked down at it. It was Dominica McCarthy. "Hey, Mac, what's up?"

She not only answered to *Dominica* and *McCarthy* but to *Dom* and *Mac* as well. *Beautiful* was another name Crawford used, but only in private.

"Got some intel for you, Charlie. On Wayne Crabb," she said.

"That was fast," Crawford said, looking at his watch. It was 5:25. "How 'bout I meet you at the par-three. We can do a working speed nine?"

"Sure. When?"

"Say, twenty minutes?"

"I'll see you then."

Crawford clicked off.

Ott, at the wheel of the Crown Vic, looked over. "I don't get the nod?"

"Nah, you're too slow."

A speed nine was a quick break from work and a form of

recreation for Crawford. In addition to going to his gym in West Palm Beach, once a week or so Crawford would play nine holes at the par-three golf course south of Palm Beach. He had dubbed it a *speed nine* because he didn't take any practice swings and anything within five feet of the cup was a 'gimme'. It never took more than an hour and his record was forty-eight minutes. So, he could break up a day with a quick round and then go back to the office. The one time he played with Ott it took well over an hour and a half, as Ott insisted on taking two practice swings before each shot and scrupulously putting out every hole. So, Ott hadn't been asked back.

Dominica, on the other hand, got the idea fast and played even faster. Plus, she was a lot easier on the eye than Ott.

"You coming back to the station after?" Ott asked.

"Yeah, I'll pick up some takeout on the way back. I figure it's gonna be a late one tonight. Want me to get you something?"

"Where you gonna go?"

"Fong's Garden." A Chinese place in West Palm.

"You all done with Chinee Takee Outee?" That was actually the name of a place on Okeechobee Boulevard.

"Yeah, it kinda sucked. Get you something at Fong's?"

"Nah," Ott said. "I feel like a pie."

"Nico's?" A good pizza joint just over the bridge.

"Yup," Ott said as he pulled up to the station.

Ott got out and Crawford slid over into the driver's seat. "Later," he said.

"Bet you don't break thirty-five," Ott said.

Par for nine holes was twenty-seven.

"Bet you're right."

THE CUSTOM WAS they didn't talk shop while playing—only afterward, over a beer in the clubhouse.

Crawford duck-hooked his first drive into the water and quickly teed up another.

"Weren't you supposed to be a big athlete in college?" Dominica rubbed it in.

He ignored her and hit a second drive. It ended up in a bunker to the right of the green, about twenty yards short of the hole.

"You're up, bigmouth," he said as Dominica teed up an orange ball.

She swung the three-wood deliberately and hit it cleanly. It ended up in the middle of the fairway, fifteen yards short of the green.

Dominica picked up her tee and pumped her fist. "I outdrove you, plus you're lying three and I've still got a shot at par."

Crawford smiled as they got into the golf cart. "Yeah, but I've seen you chip," he said. "And it ain't pretty."

She laughed. "Bite me."

"Love to."

They drove up to Crawford's ball in the trap. It was buried in the sand. He stepped up to it and attempted to strike the sand three inches behind it. He caught it too cleanly and it bounced once before flying into the water again.

Dominica laughed. "Are you going for the course record? Highest score ever?"

He shook his head. "You saw that. It was a terrible lie."

"Excuses, excuses," she said. "Sure you got enough balls to get around?"

"Never been a problem before," he said as he walked over to the drop area.

Crawford ended up lucky to card a *snowman*, an eight, while Dominica chipped it close and made her par.

Crawford's game improved slightly and at the end of eight holes they were tied, each winning four holes apiece.

It was Dominica's honor. She teed up her orange ball then stood ready to hit it.

From behind her, Crawford said, "Did I mention that's the ugliest ball I've ever laid eyes on? A little pumpkin with dimples on it."

"Are you trying to distract me?"

"No, just making an observation."

"Well, keep 'em to yourself."

Dominica began her backswing and took a smooth cut at the ball. It didn't quite reach the green but came close.

She turned to Crawford with a smile. "No pressure, Charlie."

"Nice shot," he said, grudgingly.

"Thank you." She mock-curtsied. "This is for all the marbles, big boy. You wouldn't want it getting around that you lost to a girl."

Crawford chuckled. "I've lost to girls before… just never to one with an orange ball."

He placed his ball on the tee, waggled the club a few times and swung hard. His slice was back with a vengeance.

Plunk. It skipped once across the water, then *glug-glug-glug…* Davey Jones's locker. He reached into his golf bag for another ball. Coming up empty, he checked all of the other pockets in his bag, but it seemed that ball had been his last.

He turned to her sheepishly. "Ah… I'm all out of balls, can I—?"

"Sure, Charlie," she said, pulling an orange ball out of her pocket. "Just don't lose it, huh?"

His drive stayed dry this time, but he got a seven, Dominica a four.

"Come on," she said, plucking her ball from the cup. "I'll buy you a beer. Maybe it'll soothe your bruised ego."

THEY ORDERED beers and sat down at an outside table.

"One of the divers found what was left of the drone," Dominica said. She then took a sip of her Modelo.

They were sitting at a table looking out over the course and at the ocean beyond.

It was a nice place to talk shop.

"Those guys do good work," Crawford said. "Bet it was pretty mangled."

"Yeah, it was. They didn't find every little piece, but enough."

Dominica took out her iPhone and scrolled down until she found what she was looking for. Then she handed the iPhone to Crawford. "It's called a Phantom 4 Pro V2.0. Made in Shenzhen, China."

Crawford perked up. "Suspects of mine are from China," he said, looking at the photos and description of the drone. "Investors in Sabal House."

"Don't get too excited, Charlie," Dominica said. "Turns out most drones come from China."

"How fast does it go?"

"Around twenty, twenty-five miles an hour."

Crawford nodded and took a closer look. It had a white body, above which were four rotors, and below it, a built-in camera. Crawford scrolled down and read its bullet-point specs:

- 30 Mins Flight Time
- 7 km Control Range
- 4 dB Noise Reduction
- 4K 60fps
- 30 m Sensor Range
- 5-direction Obstacle Sensing

"I don't know what half that stuff means," Crawford said. "But I'm guessing that they mounted the gun where the camera goes?"

Dominica nodded. "That's a good guess. I assembled the pieces the divers found, and that's exactly where it was."

Crawford nodded and read further. "'The Phantom 4 Pro V2.0 is equipped with a 1-inch 20-megapixel sensor capable of shooting 4K/60fps video and Burst Mode stills at 14 fps.' Not to mention, shooting a guy off a surfboard. What's an 'fps'?"

"I think it stands for frames per second."

Crawford scrolled further. "Says, 'FlightAutonomy is an advanced aerial intelligence and flight automation platform.' So these things are used for surveillance a lot."

Dominica put her beer glass down. "Yeah, not usually for picking off poor, unsuspecting surfers."

"How much does one of these cost, anyway?" Crawford asked as he finished off his beer.

"Around two grand or so. Why? You thinking of getting one?"

Crawford smiled. "Got a few people I'd like to pick off," he said. "So, if this thing can go twenty-five miles an hour and can stay in the air for thirty minutes, it could have been launched from just about anywhere within, say, a ten-mile radius."

Dominica nodded and leaned back in her chair. "It would be nice if we could find someone who saw it lift off out of their neighbor's backyard or something, but that's probably not gonna happen."

"Yeah, we'd have heard about it by now," Crawford said, peeling the label off his Sierra Nevada bottle. "Probably launched it from some deserted area. Someone was probably watching Crabb and saw him head to the beach. Or got tipped by his assistant. Ott's checking into that."

Dominica glanced at the ocean, then back at Crawford. "So at least two perps. One to see where Crabb was going, another one to launch and operate the drone."

"I guess," Crawford said. "Did it occur to you that this was a hell of a lot of trouble to go through to whack a guy? I mean, why not just pop him with a gun when he's leaving his office or something?"

Dominica shrugged. "I don't know, I guess some people just like to be creative."

"I guess," Crawford said. "Want another?"

Dominica looked at her watch. It was 7:15. "Sure. What are you gonna do for dinner?"

"Picking something up at Fong's Garden, then heading back to the office."

"General Tso's chicken?"

"You know me too well."

"That's too bad because I was gonna offer to whip up my penne alla Dominica."

Crawford sighed. "Believe me, I'd love to join you, but I gotta get somewhere on this thing. Meeting Ott back at the station."

Dominica shook her head. "All work and no play—"

"I know, I know," Crawford said, squeezing her hand. "Raincheck."

She nodded.

Crawford got up from the table and ordered another round for them both.

A few minutes later he came back to find Dominica working her iPhone.

"Whatcha doing there?" he asked.

"I was thinking," she said, "about surveillance systems that airports have."

Crawford nodded. "I like how you're thinking."

"Best I can tell—as the crow flies—the airport is only three or four miles from the murder scene, so maybe they picked up something—" She looked down at the Wikipedia article she was reading. "Says here that major airports typically track air traffic within a sixty-mile radius. I wouldn't call PBI a major airport, but wouldn't you think it covers, I don't know—" she shrugged "—ten miles, at least?"

"I would think so," Crawford said. "Why don't you talk to 'em and see what you come up with?"

"I'll get on it first thing tomorrow morning," she said, then read further. "Says, 'The primary radar typically consists of a large rotating parabolic antenna dish that sweeps a vertical fan-shaped beam of microwaves around the airspace surrounding the airport.'"

Crawford laughed.

"What?" Dominica looked up and smiled.

"Hell of an exciting date, sitting here reading technical stuff back and forth to each other."

"It's a working date," she said, patting his hand.

"Whatever it is, I'm enjoying it."

10

It was 8:30 and Crawford had just finished his General Tso's chicken. Every last delicious morsel of it.

He was on Google now. He had once calculated that he spent ten percent of his working hours online, mostly Google, but probably twenty percent on Wikipedia. He had Googled Wayne Crabb and there was a lot to read. The man was clearly sue-happy. According to an article in the *Palm Beach Post,* he had sued, or was in the process of suing, two former girlfriends for what appeared to be the same reason: they had stopped, well, *putting out.*

One, with the unlikely name of Chastity Flowers, was apparently an equestrian champion and former Miss Florida, who was supposed to be bringing rich buyers to purchase houses at Crabb's Equestra-World development. She had, according to Crabb's suit, assured him that she would deliver no fewer than fifteen buyers for his homes there. In return, he had bought her a $350,000 condo, which she had moved into and—reading between the lines—conjugally entertained Crabb there on numerous occasions. But, Crabb contended in his lawsuit, Chastity had not lived up to her part of the bargain, delivering not one single buyer. Claiming fraud and misrepresentation, Crabb had demanded his condo back. But Chastity's counterclaim was that it was a gift, along with several furs, expensive jewelry, and designer clothes, which Crabb was also trying to recover. Chastity asserted that all such gifts were for "services rendered".

The other woman, a beautician thirty-nine years younger than Crabb, Gabriella Dolan, who clearly had a relationship with him, was being sued for refusing to pay for improvements made to her house in Pahokee by a construction company controlled by Crabb. The improvements consisted of an addition in the back for a home gym and a Jacuzzi, in which it seemed apparent that Crabb and Gabriella had frolicked frequently.

Next, Crawford Googled Levi Singer, the New Jersey man alleged to have Mafia ties, who had lost out when Crabb sold his hotel in Nassau to another buyer. For starters, Levi Singer was eighty-eight years old and had served in the Korean War, during which he lost his right arm and was awarded the Bronze Star. It seemed unlikely that he was the man responsible for the drone attack on Wayne Crabb. Singer was in the hotel business, primarily in New Jersey, Delaware, and Pennsylvania, but it appeared that he spent a large amount of time supporting a variety of humanitarian and philanthropic causes. According to several articles, his two sons, Jerry and Jeffrey, had taken over day-to-day control of his hotel business, American Premier Lodging, based in Toms River, New Jersey. Another son lived in Florida.

Crawford still wanted to talk to Singer, even though the war hero didn't seem, at least on paper, to be the mobbed-up ogre Mary Beth Hudson had made him out to be. He also still needed to question Crabb's son-in-law and was typing the number of dentist Arthur Doe's office into his Reminders file when he heard the unmistakable thudding footsteps of Mort Ott as he entered Crawford's office.

Ott eyed the empty food containers on Crawford desk. "How was the General?"

"Christ. How'd you know that's what I had?"

Ott shrugged. "That's all you ever get at Fong's."

Crawford thought for a moment. "I had the Mongolian beef once."

Ott shook his head. "Smells like the General."

Crawford shook his head. "So, I got a lot to catch you up on."

Ott nodded. "Me too. Why don't you go first?"

Crawford told Ott all about his conversation with Dominica regarding the discovery of the Chinese-made drone and her idea to check with airport communications to see if they had any radar footage that might include the drone.

Then it was Ott's turn to catch Crawford up on what he had found out in the last few hours.

"So, for starters, on that list of Chinese investors, I found one guy who had paid a so-called *consultant* a million bucks to get his daughter into Stanford on a sailing scholarship."

Crawford nodded. "That shit's old news."

"Yeah, I know. I got some good stuff on Gina Platt, though," Ott said.

"Let's hear it."

"Well, in the Sabal House prospectus to the EB-5 investors, there were three or four shots of Gina standing next to movie stars. You know, like on the red carpet at the Oscars, shit like that. Next to Meryl Streep in one, Justin Timberlake in another. Turns out, according to this article in *The Post*, they were all Photoshopped, I guess to impress the foreign investors."

Crawford slowly shook his head. "What else you got?"

"I got Suarez checking manifests for Chinese names coming into PBI for the last week," Ott said.

"Good."

"Yeah, but it probably comes under the heading of 'needle in a haystack.'"

"Never know," Crawford said. "Anything else?"

"I dropped in on Mary Beth Hudson. Asked her if she'd mind showing me the phone recs of Crabb's office and of her cell."

"And?"

"Nada. She didn't make calls on either one until mid-afternoon."

"Meaning she didn't tip anyone off about her boss going surfing."

"Nope. So I'd say she's off the hook," Ott said. "Oh, also, as you suggested, I put in a call to the lawyer representing all the investors who got ripped off on the Sabal House thing."

Crawford nodded. "I want to be in on that Q&A," he said. "Based on everything we got so far, they're probably our best shot."

"I agree, but I'm still curious about the son-in-law," Ott said. "You know, Arthur 'got no dough' Doe?"

Crawford nodded. "Yeah. How about the Indian chief?"

"He's probably a long shot."

Crawford put his hand on his chin. "I got another longshot for you."

"Who's that?"

"Does the name Orchids of Asia mean anything to you?"

Ott leaned back in his chair and looked up at the ceiling.

"I'll give you a clue—where a certain NFL team owner was photographed partaking in an illegal act as recorded by a hidden camera—"

"Oh, yeah," Ott said. "That massage parlor up in Jupiter."

"And, my next question is, what possible link could there be between Orchids of Asia and the murder of Wayne Crabb?"

Ott thought for a second. "Chinese people ran Orchids of Asia and Chinese nationals were screwed in Crabb's Sabal House fleece job?"

Crawford nodded. "Bingo. And, turns out, there are a lot of other Chinese massage parlors around the state. Not just Jupiter, but all over."

"Yeah, but, as I remember, it was women running them."

"True, women managed them, but they didn't necessarily own them. Think about it: the women who worked at 'em were basically sex slaves, right?"

"Yeah. So?"

"So, someone's got to threaten and intimidate 'em to keep 'em in line. Tell 'em if they ever try to run away, they're dead meat. What got me thinking about this was an article I read in the *Post*, I think it was. About this guy—they called him an enforcer—who worked for a bunch of these places. He'd go around and tell the girls that if they ever took off, he'd go to China and kill every single one of their relatives. Death by a thousand cuts. *Lingchi*, they call it."

"Yeah," said Ott. "I read about it too."

"So, my theory—admittedly, a longshot—goes like this: a pissed-off Sabal House investor knew someone in the massage parlor business and borrowed the services of their enforcer to take out a certain surfer."

"It's a decent enough theory, Charlie, except I think of a goon like that as being handy with a gun or a knife, not a drone."

"Yeah, I hear you. I still want to look into it."

"My other question is, where you gonna find this enforcer? As you know, they shut those massage parlors down."

Crawford shook his head. "Come on, you know how it works. They close 'em down and a week later, another one pops up just down the road."

"Yeah, good point," Ott said.

Crawford looked at his watch. It was 10:15. "Okay, time to blow this pop stand."

Ott nodded. "I wish you hadn't brought up that *lingchi* thing."

"Why?"

"'Cause, guarantee you, I'm gonna have nightmares about it."

11

Instead it was Crawford who had bad dreams. First, a man—or maybe it was a woman, because he/she wore an executioner's hood and never spoke—cut into the underside of Crawford's forearm with a scalpel. Thankfuly he could barely feel it, and it didn't bleed much. Next, the blade sliced a sliver of skin between the toes on his right foot. That was a little more painful. He cried out in pain and woke up in a panic, drenched in sweat. He wasn't sure whether the cry was in his dream or he had actually cried out. He looked down at his arm and everything was intact. No cut. No blood. Then he swung his right leg out to the side of the bed and examined his toes. They were all there. He exhaled loudly.

He waited a while before he lay back down and tried to get back to sleep, unsure whether his dream might pick up where it had left off. Finally, he nodded off and had another dream. This was a good one. Well, for a while anyway. He, Dominica, and Rose Clarke were paddling a long canoe somewhere in the Adirondacks. It was apparently in the summer because Rose had just said something about how it was good to be "up here instead of in that stifling heat of Palm Beach." But then it turned dark—literally and figuratively—as thick clouds suddenly rolled in and the sky blackened. Dominica suggested they paddle harder to get to the shore and safety. They did, but Crawford realized that they were going in a circle. He pointed this out to the women, but the three were unable to keep the canoe from moving in circles. Rose suggested to Crawford that he do a J-stroke, but he had no idea what that was, having never paddled a canoe before.

Rose demonstrated a J-stroke to him and he executed it. They were headed to the shore now and to the big, eight-bedroom Adirondack "cabin" where they were staying. But then Crawford saw that they were heading straight for an enormous log floating on the water's surface. He warned the others and did a quick, newly-learned J-stroke to avoid the log. As the canoe missed it by inches, Crawford looked down and realized that it was a large alligator, watching him with big red eyes that shone. It seemed to be smiling… then it winked.

CRAWFORD'S ALARM clock went off at seven and he got right out of bed, happy to leave his dreams behind. After a stop at Dunkin' Donuts, or just Dunkin' as they were calling it these days, he was at his desk by quarter of eight. He polished off the coffee, and walked down to the crime-scene techs' offices. He could see the top of Dominica's head as he approached her cubicle.

"Hey girlfriend," he said under his breath.

She swung around with a look of panic as he walked into her cubicle. "Char-lie, you can't say that."

"Hey, girlfriend?'"

"Shh—Jesus!"

Crawford put his hands up. "It's just a figure of speech. Like saying, 'How's it goin', beautiful.' Or 'What's shakin', babe?'"

"'What's shakin', babe?' Jesus, did you grow up in the 1950s or something?"

"Funny. I just came by to ask you a few questions. I'm pursuing the

Chinese angle, since there were apparently a lot of pissed-off Chinamen who invested in the Sabal House scam. So, my first question is: You grew up in Miami. Are there any Chinese gangs down there? You know, like the Triads?"

Dominica thought for a second. "So you're thinking one of the Chinese investors contacted a Chinese gang member, offered him a few bucks to take out Crabb?"

"Yeah, something like that."

"Well, here's the line-up of gangs in Miami: Heavy on motorcycle gangs—the Mongols, the Outlaws, and the Warlocks, being the worst. Heavy on Latino gangs, too—MS-13, Sureños, and La Raza are a few. Then we got the Bloods and the Crips—as you know, black gangs. And the Mafia's still going strong down there, the Trafficante family being the biggest player. But Chinese gangs—" she shook her head "— not that I'm aware of."

"I kind of figured that," Crawford said. "So, you're gonna check in with the people at the airport?"

"Already put in a call."

"Thanks. All right, I guess that's about all I had." He turned to go.

"Hey, Charlie?"

He turned back. "Yeah?"

"Any time you want me to kick your ass again at golf, just let me know."

Crawford laughed. "One lucky victory and it goes right to your head."

"Where you going now?"

"Got a dentist appointment."

12

Except he didn't have an appointment. It was a drop-in. Which was all right because Arthur Doe wasn't pulling a tooth or putting in a crown when Crawford walked into the office, located in a strip mall. Instead, the white-coated man was snoring soundly in a dental chair, as revealed through the unoccupied dental window.

Crawford cleared his voice. "Ah, excuse me? I'm looking for Dr. Doe."

The man lurched out of the chair. "Yes, yes, that's me, who are you?"

Crawford was still looking through the reception window. "Could you let me in, please? Name's Detective Crawford, Palm Beach Police."

Doe walked over to the door and opened it.

"Thank you," Crawford said, taking a few steps forward as Doe took a step back.

"How can I help you?" Doe asked.

"I'm the lead detective on the murder of your father-in-law, Dr. Doe. I'd like to ask you a few questions if that's all right?"

"Well, okay," he said, looking at his watch. "I have a little time until my next appointment. What would you like to know?"

"First of all, my condolences."

"Thank you," Doe said. "Wayne wasn't a bad guy, in spite of the rep he had."

Not exactly a ringing endorsement.

"So, you two got along pretty well?"

Doe frowned. "Yeah. Why, what have you heard?"

"Nothing, just asking. Did your wife ever say anything about enemies he may have had? Anyone who may have… I don't know, threatened him? Someone he may have feared? Or, maybe your mother-in-law mentioned someone?"

"I heard a lot of stuff. Not necessarily from my wife and never from my mother-in-law. Wayne was always getting into it with someone. Ex-business partners, politicians, girlfriends—"

"Girlfriends?" Crawford played dumb.

"Come on, Detective, that had to be the first thing you found out."

"Got any names?"

"Just Google him in *The Post*; he was in there just about every week."

"I've put in several calls to your wife but haven't heard back from her. Is there another way to reach her?"

"Just so happens she's stopping by here in a little bit to switch cars with me."

"Did she say when?"

Doe looked at his watch. "Should be any minute."

Crawford nodded.

On the way over, he had labored over how to ask his next question. "Dr. Doe, have you ever had financial issues?" It was flat-footed, but he had decided that it was the best way to go. Just blunder forward.

Doe's frown amped up into a look of anger. "What the hell kind of a question is that? I thought we were talking about Wayne, not me."

"We are. I just—"

"I get it, I get it." Doe started nodding like a dashboard bobble-head doll hitting speed bumps. "You're suggesting that maybe I killed Wayne so Lauren and I could get at his money. Is that it?"

He wasn't going to deny that was the gist of the question, so instead he tossed Doe an old favorite. "Dr. Doe, in the course of a homicide investigation, I go all over the place trying to flush out the truth. Don't be offended. I'm just doing my job. Did you ever have financial issues?"

Doe's face had turned a light shade of red. "Nothing serious," he said. "Am I a gazillionaire? No. Am I on food stamps?" He chuckled. "Not by a long shot. Would it be nice to have a little of Wayne's money? Sure. Would I kill him to get some? Not in my wildest dreams."

Crawford wasn't sure, but he tended to believe the man.

"How did you get along with your father-in-law?"

Doe thought for a second. "We got along all right. I think, as a rule, fathers-in-law always think their daughters could have done better."

Crawford chuckled to himself. That was pretty much what his ex-father-in-law had thought.

"Okay, last question. Where were you yesterday morning between eleven and twelve?"

"Why didn't you just ask me that in the first place?" Doe asked.

"Were you here?"

"Yeah, would you like to see my schedule book? I was here all day long. Including my daily nap in the chair."

Crawford glanced over at the chair. "Looks pretty comfortable."

Doe smiled and gestured toward it. "Wanna try it out?"

"Nah, you might pull a tooth."

Just as he said that, he heard a woman's voice. "Arthur?"

Crawford heard footsteps and a woman walked in. She had flaming red hair that looked natural, gray piercing eyes, and wore a black T-shirt with an 'Under Armour' logo.

"Hey, Lauren, this is Detective Craw—"

"Hi, Mrs. Doe," Crawford said, taking a step toward her. "I'm the homicide detective who called. Working on your father's case."

She shook his hand. "I apologize for not calling you back. Kind of had my hands full."

"I understand," Crawford said. "Mind if I ask you a few questions?"

"Sure, go ahead."

Crawford took out his iPhone. "Were you and your father pretty close?"

Lauren shrugged. "Yes… I'd say very close."

"Did he ever happen to mention anyone he was… afraid of?" Crawford went to his standard questions. "Anyone who may have threatened him? Maybe a business deal went awry or some kind of personal situation that… might have escalated?"

Lauren turned to her husband. "What have you told him?"

"I told him the truth. That Wayne was always getting into it with someone. Business partners, girlfriends… hell, even an Indian chief."

"That wasn't very loyal of you," Lauren said. "The poor man was just murdered."

Doe shrugged. "I was just trying to be helpful. So the detective can catch the guy who did it."

Lauren turned to Crawford and lowered her voice. "I wish I could help, but I really don't know of anyone. I mean, he had lots of partners, most he got along with, a few he didn't…" She paused, like she didn't want to tackle the *girlfriend* issue. "His assistant would know much more than us. Have you spoken to her yet? Mary Beth?"

Crawford nodded. "Yes, I have, and she was helpful."

"She knows a lot more than me," Lauren said.

"Well, thank you both," Crawford said. "I appreciate your time."

Arthur Doe nodded and flashed his pearly whites, a good advertisement for his profession. "Happy to help," he said. "You ever get a cavity, you know where to come."

∾

CRAWFORD HAD BEEN to the Jupiter Police Station before and knew it was on Military Trail. Seemed fitting—police... military.

The guy he had dealt with in the past was the deputy chief there. Dave Somebody. It was the name of a country, Crawford remembered. Spain? No. England? No. Ireland? Bingo, that was it.

He was in luck, Ireland was in. He met Crawford at the front desk.

The guy didn't look Irish. More Mediterranean, Crawford thought. Tanned and wiry, with thinning dark hair he combed straight back. And a big red nose. Well, that part was Irish. Crawford chided himself... *stereotyping again.*

"How ya doin', Charlie?" Ireland said, shaking his hand.

"Good, Dave, how 'bout you?"

"I'm good. Got any leads on the Silver Surfer?" asked Ireland.

Some joker had referred to Wayne Crabb that way on social media, and, for better or worse, it seemed to have stuck.

"That's why I'm here," he said. "Did you have anything to do with that bust at Orchids of Asia?"

"Kind of in a roundabout way... Why, what do you want to know?"

"Well, back when it went down, I read about a guy who was working at the one...not Orchids, but the one up in Hobe Sound—"

"You talking about the enforcer they mentioned in the paper?"

"Yeah, exactly."

"I think his name is Wang Zheng."

"Reading between the lines, his job was to stop the girls from even thinking about running away, right?"

"Correct," Ireland said. "And, also, to make sure they put in eighteen-hour days. They slept there, in fact."

"Jesus, really?"

"Yeah. And we found out he was doing the same thing at three other places. One up in Fort Pierce and two in Stuart. Girls were scared shitless of the guy, 'cause supposedly he tortured one of 'em. But, of course, nobody's talking."

"Any idea where he is now?"

"Well, the one in Hobe Sound was closed down, like Orchids was, and I'm pretty sure one of the ones in Stuart, but I think the other two are still open. We couldn't find enough to close 'em all down."

"You got addresses?"

"Sure do." Ireland reached down for his office phone. He dialed three numbers and waited a few moments. "Hey, Phil, those two nail joints up in Stuart and Fort Pierce, you got the names and addresses?" He scribbled them down on a piece of paper. "Thanks… yup, that's all I need."

He clicked off.

"You called 'em 'nail joints'," Crawford said. "But weren't they—"

"Massage parlors in the back, nail joints in the front," Ireland said. "So, if you didn't know any better, you'd think it was just a place where you get manicures and pedicures. But a lot of guys… knew better."

"Gotcha."

Ireland handed the piece of paper to Crawford. "Here you go, Charlie, go get yourself a manicure."

"Thanks, I'm thinking a pedicure. My toes need help… they're pretty damn gnarly."

STUART WAS A HALF-HOUR AWAY. Crawford decided to drive up and have a look-see at one called Heaven Nail & Spa. He plugged the address into his GPS and headed north.

Twenty minutes later, he parked in front of the shop in a small shopping center called Squirrelwood Mall. That was a new one…. Was there really a type of wood or a tree called a squirrelwood? A question for Siri or Alexa….

He got out of the Crown Vic and walked in. He wondered what Norm Rutledge would say if he saw 'pedicure' on his expense report. The only time the chief had ever questioned him was when Crawford submitted a report for $22.50 for a strip club in West Palm called Puss in Boots. It included the ten-dollar cover charge and the price of two watered-down drinks—but the leads he'd tracked down were priceless.

"Hello, sir," said an Asian woman at the front desk. "Welcome to Heaven."

It'd be about fifty years before he expected to end up in the place with the same name. If he was lucky.

"Thank you," Crawford said. "I would like to get a pedicure, please."

"Absolutely," the woman said, "Have you ever been here before?"

"No, this is my first time. How much is it?"

"Twenty dollars, unless… do you have coupon?" She said it with a wide smile.

"Unfortunately, no coupon."

She handed him one that was in a stack on the side of her cash register.

"Now, only nineteen dollars," she said, pointing. "You go right over there—" She indicated an open chair in between two Caucasian women. "Then you take off your shoes and socks, please, sir."

He walked over to the empty chair, sat, and took his shoes and socks off. A young Asian woman came over. "Hello, I am Mimosa, I give you pedicure."

"Okay, great. I've never done this before, so just tell me what to do."

"Yes, sir, you do nothing. Just sit, relax, and enjoy." She placed a plastic tub in front of him. "Please put your feet in here and I wash."

He did as he was told. She looked at his feet disapprovingly, her smile melting away. His toenails were jagged, because when you're six-three, as Crawford was, it was a long way down to clip your toenails. When he did clip them, which was infrequently at best, he did it fast and inexpertly. On his right foot, his second smallest toe was crooked and partially wrapped under the middle toe, so he could barely see the toenail. On his other foot, all his toes—though perfectly functional—looked a little like old vines that had twisted around each other.

The front door opened, and an older man with a Miami Dolphins cap entered. He gave the receptionist a quick nod and walked through to the back, where he opened a door and slipped through it.

Mimosa smiled and started scrubbing his feet. "Don't worry, sir, you will leave Heaven with beautiful feet."

"Great," he said. *That would be no small miracle.*

After thoroughly washing both feet, she dried them with a fluffy, white towel.

"Now, I buff," she said.

The only buff he was familiar with was back in New York when he got his leather shoes shined. But that had been years ago. Leather shoes were history now; he was a slip-on Skechers man all the way.

Buffing involved Mimosa running a little machine along the soles of his feet. It kind of tickled.

She looked up at him. "You like?"

He smiled and nodded.

Next, she clipped his nails, fast and neat, until—to Crawford's surprise—they looked a hundred percent better. She did the same with his cuticles, pushed them back so he could barely see them. There wasn't much she could do about his twisted toes, but Crawford was feeling better about the prospect of getting into a bathing suit again and not hiding his feet in his tacky yellow Crocs. He wasn't self-conscious about his body—he was, for the most part, well-toned and, to use the word in a different context, *buff*—but his toes had always been the weak link in his look.

Mimosa looked up and gave him a mischievous smile. "Would you like toenail polish?"

"Me?" Crawford was incredulous.

"Why not? It look nice on everybody."

Crawford smiled. "Sure. Why not."

She walked over to the rickety built-in that held her buffer, clippers, and supplies and brought back a laminated nine-by-twelve sheet. "What color you want?" It was a color chart dominated by various shades of reds, pinks, and oranges, but there were others, too.

He didn't hesitate. He pointed at the color that looked like Dartmouth green.

"Ah, very pretty," Mimosa said.

As she was applying the polish, he noticed the woman sitting in the chair next to him glance over several times. Her look was barely-concealed disapproval; at one point, she shook her head and mumbled something that sounded a lot like *tsk-tsk*.

Crawford was undeterred. "You like?" he asked her, pointing at his toes.

She turned and rolled her eyes. "A man with green nail polish?"

He chuckled. "So, I guess that means you do."

She didn't answer.

The door behind him opened and the man with the Dolphins cap quickly stepped out and walked back through the manicure and pedicure section of Heaven.

As Mimosa started applying polish to his left foot, Crawford leaned forward and lowered his voice. "I have a question."

"Yes?"

He dropped his voice even lower. "Is Wang Zheng here?"

Her hand jerked and she painted the skin below his nail accidentally. "Oh, sorry."

She dabbed at it with a Kleenex.

"Is he?" Crawford asked.

"Why you want to know?"

"Because I'm a cop and I don't want him to hurt anyone."

The *tsk-tsk* woman next to him leaned in their direction, trying in vain to listen in.

"You are too late," Mimosa said, her lip trembling as she concentrated on doing her job.

"Tell me what happened," he asked, leaning even closer to her.

"I cannot say," she whispered.

"Even for a nice, big tip?"

She sighed.

"Come on, Mimosa."

Glancing up at the woman next to them, she mumbled something inaudible.

"What?"

She didn't look up. "He comes here at night. Around eight."

"What else?"

"He is dangerous man."

"What else?"

"He did something very bad to a girl named Guan-yin."

"Who?"

She looked up and whispered. "Guan-yin."

"Tell me—"

"That's all," she snapped.

He looked down at his toes. She only had one to go.

"You do good work."

She didn't respond.

He left five minutes later, wondering whether Norm Rutledge seeing a fifty-dollar tip for Heaven Nails & Spa on his expense report would make him choke on his donut.

13

It was only four o'clock. Hanging out at the Squirrelwood Mall, killing four hours so he could have a heart-to-heart with Wang Zheng, Crawford decided, was not the best use of his time. He would have done it, though, if Zheng were his primary suspect. But he wasn't. He could wait until tomorrow night. Or the next. He had plenty else to do.

He called Ott, who picked up right away.

"So we got Bartey at one, right?" Crawford asked, referring to the lawyer for the Sabal House investors.

"Yup."

"After that, let's go down our lists in my office."

"Sounds good."

"See you then," Crawford clicked off.

His phone rang as he merged onto 95 South.

"Hello?"

"I'm lonely, Charlie." It was Dominica.

"I love it when you get like that."

"So, what are you going to do about it?"

He exhaled. "Not much, 'cause I gotta work late."

"Well, then come by late," Dominica said. "By the way, I contacted one of the air-traffic controllers at PBI."

"Yeah, and?"

"Nothing so far. I had an appointment to see him but he canceled it. Seem like these guys don't have time for anything but watching little blips go across radar screens. But don't worry, I'm on it."

"Yeah, that could be the key. You want me to call 'em too?"

"Nah, you got enough on your plate. I'll make it happen."

"Okay, so is nine okay?"

"That's good."

"And speaking of 'on my plate,' would penne alla Dominica be too much to ask for?"

"You're on. And a chilly Sierra Nevada Torpedo will be waiting for you."

"I'll pick up a bottle of wine. I know what you like."

"You certainly do."

AS HE HAD with Arthur Doe, Crawford decided to just show up at the house at 61 Granada Road, now owned by the estate of Wayne Crabb, where Sunny Hedstrom still lived. Mary Beth Hudson had told him that Sunny had until the end of the month to vacate. It was a small, two-story, Spanish-style house that had green shutters and peeling paint in front. Crawford parked on the street, crossed the lawn, and knocked on her door.

A bleached blonde in a polka-dot tank top opened the door and shaded her eyes. She was holding a poodle that was squirming like it wanted to make a run for it.

"Ms. Hedstrom?"

"Yes, who are you?"

Crawford flashed his ID. "Detective Crawford. Palm Beach Police Department."

"This is about Wayne, right?"

He nodded.

"Look, I'm not happy he's dead, but he killed my dog, you know."

"I heard about that, and I'm sorry," Crawford said, smiling at the poodle in her hands. "So, you had two?"

"No, actually, I just got this little guy from the shelter," she said. "A rescue."

The dog was wriggling around like it wanted to be anywhere but in Sunny Hedstrom's arms.

"Cute little fella," Crawford said.

"Let me just put him in his crate," Sunny said. "I'll be right back." She walked away.

A few moments later she was back. "So, I'm guessing that bull dyke Mary-Jane-whatever told you about me coming into Wayne's office loaded for bear."

"Yes, she did," Crawford said. "What did you do after you left Crabb's office yesterday, Ms. Hedstrom?"

She sighed. "I was so pissed, I wanted to kill that guy—" she laughed "—but, don't worry, I didn't. Newspaper said he was killed by a drone with a gun on it, is that true?"

Crawford nodded.

"That's a little above my skill level. If I was going to do it, I'd have just gone into his office and given him both barrels of a shotgun. Not that I own one or anything."

"What did you do?"

She thought for a second and her eyes got misty. She was choking up. "Well, first thing I did was go to a U-Haul place. I got a little box —" she spread her hands "—and put poor Winston in it. Took him up to this little family burial plot up in Palm City and buried him. Wanted him to be near me when my time comes. He was such a lovable little guy."

She looked down as tears slid down her cheeks.

"I'm really sorry about what happened, Ms. Hedstrom." He patted her lightly on the shoulder. "I'm sure your new pup will give you many years of love and enjoyment."

He crossed Sunny Hedstrom off his list.

14

Crawford and Ott were in the office of the attorney Lloyd Bartey, a man with a reputation as a bare-knuckled litigator. Bartey probably could have made O. J.'s legal team, except he would have been only about fifteen at the time. He reminded Crawford of the New England Patriots player, Julian Edelman, both in his looks and the scrappy pugnaciousness of a smaller man who'd spent his life needing to outwit and outmaneuver bigger men. He was no more than five-seven but carried himself as if he were six-three.

Bartey asked the first question, cutting right to the heart of the matter the moment Crawford and Ott sat down in his office.

"You guys suspect one of my clients had something to do with Wayne Crabb's death? Otherwise you wouldn't be here, right?"

How else could Crawford answer?

"Let's say *might have had something to do* with Wayne Crabb's death. Probably a lot of 'em figured Crabb got what he deserved."

Bartey chuckled. "Hey, it's not like they popped champagne and celebrated. But, I mean, the guy was a bad dude. My clients worked hard for the money they entrusted to him."

Crawford nodded. "Even if you had a strong suspicion one of your clients had something to do with what happened to Crabb, you wouldn't tell us, would you?"

"No, I wouldn't. My loyalty's to my clients. Not the Palm Beach Police Department."

Crawford nodded. "Okay, just wanted to make sure where we stood."

"Now you know."

"So, have you met many of these guys before? Your clients on Sabal House?"

"Only two of them in person. One was from China, one was an Iranian."

Ott leaned forward and asked his first question. "So, they both came here?"

Bartey nodded.

"How long ago?"

"The guy from China, about a month ago. The Iranian, just a few days ago, matter of fact."

"Are either of them still around?" Ott asked.

"The Chinese guy left town, but may still be in the States. The Iranian, I'm not sure about."

"What are their names?" Ott asked. "And do you know where the Iranian was staying?"

"Yu Jintao is the guy from China—"

"Spell it, please?"

Bartey did. "Mahmoud Abdi's the Iranian. He was staying at the Hampton Inn near the airport." The lawyer shook his head. "Told me he would have liked to have stayed at the Breakers, but couldn't afford it anymore."

"What exactly were they doing here?" Crawford asked.

"Mahmoud, who's an engineer, told me the 500K he put up was about eighty percent of his net worth. I think he figured that by coming here he might be able to get the money back. Some of it, anyway. I'm not sure why he thought that."

Crawford looked out the window, then his eyes drifted back to Bartey. "So, I'm guessing that meant… confronting Wayne Crabb?"

"Sure, I mean, how else would he do it?" Bartey answered without hesitation.

"And what about—" Ott looked down at the name he had written down "—Yu Jintao? You think he might have come here to try to… have a little chat with Crabb too?"

"Jintao couldn't even have a little chat with me. He spoke about five words of English."

"You said he might still be in the States. Any idea where?"

"He had either a brother or a cousin up in Atlanta he planned to see next, as I recall."

"He still could have confronted Crabb," Ott said.

"Could have, but unlikely," Bartey said. "I mean, what's he gonna do? Show him a note that says, 'I want my money.' It would be like you going over to China—I'm assuming you're not fluent in Mandarin—and trying to twist someone's arm. How do you think that would go?"

Ott nodded.

"Any other investors we should look into?" Crawford asked.

"I'm thinking you're barking up the wrong tree. In my experience, people who get screwed on business deals don't suddenly turn into killers."

"Usually not," Crawford said. "But it happens."

Bartey shrugged. "Okay, but I'd put Jintao and Abdi in the hundred-to-one category."

"Maybe, but we still want to talk with them," Crawford said.

Bartey shrugged again. "If I hear from them, I'll tel' 'em."

"If Abdi's still around, we'd like to talk to him," Crawford said. "You got a cell number for him?"

"Yeah, matter of fact, I do." Bartey pulled out his iPhone and read them a number.

"Well," Crawford said, getting up, "we appreciate your time. Thanks for the information."

"No problem," Bartey said. "Good luck with your investigation."

Crawford nodded, and the men shook hands.

They walked out into a long hallway and up to a bank of elevators.

"You got the lady golf pro now?" Crawford asked.

"Yeah, she's coming up to the station from Delray. Judging from her Facebook page, she's pretty hot."

"Yeah, so?"

"Well, it just always seems to work out that you interview the hotties, and I always get the matronly babes."

Crawford shrugged. "Luck of the draw."

Ott snickered. "No sale, Charlie."

CRAWFORD DROPPED Ott at the station for his interview and grabbed a quick lunch at Green's Pharmacy.

Ott was waiting for him in his office when he returned, banging away on his iPad.

"Whatcha workin' on?" Crawford asked as he walked in.

"Checking out this guy, Merle Bolling."

Crawford sat. "That's the golfer's husband, right?"

"Yeah," Ott said. "He works at a car dealership in Kansas City."

"Got anything else on him?"

"Dude's got a sheet."

"What did he do?"

"Nothing major. Couple misdemeanors. Got into it with a guy over a parking spot, the report says. Beat the shit out of him. In 2017, he got booked for a barroom brawl."

"Anger-management issues, huh?"

"Yeah, seems like it. I got the sense from the wife that she's scared of him."

"Who can blame her?"

Ott nodded. "I saved the best for last. Bolling was *here* when Crabb got droned."

"No shit," Crawford said. "So that's a verb now?"

"Yeah, as in *to drone someone to death*," Ott said. "Then he flew back that afternoon."

"We need to have a conversation with ol' Merle."

"You thinkin' of goin' to Kansas City?"

"I don't know. Pretty flat out right now. I can't see getting away anytime soon."

"So, what did you come up with? The dentist and the guy at the spas?"

Crawford leaned back in his chair and filled Ott in. He was dying to pull off his shoes and show him his Dartmouth green toenails, but he figured Ott would have it all over the stationhouse in five minutes. He didn't need the distraction.

"Let's go down the list and figure out our next few moves," Crawford said.

They did and agreed on a plan of attack:

Ott was going to meet with Levi Singer at either the station or Singer's house up on the north end. Same with Gabriella Dolan—one of the two women who was being sued by Crabb. Ott still had to track her down before he could interview her. They agreed that for now they were going to do nothing further with Arthur Doe, Crabb's dentist son-in-law, and Preston Platt, the Sabal House developer. That left Merle Bolling in Kansas City, Mahmoud Abdi, and Wang Zheng. Crawford told Ott he planned to go back to Heaven the next night, call Merle Bolling—for now, at least—and do what he could to track down Mahmoud Abdi. He had now called Abdi twice at the Hampton Inn and had not connected. He planned to show up at the motel at the crack of dawn tomorrow.

"So, is that everybody?" Crawford asked. "Oh, wait, I forgot the Indian chief."

"Leroy Mack? You got enough to do already. Why don't I add him to my list," Ott said, then, with a grin: "Go see him in his teepee, pass the peace pipe, talk about Custer and shit."

THE TWO MEN broke up a little while later and Ott went back to his cubicle. Crawford read about Merle Bolling's two misdemeanors and tried to find something about the Chinese investor, Yu Jintao, and the Iranian, Mahmoud Abdi, but he couldn't find a thing, beyond the fact that they were both plaintiffs in the suit against Wayne Crabb. He didn't come up with anything on the spa enforcer, Wang Zheng, either, though he planned to call Officer Ireland in Jupiter and see if he knew anything more about the man. He looked at his watch. Spur of the moment, he decided to go to the Hampton Inn and try to track down Mahmoud Abdi now instead of waiting until morning.

On his way, he stopped at ABC Fine Wines & Spirits and got a bottle of Santa Margherita wine. The guys there knew he was a Palm Beach cop and liked to talk shop with him.

"You get the perp who whacked the surfer yet, Charlie?" the skinny, chinless clerk asked.

Crawford thought his name was Earl. "Not yet. You hear anything, let me know."

"Be your C.I., you mean?" Everyone who owned a TV and watched *Law & Order* knew what a C.I. was.

"Yeah," Crawford said, "maybe get a medal from the mayor of Palm Beach."

"Whoopee," said the man with a smile.

Crawford thanked him, walked out, and headed over to the Hampton Inn.

He parked, went to the front desk, identified himself, and said he needed to speak to Abdi. The desk clerk said he couldn't leave but gave Crawford a keycard to Abdi's room. Crawford went to Abdi's door and listened for a TV or other noise inside. Hearing nothing, he opened the door with the key. No Abdi. He did a quick search of the room and found nothing except a Kit Kat bar wrapper on top of the dresser. He walked out of the room, still eager to speak to Abdi.

His work done for the day, he drove over to Dominica's.

What Dominica always did, knowing Crawford liked his Sierra

Nevada Torpedo beer just shy of freezing, was pop one in her freezer fifteen minutes before he was to arrive.

"You're the best," Crawford said, kissing her and exchanging the bottle of Santa Margherita for the Sierra Nevada. He took a long pull. Four ounces or so. *Ah...* it hit the spot.

"So, anything new on Crabb?" she asked.

"Not really. Still got an international line-up of suspects to interview," Crawford said, not in much of a mood to talk shop.

He sat down in his favorite couch. It was made of soft brown leather. He picked up a TV clicker on a side table.

"The *Tank?*" he asked.

They liked to watch *Shark Tank* together.

"Yeah, let's see who Mr. Wonderful is going to humiliate tonight." The show came on the screen.

"I've seen this one before," Crawford said.

"Yeah, me, too," Dominica said. "Wanna watch a movie?"

"Not sure I'm going to last that long."

"Food'll be ready in about fifteen minutes."

"I can't wait," he said, taking another pull on his Sierra.

He put his arm around Dominica. She smiled, and he drew her closer and kissed her.

He pulled back. "I've missed those big, luscious lips of yours."

"They've missed you."

They kissed again. This time it went on for a while and they shifted on the sofa so Crawford was above her.

"Come on. I can't wait," Dominica said as she grabbed his hand and stood up.

"What about—"

"It can wait, we'll do a quickie," she said, giving him that sexy little smile he found totally irresistible.

He stood, slipped his hand under her skirt and grabbed her tight ass.

"Hurry up," she said, taking off her top and tossing it on a chair.

He did the same as he followed her into her bedroom, flipping his shirt onto a chaise. He kicked off his shoes and socks as Dominica stripped to her panties and bra.

She looked down at his bare feet and laughed. "What in God's name…?"

Crawford looked down at his feet. "It's a long story," he said. "You like?"

She was still laughing. "Yeah, I do, but I pictured you as more of a shocking-pink guy."

"What can I say? It's my school's color."

CRAWFORD HAD a plateful of penne alla Dominica in his lap. "You might say we had dessert first."

"You might," Dominica said, "and it was delicious."

15

Crawford and Ott had decidedly different interrogation styles. Ott was more impatient. Less willing to let an interview ramble. A natural "bad-cop" practitioner.

Crawford, on the other hand, found that the unexpected twists and turns of a rambling interview sometimes resulted in case-busting revelations. So he'd let people meander and zig zag, while Ott tended to keep them on a tight course.

Ott had reached Levi Singer the night before and set up an interview. Singer said he was going to his bank on South County not far from the station the next morning and would stop by afterward. Just before ten, Singer walked in. The woman at the desk buzzed Ott and he came out, met Singer, and took him over to the far corner of the reception area.

"I don't have all day," Singer said, sitting.

Ott smiled. "That makes two of us." He took in the tall, one-armed, older man with dyed-black hair who seemed to breathe with difficulty. Why an eighty-eight-year-old man would bother to dye his hair was Ott's first question, but he skipped it and instead asked: "You were acquainted with Wayne Crabb, right, Mr. Singer?"

"Yeah, I had a few business dealings with Wayne, none of them very agreeable. Guy was a total fuckin' scuz bucket."

Whoa. Ott had always assumed that when you reached a certain age you expunged the f-bomb and other foul language from your vocabulary... Apparently not. 'Scuz bucket' was certainly original, but just what in God's name was a scuz bucket anyway, he wondered?

Singer was not done. "Guy was a complete schmendrick, too. Told me I had a deal on this hotel, then reneged. The bastard." So much for speaking well of the dead.

"A schmendrick?"

"Yeah, you know, a schmuck," Singer said, eyeing Ott a little more closely. "I thought with a name like 'Och' you might be Jewish."

Ott shook his head. "It's Ott, and I'm Bavarian. You know, like Otto von Bismarck."

Singer nodded. "Oh, yeah, the Iron Chancellor." Then, like it was an afterthought, "Your people weren't too nice to my people."

They were way off-track now and getting more so by the moment. Crawford might have indulged the disagreeable old miscreant, but Ott had no such intention.

"Mr. Singer, do you have any knowledge about the death of Wayne Crabb?" Then, before Singer could respond, Ott raised a hand to stop him. "Let me cut to the chase. Did you, personally, have anything to do with the death of Wayne Crabb?"

Singer shook his head and smiled for the first time. "You mean, was I the drone pilot who picked him off on his surfboard? Listen, my friend, if I was going to do something to that guy, I'd have done it the old-fashioned way—gone up and put three bullets in his kisser. Why the hell would someone go to all that trouble?"

That was a very good question. One that both Ott and Crawford had, thus far, failed to answer.

"Also," Singer continued, "what was a sixty-year-old guy doing out on a surfboard in the first place?"

Rather than answer, Ott fired off another direct question, even though he already felt sure the octogenarian was probably innocent.

"Where were you between the hours of eleven and twelve o'clock two days ago?"

"At the Palm Beach Country Club. A bunch of us play gin there every day from ten to twelve. We have lunch and a couple shooters, then most of us go home and count sheep on the sofa."

Ott looked at his watch. It was 10:30. "How come you're not there now?"

Singer squeezed off a smile. "When you called last night, I thought it might be more fun coming down here and shootin' the shit. Gets really old playing gin with a bunch of old buzzards in Pampers."

OTT CROSSED the old man off his list, along with Gabriella Dolan a little later. She flounced into the station wearing the shortest skirt and biggest diamond on her finger that Ott had seen since breaking his addiction to *The Real Housewives of Beverly Hills*. She had apparently bounced back from her rocky fling with Wayne Crabb and had little or no concern about the lawsuit he had brought against her. She dismissed it with a swoosh of her hand. "Oh, that's nothing. Carl will take care of it."

When Ott asked her who Carl was, she flashed her ring. "Only the third richest man in Athens."

Ott asked, "Oh, so he's Greek?"

Gabriella looked at him funny. "Greek? Hell no, he's American. From Athens, Georgia. Has a house down here on Australian, too."

The geography was a little confusing, but Ott had no doubt Gabriella was innocent.

Next up was the chief with the un-chief-like name of Leroy Mack. When Ott reached him, the chief said his car was in the shop, so Ott volunteered to come to him.

Royal Palm Beach, on former Seminole Indian hunting grounds, was neither on a beach nor particularly royal.

Leroy Mack lived in a double-wide on Shawbilly Road, just

outside of downtown Royal Palm. The chief began by giving Ott a tour of the kitchen of his trailer. It had a Subzero refrigerator, a Viking stove, and quartz countertops, all of which the chief took obvious pride in.

He was a short man—maybe five-six—with beady, snake-like eyes and an Elvis pompadour hair-do. He wore black jeans and one of those dorky string ties that men who were trying to prove they were either a cowboy or an Indian felt obliged to wear.

"Know who owns the company that made this little beauty?" the chief asked, referring to his trailer.

Ott shrugged. "No clue"

"Warren Buffet. Yup, Clayton Homes is owned by that company of his, Berkshire-Hathaway."

"No kidding."

"Yeah," the chief said with a chuckle. "Pretty sure Warren doesn't live in one, though."

They walked into the living room and the chief pointed at a chair. "Have a seat."

Ott sat as the chief slid into a Barcalounger with twin cup holders and what looked like a gear shift. "So, what do you want to know about Wayne?"

Once again, Ott cut right to it. "Well, first of all, it came to my attention that you threatened to kill him."

"That's bullshit," said the chief. "Where'd you hear that?"

Ott decided not to say he heard it from Crabb's wife. "I heard there were a couple of people there when you said it."

"Look, man, I don't know who's feeding you this bullshit, but at the time Wayne was killed we were still going forward with the deal, trying to make the casino thing happen."

"Really? Way I heard it was you two had busted up your partnership and it was a dead deal."

"Well, now it is, but it wasn't until Wayne got killed," the chief said. "For me, Wayne getting dead was the worst possible thing that could happen."

Ott pondered that for a few moments. Pauses were always good for making interviewees uncomfortable.

"Hey, you don't believe me," the chief blurted out, "talk to the head of the town council in Wellington. Guy's totally against the casino, but he told his lawyer he thought it was going to get voted in."

"How do you know that?"

"A reporter from WPEC overheard him say it," the chief said. "I'll tell you the guy you should be talking to… Ricky Slashpine."

"Who's he?

"Head of the Miccosukee tribe. You ever hear of Buffalo Tiger?"

Ott, scribbling in his leather-bound notebook, looked up with interest. Finally, an Indian with a cool name. "No, who's he?"

"He was the head of the Miccosukees before Ricky."

Ott nodded, writing the second name down.

"Anyway, the Miccosukees own a casino in Miami and were trying to get another one. Slashpine was negotiating with Wayne before me, but it broke down, then Wayne contacted me. The way Ricky told it, Wayne screwed him out of three hundred thousand dollars that was going to local politicians to help make the casino fly. You know, grease the skids."

"Sounds more like grease the palms," Ott said. "In other words, bribes?"

The chief shrugged. "Your words, not mine."

Ott tapped on his chair's arm. "Let me ask you something, chief. Are you sure you didn't contact Crabb when he was dealing with this guy, Slashpine, and offer him a better deal?"

The chief quickly glanced away. "Well," he said after a long pause, "Slashpine and the Miccosukee thing had just about run out of gas. And along I came."

Ott wrote down: "Just like Singer's hotel deal." Leroy Mack's story bore a striking resemblance to Wayne Crabb's sale of the Caribbean hotel, in which he jumped ship from one buyer to another for a higher offer. The buyer in that case, Levi Singer, had assumed he alone was negotiating with Crabb only to get, in real estate jargon, "gazumped" by a higher offer.

"So the thing fell apart with Slashpine. Why are you suggesting that I talk to him?"

"Because, unlike me, he really did threaten to kill Wayne."

"According to who?"

"According to me. Because I was there when he said it. I was meeting with Wayne and I guess Ricky heard about the meeting, so he comes charging into Wayne's office and says he's gonna cut him up into a thousand pieces."

Ott looked up. "Is that an Indian thing?"

The chief laughed. "Not that I know of. Maybe a Slashpine thing."

Next, Ott asked the inevitable 'Where were you between the hours of eleven and twelve?' question.

The answer was as disappointing as Leroy Mack's name. He claimed to be doing a workout with a trainer named Roger, followed by a Zumba class at the Zoo Health Club on Okeechobee Boulevard in Royal Palm Beach.

Mack didn't even seem embarrassed to admit it.

Oh, how the mighty red man had fallen.

16

Crawford woke up with Mahmoud Abdi on his mind. Dominica woke up with sex on her mind. So Crawford, being an accommodating man and a gentleman, let her have her way. Then he quickly dressed and swung by the Dunkin' Donuts—he'd be damned if he'd ever call it just plain Dunkin'—and got his usual—a regular extra-dark coffee and two blueberry donuts.

He had now called Mahmoud Abdi six times at the Hampton Inn and left him five messages. It was hard not to be suspicious of the man. Fortified with caffeine, he returned to the Hampton Inn.

He arrived at 7:15 a.m., stepped up to the reception desk, ID'd himself again, and asked the desk attendant if Abdi was in his room. The woman desk clerk didn't know but volunteered to call him. He asked her instead to make him a copy of the room's keycard.

Once more, he found Abdi's room, put his ear to the door, and listened for signs of life. He thought he heard voices coming from inside. Maybe the TV. He banged hard on the door. "Open up. Police."

The voices stopped, followed by footsteps. He pulled out his Sig Sauer.

"I am opening the door," an accented voice said from inside.

"Open it and come out with your hands up."

"Okay," said the voice, and the door opened.

"Let me see your hands," Crawford said.

A man walked out wearing only pants, hands in the air. "I did not do anything."

Then a boy, ten years old at most, walked out with his hands up. He looked absolutely petrified.

"Okay," Crawford said to them, "you can put your hands down. Are you Mahmoud Abdi?"

"Yes, and my son, Jafar."

The boy still had his hands up. Crawford caught his eye and smiled. "It's okay, Jafar, you can put your hands down."

The boy did.

Then, to Abdi: "Let's go in your room and talk."

Abdi shrugged. "Okay."

Crawford followed the two in, and they turned and faced him. "I have left you many messages, Mr. Abdi. Why didn't you call me back?"

"Because we were up at Disney World. I never got your messages until we got back late last night. I am sorry. I was going to call you back this morning."

Crawford nodded and looked down at the boy. "Did you like Disney World?"

"Oh, yes, it was so cool," the boy said in perfect English. "It was the best place I have ever been in my life."

Crawford had never been there. "That's what everyone says." Then to Abdi, "I'm sorry about this, Mr. Abdi. So, you came to Florida to go to Disney World?"

"Well, I also had some business," Abdi said.

"I see, and I hope that went well?" Crawford probed.

Abdi frowned. "Not so well, actually... but it's okay because Jafar and I had a trip we'll never forget."

"I'm glad to hear that," Crawford said. "But let me ask you a few questions about Wayne Crabb. I know you invested in his Sabal House property."

Abdi sighed deeply and shook his head. "It was the worst decision I ever made."

"I've heard a lot about it." Crawford glanced at Jafar. "Mr. Abdi, do you mind if we go back outside?"

Abdi shook his head. "Not a problem," he said. Then, to Jafar, "I'll be back in a little while. Why don't you just watch TV?"

Jafar smiled and nodded as Crawford followed Abdi out the door.

"This is good right here," Crawford said.

They were standing on an asphalt walkway.

Crawford looked Abdi in the eyes. "I'm just going to ask you one question, Mr. Abdi. Did you have anything to do with the murder of Wayne Crabb?"

Abdi stared back, unblinking. "No, I did not. I have never laid a hand on another man in my entire life."

Crawford had a good track record at spotting liars. He was convinced Abdi was telling the truth.

"Okay, Mr. Abdi, let's go back inside."

Crawford followed Abdi back into his motel room.

Jafar got up and walked over to them.

Crawford leaned down and put out his hand to the boy, who shook it.

"Nice to meet you, Jafar."

"Nice to meet you, too, sir," Jafar said.

Then he shook Abdi's hand. "Well, I hope the rest of your stay is enjoyable. Again, my apologies."

MERLE BOLLING WASN'T NEARLY SO pleasant as Jafar and Mahmoud Abdi.

In fact, he acted insulted that Crawford had even called to ask him questions.

"You're asking me about a murder that took place in Palm Beach?" Bolling said, outraged.

"I'm asking why you came here."

"To see my wife. Got a problem with that?"

"And how long were you here?" Crawford pressed, ignoring the man's aggressive stance.

"Three days."

"And where exactly were you three days ago between eleven and twelve o'clock noon?"

"Look, pal, I resent that question. Maybe you don't know any better, but I'm part owner of a large car dealership here in Kansas City."

Like that had anything at all to do with anything. This was not the first time Crawford had encountered this reaction: The logic was, I'm rich and rich people don't kill people. But was a guy who was "part owner" of a car dealership really rich? And, even if he was, Crawford had plenty of evidence that, yes, in fact, rich people do kill. Then there was being called *pal*... was there anything lower than being called *pal* by a dipshit named Merle?

"I asked you a question. Where were you, Mr. Bolling?"

Long, painful sigh. "My wife and I played golf in the morning. Then we had lunch at Sant Ambroeus." He totally butchered the name of the restaurant, pronouncing it *Saint Am-bro-shush.*

"And where'd you play golf?"

"Mayacoo."

"And are there people at Mayacoo and that restaurant who could say they saw you at those times?"

"Yeah, I guess," he said. "I don't know. Hey, look, I'm getting sick of your questions—"

And Crawford was sick of his attitude.

"Mr. Bolling, we wouldn't be having this conversation if you hadn't threatened a man who is now dead. His name is Wayne Crabb and, as you well know, he sponsored your wife on the tour. Just in case you were going to pretend you didn't know who I was talking about." Crawford refrained from asking why someone else would sponsor his wife... given Bolling's car-dealership millions.

"I knew exactly who you were talking about, Detective. The biggest sleazeball in Florida." Crawford didn't have an accurate, up-to-the-moment count on how many people had called Crabb a sleazeball—or words to that effect—so far. But it was more than three and less than a hundred. Also, by his count, six people had threatened Crabb's life, but that number was sure to rise.

"All right, Mr. Bolling, I'll check your story very carefully. If I find any holes in it, I'll come out there and pay you a visit."

"That'd be great. Maybe I'll hook you up with a nice, new Lincoln Town Car… Or maybe you're more of a Ford Escort kind of guy."

Ouch. It was a not-very-subtle putdown.

"Thanks," Crawford said, patting the wheel of the Crown Vic, "but I've got a nice Crown Victoria I'm pretty attached to."

CRAWFORD LEFT the station at 7:30 and headed up to Stuart. He got to Heaven Nails & Spa at 8:10. A different woman was at the desk this time, but he saw Mimosa at the same station as before and gave her a wave. Her eyes flitted away from his and her posture turned tense.

He spotted a man near the door in the back of the manicure-pedicure area. He started to go toward him but the woman at the desk held up her hand and stopped him. "Can I help you, sir?"

"I need to see Wang Zheng."

The woman's eyes shot to the man in back. "Does he know you?"

"He's about to," Crawford said, pushing past her and walking toward the back.

The woman shouted something in Chinese. Crawford saw the man make his move for the back door. Crawford started running. "Stop! Police!"

The man pushed open the door.

"Stop or I'll shoot," Crawford bluffed, drawing his Sig Sauer to give his threat teeth.

The man did not hesitate but sprinted through the door, Crawford on his heels.

"Stop!" Crawford yelled. "Unless you want a bullet up your ass."

The man stopped but didn't turn toward him.

Crawford's heart was racing. It had been a long time since he'd pulled his Sig twice in the same day. He stepped up to the man, pulling out a set of handcuffs with his other hand.

"Palm Beach Police. Hands behind your back."

The man did as he was told.

Crawford cuffed him. "Wang Zheng?"

The man stiffened but didn't answer. Crawford spun him around and looked into the hard-planed face of an Asian man in his thirties or forties.

"All right, then, we're going to have a little talk in my car."

Crawford marched Zheng past Heaven to the front of Squirrelwood Plaza, where he opened the passenger door for Zheng. He got in and Crawford slammed the door. He walked around to the driver's side and got in.

"So, first question, where's Guan-yin?"

"Guan-yin?"

"Yeah. Lose the dumb act."

A frown cut across Zheng's face. "I don't know. She went away. I don't know where."

It was bluffing time. "Something happened to her and I know you know what."

Zheng shook his head, violently almost. "I don't know. I don't—"

"What about Wayne Crabb?"

Zheng shrugged. "Who is he?"

Crawford shook his head. "I ain't buyin' your act, Zheng."

"I never heard that name."

"And I suppose you know nothing about a drone?"

"A drone? I have no idea what you're talking about."

Crawford looked him in the eyes for a full ten seconds. Zheng didn't blink or look away.

"Don't fuck with me, man. Who hired you? Was it Yu-Jintao?"

"I never heard that name, either."

Crawford eyeballed him again and concluded Zheng would win most staring contests, hands-down.

Crawford's phone rang. He looked at the caller ID. Dominica. He clicked it. "Can I call you back in a few minutes?"

"No!" Dominica almost shouted. "Rose was hit by a car. A hit and run. She's in bad shape."

"Oh, Jesus," Crawford said. "Where is she?"

"Good Sam." The hospital in West Palm Beach.

"I'll be there in twenty minutes." He clicked off, unlocked Wang Zheng's handcuffs, roughly pulled him out of the Crown Vic, and shoved him away from the car. "To be continued."

17

Rose Clarke was unconscious with a tube in her nose, and her face was marshmallow-white when Crawford walked in. Dominica got up from a chair and gave Crawford a kiss.

"She okay?" he asked, out of breath from the run from his car.

"She's got a broken hip, three broken ribs, and a lot of internal bleeding," Dominica said. "But she's gonna make it."

"Thank God," Crawford said. "You know how it happened?"

"It happened in front of her office. Apparently, she was working late, left her office, walked outside, and boom, got hit."

Crawford winced, visualizing the collision in his head. "And the driver just kept going?"

"Yup. It was a good thing another agent from her firm was there. Heard Rose scream."

"Do you have her contact info? The other agent?"

"Yeah, right here," Dominica took out her iPhone. "Rita Butler." She read Rita's number.

"Thanks." Crawford typed it into his phone. "What else do you know?"

"That's about it. Rob Shaw investigated. Didn't find any eyewitnesses, so no description of the car."

"I'm just wondering the obvious: why was a car going fast in Royal Poinciana Plaza? Not like it's a street or anything."

"Yeah, I know, I thought the same thing."

Royal Poinciana Plaza was a high-end shopping strip that had parking on three sides and two lanes around its perimeter for cars driving around it.

"I mean, how fast would someone normally be going?"

Dominica shrugged. "I don't know. Twenty, twenty-five, max?"

A woman in a white coat walked in.

"This is Doctor Yaris. Doctor, Detective Crawford," Dominica introduced them.

"Hi, I'm a friend of Ms. Clarke."

The doctor smiled and shook his head. "Nice to meet you. Your friend's pretty tough."

Crawford smiled. "I could've told you that. How's she gonna be?"

"Too early to tell for sure."

"Do you have any idea when she'll regain consciousness?"

"Impossible to say. Probably best to come back in the morning."

Crawford nodded. "Let me ask you this—judging from her injuries, is there any way to guess how fast the car was going that hit her?"

Yaris glanced over at Dominica. "Your friend asks hard questions." Then back to Crawford. "The short answer is no. The longer answer is that it's all about impact. I think Ms. Clarke may have turned at the last moment, so the car hit her on the hip, which, generally speaking, is better than being hit head-on."

"Got it," Crawford said. "Better not to get hit where your organs are?"

"A bit of an oversimplification, but that's the general idea."

The doctor turned to Rose, leaned over, and studied her face, then took her pulse.

Crawford looked on apprehensively. "So?"

"She's okay. Temperature's normalized," Yaris said, looking back down at Rose, "and the good news is, nothing happened to that beautiful face of hers."

Dominica smiled.

"Well, thank you, doctor," Crawford said.

"You're welcome," she said and walked out.

Crawford stepped to Rose's side and held her hand. Then, he turned to Dominica. "Something tells me she'll still be banging out real estate deals from her hospital bed."

Dominica nodded. "Oh, yeah, no doubt about it. She'll get her assistant to do the showing, and she'll do the rest."

"A little thing like this?" Crawford said, still holding her hand. "Ain't gonna slow her down one little bit."

18

D ominica left Rose's room a little after two in the morning. Before she left, Crawford asked her if she was having any luck with the air-traffic controllers and she said she had a meeting scheduled for the day after next. If they tried to cancel on her again, she said, she planned to show up at the airport, barge in on them, and insist they answer her questions.

At 2:45 a.m., Crawford walked over to Rose's bed and looked down at her. She was still out and hadn't shown any signs of waking up. Her breathing remained regular, which he took to be a good sign. He leaned down and kissed her on the cheek. "I'll see you tomorrow morning," he said, and added, "Feel better, kid."

He drove back to his condo, set his alarm, and conked out in minutes.

Four hours later, he walked into the station. Ott was waiting for him in his office, a big mug of office rotgut in his hand. "I heard about Rose," he said in a concerned voice. "You seen her yet?"

"Yeah, I went to Good Sam soon as I heard."

"How's she doin'?"

"Broken hip. Bunch of broken ribs."

"Jesus. Anything on the driver?"

"Not a damn thing," Crawford said. "I'm going back over in a little while."

"I'll go with you."

Crawford nodded. "We haven't talked about what you found out yesterday."

"Yeah, I know," Ott said. "You come up with anything?"

"Well, our Iranian suspect's in the clear. I don't know about Merle Bolling or the guy from the massage joint."

"Wang Chung?"

"Zheng."

Ott scratched his head. "Who's Wang Chung?"

"A one-hit-wonder British band."

"Oh, right."

"What about you?"

"Well, Levi Singer is one crude old sumbitch, but I ruled him out pretty fast. Gabriella Dolan, too. But then it got interesting. I got one Indian chief, Leroy Mack, telling me another Indian chief named Ricky Slashpine had a real motive."

Ott spent the next ten minutes recounting his conversation with Leroy Mack in the chief's upmarket double-wide. He added that he'd already put in a call to Ricky Slashpine but hadn't heard back yet.

They were interrupted by Chief Norm Rutledge as they were preparing to leave for the hospital. Crawford glanced at his watch. 8:45. This was a first; as far as Crawford could remember, Rutledge had never set foot in the station before 9:00.

Rutledge didn't believe in hellos; he simply barged into Crawford's office. "This Crabb thing made national news, boys. That's not a good thing."

Except for a brief conversation immediately after the murder, this was the first contact Rutledge had made with the detectives since Crabb's death. Crawford was pretty sure the "national news" he was referring to meant the *New York Times*; he'd seen a digital-edition article about the murder the day before. He guessed the only reason it had made the *Times* was because of the unique method of execution.

Crawford glanced over at Ott. He could read what Ott was thinking—that Norm was about to launch into his standard 'this kind of press is really not good for the local tourist trade', or words to that effect.

"In case it's not obvious, boys, we really don't want people thinking we got machine-gun drones flyin' around down here taking out the local citizenry," the chief said. "Fact is, we don't want drones flyin' around period. It's against the law, them in our airspace."

"I didn't hear a question, but is that your way of asking how the case is going?" Crawford asked.

"Hey, look, I know you're on top of it, but catch me up. Whaddaya got?"

Crawford looked at Ott, smiled, and turned back to Rutledge. "Well, let's see, we got Chinese, we got Iranians, we got not one but two Indian chiefs. We got car salesmen, we got real estate developers, we got accountants, we got ex-girlfriends, we got executive assistants, we got mafiosi, we got Triads—" he glanced back at Ott "—I leave anybody out, Mort?"

"You forgot the chick whose dog got hung from the garage door."

Rutledge's face morphed into a bewildered frown. "What?"

"I believe it's 'hanged'," Crawford stage-whispered to his partner. Ott shrugged.

"Then there's the cuckolded wife," Crawford added.

"Though she's not high on our list," Ott said.

Crawford nodded.

"Jesus…" was all Rutledge could come up with.

"No," Ott said. "He's not on it."

"Very funny," said the chief, shaking his head.

"Norm, I want to ask you a favor," Crawford said.

Rutledge's wary look was a combination of squinty eyes and a hardened jaw. "Okay, what is it?"

"Last night, Rose Clarke got run down by a hit-and-run driver."

Rutledge got very serious. "Oh, Christ. Really?"

Crawford nodded. "She's in pretty bad shape. We want to work the case. We'll put in extra hours and won't take a minute away from Crabb."

Rutledge cocked his head to one side. "Is she gonna be all right? I mean, how'd it happen?"

Crawford explained, repeated his request, and once again emphasized that Ott and he would maintain full focus on the Crabb case. Rutledge agreed to let them take the lead on Rose's hit-and-run, then offered Rob Shaw and Ronnie Suarez to back them up on it.

Crawford agreed, though he planned to tell Shaw and Suarez that he and Ott had it covered. Adding another team would be overkill, since—so far, anyway—they had no witnesses to interview and no evidence to examine.

"Okay, thanks, we'll keep you up to speed on both," Crawford said.

Rutledge nodded. "Okay, tell Rose I wish her a speedy recovery."

19

When they walked into Rose's room at Good Samaritan, Ott and Crawford found her conscious. She even had a little color in her face.

"Hey, honey." Crawford went up to her and planted a light kiss on her cheek.

"Hello, boys," she said, mustering a smile but sounding groggy.

"Hey, Rose, how ya doin'?" Ott asked.

"Hi, Mort. Well, all I can say is thank God for morphine, or whatever they got me on."

Crawford got a chair and pulled it over close to Rose. "You look a lot better than you did last night. Any idea how long you're going to be here?"

"The doc said they've got to play it by ear. Thanks for coming last night. Sorry I wasn't a better hostess."

Crawford smiled. "You were as white as a ghost. You feel up to answering some questions about what happened?"

Rose gave a nearly imperceptible nod. "So, you guys'll be on it? Find the son-of-a-bitch who hit me?"

Crawford leaned forward and patted her arm. "Yup. We're on it.

That's the good news. The bad news is, you seem to be our only witness."

Rose smiled. It looked like a painful gesture. "What do you want to know?"

"Go through the whole thing, if you would, step by step," Crawford said. "You were working late at the office, then what?"

Ott took out his leather-bound notebook.

"Okay, so I got up from my desk—"

"What time was this, Rose?" Ott asked.

"Um, eight-fifteen or so… said good night to Rita Butler, another agent, then headed to the front door. I opened it and walked toward my car—"

"Did you see or hear anything at that point?" Crawford asked.

"No."

"And then what?"

"I glanced to my right and suddenly this car was maybe ten feet away, and boom… lights out."

"Do you remember anything else? Like the sound of brakes or a horn, anything at all like that?"

Rose shook her head.

"You don't know what kind of car it was, do you?" Ott asked.

"Sorry, no idea. Just that it was black."

Crawford raised his hand. "What were you wearing when it happened?"

Rose looked over at a chair and pointed. "That red skirt." There was also a silver top with blood on it.

Crawford scratched his head and thought for a moment. "There are two restaurants at the Royal Poinciana Plaza, right? Palm Beach Grille and what's the other one?"

"The Honor Bar," Rose said.

Crawford nodded.

"What are you thinking?" Ott asked.

"Somebody, who maybe had a lot to drink, got in their car a little drunk," Crawford said.

Ott nodded. "Coulda been."

"You're thinking a drunk driver?" Rose asked.

"It's a possibility," Crawford said. "So, you were unconscious immediately?"

"Yes, next thing I remembered was waking up here. No getting lifted onto a stretcher, no ambulance ride, just looking up and seeing the doctor."

"Have you seen cars speeding in the Plaza before?" Ott asked.

Rose thought for a second. "Not really. I'd say drivers take it pretty slow there generally."

"That's what I figured," Crawford said. "Do you know any other businesses there where people work late?"

"Well, let's see, there's that law firm, Alley Maass. Sometimes I see lights on late there. Oh, and the Pilates place stays open some nights."

"What's the name?" Ott asked.

"Squeeze. I go there," Rose said. "And, also, there're two other real estate offices."

Rose gave them the names and Ott wrote it down.

"Has it crossed your mind that this might possibly be intentional?" Crawford asked.

Rose inhaled. "No, I mean… why? Everyone loves me." She smiled. "But seriously, the worst I've ever done is piss someone off over a real estate deal."

"To the point where someone may have felt you cost them big money?"

"Or the entire deal?" Ott asked.

"Let me think about that," Rose said, and she did for a few moments. "You know, it really depends on your perspective."

"What do you mean?"

"Well, like there was a builder from Jupiter who bid on, but didn't get, a house he was going to tear down and build a spec house on," Rose said. "I heard later on he figured he was going to make a million bucks on it."

"Why would he blame that on you?" Crawford asked.

"Because I advised the seller not to take his offer. I didn't like the contingencies he had in his offer. Then along came a nice, clean offer, and the seller took it instead."

"And the builder was pissed?"

"So I heard. Really pissed," Rose said. "So, there were a few things like that. But, hey, all's fair in love and real estate."

Ott chuckled. "Hardly sounds like a reason to run you down. What's this guy's name?"

"Jack Nestor. Nestor Homes."

"I'm still thinking the driver may have been drunk," Crawford said. "Made the snap decision that the last thing he wanted was to deal with cops. Lose his license and get into all kinds of trouble."

Ott nodded.

"So, that's a possibility," Crawford said, patting the arm of his chair. "And I just came up with another angle, too."

"What's that?" Ott asked.

"What if the driver had drugs in the car? Or an illegal weapon. Or… someone else's wife."

Ott nodded. "Plus, he could've been drunk, too. Those would be damned good reasons to beat it out of there."

"Wow," Rose said. "I never thought of half this stuff."

"Ain't your job, girl," Ott said. "Why you think we get the big bucks?"

20

Ricky Slashpine called Ott back while he and Crawford were in Rose's hospital room. Ott, after checking with Crawford, made an appointment for them to meet Slashpine at eleven o'clock at his house in Hallandale Beach, twenty miles north of Miami.

They left Rose after assuring her they'd be in touch if they had any information about the hit-and-run. She thanked them, saying, "Yeah, let me know. I've gotta get the guy to pay my hospital bills. Something tells me it ain't cheap here."

They were headed down to Hallandale Beach now. "What's your read on Slashpine calling back right away?" Crawford asked Ott, who, as was their custom, was at the wheel of their Crown Vic. They had just passed Pompano Beach; next came Fort Lauderdale and after that, Hallandale Beach.

"I was just thinking about that," Ott said. "I can't think of anyone ever calling back who ended up being the perp."

"Yeah, it's pretty rare. There was that one guy, Johnny Cotton, remember? Couple years back. But he was just so damn cocky. Figured he was too smart to ever get caught."

"Oh, yeah, I forgot him," Ott said.

"Have you checked out Slashpine? He have a sheet or anything?"

"Couldn't find much. But the Miccosukees have a very slick website, complete with a logo, history of the tribe, the whole deal. There's a photo of the tribal leaders, too. Five out of six of them being Slashpines."

"Family monopoly, huh?"

"I guess, and the family business is the casino. Not only that, they also have a twenty-seven-hole golf course and country club."

Crawford chuckled. "Now that's a tribe I want to join."

CRAWFORD DID NOT END up eating his words.

Ricky Slashpine lived in a 11,500-square-foot British Colonial stucco mansion with 150 feet of ocean frontage. The casino and golf course had apparently been very good to him.

They walked up the steps of Slashpine's front porch and Ott pressed the doorbell. An older black man in a perfect-fitting suit and well-shined shoes opened the door.

"Gentlemen," the man said in a crisp English accent, "welcome to Whispering Willows."

Crawford glanced around and, sure enough, impressive weeping willow specimens stood on either side of the house.

"Thanks," Crawford said. "Detectives Crawford and Ott to see Mr. Slashpine. He's expecting us."

"Yes, I know," the man said. "I'm Henry Wentworth. If you'll please follow me?"

The man was a central-casting butler if Crawford ever saw one.

Wentworth led them through a massive living room with a sixteen-foot ceiling and dark, English furniture, up to a mahogany door. He knocked on it.

"Yes?" came the voice on the other side.

"Sir, I have the detectives here."

"Come on in, Henry."

Wentworth turned the knob and ushered Crawford and Ott in.

It was an office dominated by framed newspaper and magazine clippings on all four walls. Ricky Slashpine stood up. Though not young, he looked solidly built, extremely fit, in fact. Come to think of it, he looked vaguely familiar, Crawford thought.

"Hey, welcome," Slashpine said, shaking Crawford's hand and then Ott's.

"I'm Detective Crawford."

"Detective Ott," said Ott. He then wagged a finger at Slashpine. "I recognize you. You used to play for the Florida Gators, right?"

Slashpine nodded. "Way back when," he said with a smile.

"Oh, yeah," Crawford said. "Now I remember. Danny Wuerffel was your quarterback, right? But you went by the name 'Slash Pine'."

"Yeah, compliments of my coach. He dropped the Ricky and made Slash my nickname."

Ott nodded. "Perfect for a running back."

"Well, thanks." Slashpine smiled.

"I remember you made the cover of *Sports Illustrated*," Ott said.

Slashpine turned in his chair and pointed to the framed cover on the wall.

"Oh, yeah," Ott said. "And didn't you get married to someone famous?"

Slashpine chuckled. "Yeah, Miss Universe," he said. "Matter of fact, she's in the kitchen right now."

"Wow," Ott said, bending his usual rule about immediately cutting to the chase. "But you never went to the NFL, right?"

Slashpine shook his head. "I got made Chief of the Miccosukees when I was twenty-one. My old man, who was chief, died and there was no getting out of it. I would have rather played ball, but…"

"I never thought of being a chief as a job," said Ott.

"Don't kid yourself," Slashpine said. "It's nonstop."

"Looks like it worked out pretty well for you."

"Yeah, well," Slashpine said, "how can I help you boys? I got an inkling what this is about."

"What's your inkling?" Crawford asked.

"Wayne Crabb."

"You got it," Crawford said. "We heard that you were talking to Wayne about building a casino together on his golf course property in Wellington, but that he ended up going with another tribe."

"Wait a minute," Slashpine interrupted. "First, of all, who'd you get this from?"

"Leroy Mack."

"Well, let me tell you something. Leroy Mack is a liar and a cheat and a conman. Wayne Crabb found that out the hard way and came crawling back to me to do the deal with him. Right after he got screwed by Mack. By the way, for the record, Leroy Mack sure as hell ain't no chief, and I'm not even sure he's an Indian."

"Really?" said Crawford.

"Really. I think he got his chief badge in a Crackerjacks box or something."

Crawford and Ott laughed. "So, as far as the casino—"

"Dead as a door nail," Slashpine said. "But it had nothing to do with me or Crabb; it was the last thing that the town of Wellington wanted. They were never going to pass it. I blame myself for even getting involved and wasting my time on it." He laughed and pointed to his framed diploma. "As a magna cum laude graduate of the University of Florida, I should have known better."

They asked him a few more questions, but it became obvious to Crawford that the chief was not their man. He could tell Ott felt the same way. After closing eight major cases with the man, he could read his partner's body language like a children's book. It was partly the eyes—a little slitty with disappointment—and partly the light toe-tapping, which signaled, 'Come on, let's get outta here,' and partly Ott's faint sigh, which —if he missed the first two signs—said 'This is a dead end,' loud and clear.

"Well, thank you for the information," Crawford said.

"You're welcome."

"I understand you have a golf course in Kendall," Crawford said.

"Sure do," Slashpine said. "Last time I played, I hit six balls in the water."

Crawford held up his hands. "Say no more. I better stay away from it."

"Why's that?"

"'Cause I got a nickname kinda like yours."

"Oh yeah? What is it?"

"Guys where I play call me Splash."

21

"So, what did you think?" Ott asked as he drove up the exit ramp onto I-95 North.

"Same as you. Man's probably a good chief, devoted husband, and I know for a fact, could've been a star in the NFL."

Ott nodded. "Yeah, definitely not our guy. Plus, his alibi seemed rock solid."

Slashpine had told them that his tribe council and he had been meeting with the Miami Chamber of Commerce the morning Crabb died, after which he'd had lunch with several of the members. Ott was going to check it out, but they knew it would stand up.

"Who else famous played for the Gators?" Crawford asked. Ott was a big college football fan, Crawford was only a New York Giants fan.

"Well, let's see. Steve Spurrier way back when—"

"Coach and player?"

"Yup. Then there was Cris Collinsworth, who's an announcer now."

"He was a receiver, right?"

"Started as a QB, actually, but yup. Oh, and Emmitt Smith played there."

Crawford shook his head. "We don't talk about him."

Ott frowned. "Why not?"

"He was a Cowboy. Bitter enemy of my Giants."

"Oh, right. Then there was Tim Tebow. Last thing I heard he was playing Triple A baseball."

"Gotta hand it to the guy," Crawford said. "He never gives up. Hey, what about Burt Reynolds? Didn't he play for them back in the leather-helmet days?"

"Close. He was a Seminole. Running back, just like Slashpine, but he was always getting his knees bunged-up"

"Didn't seem to slow him down in *Smokey and the Bandit*."

Ott chuckled and shook his head at the memory. "One of the greatest movies of all time," he said. "So, what do we do now, hoss? We're kind of running out of suspects. At least viable ones…"

Crawford thought for a moment. "Dominica called me and said she's got a meeting with an air-traffic controller later today."

"Finally, huh?"

"Yeah, she's been on this guy for the last few days."

Ott nodded as he flicked his blinker. "Maybe she'll come up with something."

"Let's hope so," Crawford said. "I'm going to check for security cameras at Royal Poinciana Plaza a little later. There's gotta be something on one of 'em."

"But for now, all we got is a black car, right?"

Crawford nodded. "Yeah, I'm also gonna go to the two restaurants there and ask around. Same with the Pilates place, the law firm there, and the real estate offices."

"You want a hand with any of that?"

"Nah, you stay on Crabb. Gotta be something we've overlooked."

"Yeah, I was thinking I'd try to find out where that Chinese investor on the Sabal House went after he came here. That lawyer Bartey seemed to think he might have gone up to Atlanta."

Crawford nodded. "Also, see what you can find on Weng Zheng, will you? I haven't had a chance yet."

"I'm on it."

"First, though, I'm gonna look into another angle."

"What's that?"

"Well, I was reading some old stories in the *Glossy*, and one of the articles mentioned that Crabb and Platt stiffed a bunch of contractors. For big money. Couple of million, supposedly."

"I see where you're going. Coulda pissed off the contractors big time. Wouldn't be the first time a guy got killed for not paying his bills."

CRAWFORD AND OTT split up when they got to the station. Crawford drove over to the main courthouse on North Dixie in West Palm, where he knew claims paperwork was filed. There was an extensive file on Sabal House. It seemed that at some point Wayne Crabb and Preston Platt had just stopped paying their contractors. There were mechanic's liens from electricians, plumbers, the HVAC contractor, the roofer, and the window company, but the biggest one of all was the concrete and stucco company—L. Singer & Sons Construction.

Crawford rushed out to the wide corridor of the courthouse building and dialed Ott on his cell. Ott picked up after the first ring.

"What do you know about L. Singer & Sons Construction? That's the old guy, Levi, right?"

"Yeah," said Ott. "About ten years ago, Levi moved down here. For tax reasons, I'm guessing. He's got two sons up north who run the hotel business and—I just found out a little while ago—one son here who runs the construction business. He and the old man started it. They specialize in big cement jobs. I think they're either the biggest or second biggest in Palm Beach County. Why you asking?"

"Guess who's the largest creditor on Sabal House?"

"L. Singer?"

"Yup."

Ott fell silent for a moment. "There's a hell of a lot of cement and stucco in that building."

"Try 885,058.32 dollars' worth."

"Holy shit. That's the lien Singer's got on it?"

"Yup."

"Funny how the old man never brought that up."

"Maybe 'cause he's not so involved with the company anymore? Or could be because his son doesn't talk to him about stuff like that?"

"Could be. He seems more into his gin game now than hotels and cement. Want me to go talk to the son?"

"Yeah. Why don't you set it up? Then we both go."

"I'll call him right now. You find anything else at the courthouse?"

"Just that Crabb and Platt owed a lot of people a lot of money. But nothing close to what they owed L. Singer."

"It must be nice…"

"What's that?"

"To stiff all your creditors, then go buy a yacht."

22

Crawford crossed the north bridge from West Palm and took a right into the Royal Poinciana Plaza, where Rose had been hit the night before. It was 3 p.m., and he was hoping some of the same staff working now had been on duty at the Palm Beach Grille and The Honor Bar when Rose was struck during their shifts.

He wasn't exactly sure how he would frame his questions because he wasn't exactly sure what he hoped to find out. Who had left the restaurants drunk and, therefore, might not have seen Rose crossing the street until it was too late? He deemed it unlikely that whoever had hit Rose was in a large group or else someone would have insisted they stop and try to help her. That was his reasoning, anyway, but it wasn't necessarily the case. He figured it was most likely that a single person or a couple was at the wheel. He theorized that if it was a couple, the driver might have overruled the passenger if the passenger insisted the driver stop and face the music.

Crawford started with the maître de at the Palm Beach Grille. He had asked the bartender for the person in charge and was directed to a tall man with sagging shoulders and a Hitler-like mustache named Louis. Crawford approached him in the back of the dining room.

Louis said he had heard and seen nothing and acted like he was extremely busy, even though there were only two tables with customers. Crawford quickly realized he was going to get nothing out of the man. So he directed his questions to two idling waitresses and the bartender, but it was apparent that none of them had anything to offer, either.

Next stop was the restaurant one door down. The Honor Bar served sandwiches and salads as opposed to the full menu of the Grille. It was another place where Crawford had never set foot in. His policy was to avoid restaurants and bars in Palm Beach except as needed for business purposes. He spoke to a few staffers working there, and, although they had heard about the hit-and-run, none had anything helpful to offer. As he was on his way out, though, a man came running up behind him.

"Hey, Detective, hold up."

Crawford turned to see a man, mid-twenties or so, with a sleeve full of tats on his left arm.

The man smiled. "One of my coworkers said you were looking for info about what happened last night. That woman who got hit, I mean."

"Yes, I am. What do you know about it?"

"Me? Nothing. But my girlfriend works at Squeeze. Told me she got off and was heading back to our place when this black car passed her going like a bat out of hell. No one drives like that in the Plaza."

"What's your girlfriend's name?"

"Anna. She's there right now if you want to speak to her."

"Thanks, man, I appreciate it."

"No problem. Hope you catch the guy."

"Thanks."

Crawford walked down to Squeeze, the Pilates place. Inside he saw what, on first glance, looked like a room full of medieval torture machines. Women in various poses and stretching positions were using the complex-looking machines. He had never gotten how Pilates worked. It seemed like it was pretty passive, non-sweaty exercise. But then, both Dominica and Rose swore by it, so what did he know?

A woman in black Nike tights and a tank top came beelining up to Crawford.

"Are you the detective?"

"Yes. Detective Crawford. Anna?"

She nodded. "My boyfriend just called and said you were heading over."

He nodded. "Yes. He said you saw a black car going really fast, around the time a woman was hit last night."

"Yes, I did. The woman, how is she?"

"She got pretty badly injured, but she's going to be all right," Crawford said, taking out his notebook.

Anna put a hand to the side of her head. "Oh, thank God. She's a member here. Rose Clarke. One of the nicest women I've ever met. Anyway, yes, I was at the stop sign, leaving the Plaza, and this black car came up behind me really fast, didn't even stop, just went skidding right onto Cocoanut Row."

"And you didn't hear any kind of a thump sound or anything before? Or the car's engine?"

"Not a thing. Just all of a sudden it was right behind me."

"How fast do you estimate it was going?"

"Well, I don't know for sure, but fast. Maybe forty or forty-five," Anna said. "I wondered afterward why I didn't hear anything."

Crawford wrote something in his notebook. "So, again, just to make sure I got this—you just heard the tires squealing as it skidded onto Cocoanut Row?"

Anna nodded.

"And about what time was this?"

"Umm, right around 8:15," Anna said. "Where is she…? Rose. Do you know?"

"Good Sam," Crawford said. "It was a good thing the hospital was so close."

Anna nodded. Good Samaritan Hospital was no more than a mile away as the crow flies.

"I'm going to send her some flowers."

"I'm sure she'd appreciate that," Crawford said. "So, the driver, did you get a look at him… or her, at all?"

Anna shook her head. "No, sorry, I didn't. Don't know if it was a man or a woman."

"And no license plate number?"

"No, I thought about it too late."

"And the car, do you remember if it was one you had seen in the Plaza before?"

"Sorry, I don't even know what my co-workers drive. You know, we just park and come in."

Crawford nodded. "Well, thank you, and do you remember whether it was an SUV or a car?"

"A regular car."

"And big, little, or did you notice the make or model?"

"Sorry, just medium-sized and black was all I noticed."

Crawford nodded. "Well, thanks, I appreciate it. You've been very helpful," he said, handing her a card. "If you think of anything else, please give me a call."

"I sure will."

"And, if you would, what's your number?"

She gave him a cell number.

"Thanks again," he said, and walked out.

Next, he tried the law firm Alley Maass. The manager hadn't heard about any of the firm's employees seeing or hearing the hit-and-run, but he did say he'd put out an email to contact Crawford if anyone had any information at all. Then Crawford went to the Douglas Elliman and Brown Harris Stevens real estate offices and had similar results.

He drove back to the office, hoping that Ott and Dominica had better luck than he had.

23

Dominica McCarthy had had numerous conversations with an air-traffic controller named Sam at Palm Beach Airport. Her objective was simple—to ascertain whether radar or any other technology had caught footage of a drone launch within a half hour of Wayne Crabb's murder. On the phone, Sam couldn't have been more pleasant, but at the same time, more evasive. She got it: making sure large airplanes didn't crash into each other was a stressful, time-consuming job. But Dominica was as persistent as Sam was evasive; finally, she was sitting across from him at the airport while he was on a break.

"I might have something for you," said Sam, seeing she had no ring on her finger, "but first, how 'bout going out on a date with me?"

Dominica smiled at the man who was an inch or two shorter than her, had badly dyed blonde hair—which was quite possibly a wig—and looked to be nearly her father's age.

She resisted an urge to pat him on the head. "Sorry, but my boyfriend might have a little problem with that." She wasn't sure she could officially call Crawford her boyfriend, or how he'd feel about that, but for the purposes of ducking the man's advance, she was going with it.

Sam sighed. "Your boyfriend's a lucky man."

"Thank you, that's very sweet," Dominica said. "Now can you show me what you found?"

"Sure," he said, motioning her over to a desk. "My coworker went back to the time you told us the drone attack occurred and found absolutely nothing." As Dominica frowned, Sam held up a hand. "But wait. Since Fletcher—that's my coworker—isn't always as observant as ol' eagle eyes—that's me—I took a good hard look myself."

Dominica's frown morphed into a look of hope. "Yes, and?"

"Do you know what ASR-9 is, Dominica?"

She shook her head. "Something to do with radar, right?"

Sam nodded. "Stands for Airport Surveillance Radar, and it monitors and tracks aircraft below 25,000 feet and within roughly forty to sixty miles of an airport. Airplanes show up as blips, moving slowly across the radar screen."

Sam reached into the manila envelope he was holding and pulled out a 9 x 12 black and white blow-up of a photo. He held it up so Dominica could see it.

"I found a really small blip on the screen, barely noticeable, in the same timeframe you mentioned—" he pointed at the blip, then put the photo down and held up another one "—and here's the kicker: it started out very low, headed north from south of Palm Beach. Then it veered out a little, just barely to the ocean—" he pointed at the tiny blip, then he put the photo down and showed her a third one "—and then it disappeared."

The blip was not visible in the third photo.

Dominica leaned forward and her eyes got big. "Oh my God, that's got to be it. What time did it disappear?"

"11:46 a.m."

She pumped her fist. "Exactly when the victim was shot."

Sam shrugged, all false modesty. "Must have been the drone."

Dominica nodded. "Any way of telling exactly where the blip originated?"

"Thought you might ask that," Sam said. "It was going due north when we first picked it up down here—" he held up a fourth photo with a barely discernible blip "—and it was low enough that we could probably assume it launched from the parking lot of one of those condo buildings down in South Palm Beach."

Dominica knew the buildings he was referring to. They were high-rises that ran along the ocean for about a mile. Close to the par-three golf course. "Is it possible to narrow it down a little? I mean, to a specific building?"

Sam beamed like a kid in grade school who knew the answer to a teacher's tough question. He took a photo out of a second manila envelope and pointed. "This is a satellite shot of where the blip originated."

Dominica studied the photo. "So... from the back parking lot of that building."

"Ah-huh."

"And do you know the address of that building?"

Sam nodded and smiled. "Just so happens I do. 3524 Ocean Boulevard. A new seven-story building built a few years ago."

Dominica's first thought was that a new building was likely to have a state-of-the-art security system. She intended to go straight down there.

She thrust out her hand. "Sam, you're the best. I can't thank you enough. Can I stop by and check out that ASR-9 of yours one day?"

"Sure, how about Tuesday afternoon?"

"It's a date," she said. "Well, not exactly... a date."

DOMINICA, Crawford, and Ott were in Crawford's office, huddled around the photos that Sam the air-traffic controller had given her. She now had some of her own, too.

"So, right after meeting with Sam I went down to the building, 3524 Ocean Boulevard, and looked at miles and miles of really boring footage… until this." She showed Crawford and Ott a grainy photo of a man and a woman on what appeared to be a sand dune just to the side of a black-topped parking lot. "This is the best one."

The man, wearing a baseball cap, was glancing up at something—which on closer study appeared to be a drone—maybe ten feet over his head. Both of their faces were blurs. The woman's dark hair was in a ponytail.

Ott patted Dominica on the shoulder. "Good goin'," he said. "Too bad we can't see their faces."

"Is that the best shot you got?" Crawford asked.

"Jeez, Charlie, you got something better?" she said, shooting him a three-quarter stink eye.

"Sorry, I didn't mean it like that," Crawford said, patting her hand. "This is really helpful."

"Yeah," Ott said. "We know it's a couple, not a lone wolf."

"I tried looking at it with a magnifying glass, but it just made it grainier."

Crawford nodded. "We'd have this thing wrapped up if the condo didn't cheap out on their damned security cams."

24

Dominica had just left Crawford's office to go work on the evidence collected in a burglary case.

"Good to know it was a couple," Ott said.

"Yeah, I know, but there are lots of couples in this world," said Crawford.

Crawford and Ott were both eager to interview Levi Singer's son. "The hell with waiting around for a call-back," Crawford said, getting up from behind his desk. "Let's just go to Junior's office, give him the third degree."

Ott stood. "I agree. But it's not Junior, it's Uri."

"Okay, let's go see Uri then."

Ott was already scrolling on his iPhone for the address of L. Singer & Son, LLC. "411 North Congress Avenue," he said.

Ten minutes later they were there. It was a no-frills, one-story, cement-block building with trucks of all shapes and sizes parked in its pot-holed parking lot. They walked into a cavernous office space.

There was no reception desk, but a woman at a desk in front got up and walked toward them. "Hey, guys, can I help you?"

Crawford smiled. "Yes, I'm Detective Crawford and this is my partner, Detective Ott—" Ott nodded. "We'd like to see Uri Singer, please."

She cocked her head. "We don't have a lot of detectives dropping by… can you tell me what you need Uri for?"

"Just some answers to a few questions," Crawford said.

"Oh well, that clears it up," she said with a little laugh. "Questions about what, may I ask?"

"Ms.—"

"Pamela."

A man approached them from the other side of the large space. He wore a blue sports shirt with a large polo player on the breast pocket and tight beige chinos. Crawford glanced at him, and Pamela turned as the man got closer.

"I was trying to find out what these men—"

"Mr. Singer?" Crawford asked.

He nodded.

"I'm Detective Crawford. This is my partner, Detective Ott. We'd like to speak to you."

Singer nodded again. "So, speak."

"It's about the murder of Wayne Crabb four days ago," Crawford said. "We know he owed your company close to a million dollars for work you did at Sabal House and you filed a mechanic's lien against him."

"Yeah, so? Liens like that are filed every day," Singer said, a frown surfacing. "One of your guys hassled my father, right?"

Crawford watched Ott bristle. "I had a nice conversation with your father. He was very cooperative." *Unlike the way you're acting, dumbass,* said Ott's expression. Crawford had gotten really good at reading his partner's face.

"He's eighty-eight years old, you know."

"Yeah, he told me. So?"

"Let's talk about you," Crawford said. "Do you know anything about what happened to Wayne Crabb?"

"Not a goddamn thing—" a little bile in his voice now "—I don't go around killing people who owe me money or else the streets would be littered with bodies." He seemed happy with his turn of phrase. "I'm of the school that believes in letting the system take its course. One day I'll get my money… with interest. Anything else?"

Crawford wasn't warming up to Uri. "Where were you four days ago between the hours of eleven a.m. and noon?"

"Right here, making calls and paying bills." His eyes blinked rapidly. "Why do I get the impression that because I'm Italian and in the cement business you think I'm some goombah who goes around whacking people who owe me money?"

Crawford glanced at Ott and smiled. "First of all, who knew you were Italian?"

"On my mother's side."

"And second, who gives a damn?" Crawford said.

"When someone gets killed in Palm Beach, Mr. Singer," Ott said, "we ask a lot of people questions. That's our job. You make cement, we ask questions."

Uri Singer slowly shook his head. "I don't know, strikes me that we got a little stereotyping thing going on here. Racial profiling. Like maybe you think I go around burying bodies in cement."

Crawford sighed and dialed up his *you're wearin' me out with this shit* look. He turned to Pamela, who was standing next to Singer. "Were you here four days ago between the hours of eleven and twelve?"

She thought for a few moments, then nodded.

"And do you remember Mr. Singer being here between those hours?"

She turned to Singer. "I think you were here all day, right?"

Singer nodded. "Yup. Eight to six, nose to the grindstone."

Crawford realized that even if they both were lying through their teeth, he couldn't prove it. "Okay, Mr. Singer," he said, turning to go. "Thanks for your time."

"So, that's it?"

Crawford turned back. "Ah-huh, 'cause I believe you." He chuckled. "You have a very honest face."

"You mean, for an Italian?"

Crawford took two steps into Singer's space. "Jesus, man, you gotta give this Italian thing a rest. Just so happens, *paesan*, I'm one-quarter Italian myself."

25

O tt turned to Crawford on the way back to the station.

"Since when are you one-quarter Italian?"

"Since never, but I had to shut that asshole up," Crawford said. "Actually, come to think of it, my great grandfather on my mother's side was half Italian, so what's that make me?"

"Fuck if I know," Ott said. "Call Ancestry.com."

"Hey, we're all basically mutts, right?"

Ott chuckled. "Actually, my Bavarian ancestry is pretty damn pure."

"You and Hitler, huh?"

"Achtung, baby," Ott said. "So this mysterious couple launching the drone down south, where do we go with that?"

"That's a good question. I can't see anyone recognizing them with the photos we got."

"Yeah, I agree."

"I mean, I'd show 'em around if I thought it would go somewhere." Ott nodded.

Crawford's cell phone rang.

"Crawford," he answered.

"This is Doctor Moulton at Good Sam Hospital. I was given your name as contact for my patient, Rose Clar—"

"Something happened?" Crawford blurted.

"Ms. Clarke has been stabilized, but an hour ago she began experiencing seizures, convulsions, and cardiopulmonary arrest."

"Jesus, that sounds bad. What the hell happened?" Then to Ott. "Good Sam, floor it." To the doctor, "Is she gonna be all right?"

"She's been stabilized. We don't know the cause yet. We're working on it."

"I'll be there in ten minutes."

"Five," said Ott, who suddenly was doing seventy-five.

"What room, Doctor?"

"Four-Fifteen."

A few minutes later, they ran into the hospital, through the reception area, holding their ID above their heads, and up the stairway to the fourth floor, bypassing the elevator. They raced down the hallway and into Rose's room, where two doctors and two nurses were huddled around Rose's bed.

One of the doctors turned. "Detective Crawford?"

"Yes, and my partner, Detective Ott," he said, out of breath, looking down at Rose. "She okay?"

"Yes," Dr. Moulton said. "As I said, we stabilized her, but, of course, the big question is, what caused it?"

The other doctor turned. "Seems to have nothing to do with the injuries sustained in the hit-and-run. I'm Doctor Crais, by the way."

Crawford nodded to him.

"Do either of you know whether she ever had convulsions or seizures in her medical history?" asked Dr. Moulton.

"Not as far as I know," Crawford said. "Long as I've known her, she's always been really healthy."

"So, no epilepsy or respiratory problems. How 'bout high blood pressure?"

"Again, not that I know of," Crawford said, glancing at Ott.

Ott shook his head.

"Let me ask you all a question," Crawford said. "When you've seen these symptoms before, what usually causes them?"

Moulton looked at the other doctor. "What do you think, Ben?"

"Well, it's usually a condition that the patient has experienced before. Like you mentioned, epilepsy or something."

"But, see, I'm ninety-nine percent sure she's never had anything like that." Crawford turned to Ott. "Can you call Dominica, ask her what she knows about Rose's medical history?"

Ott nodded, walked over to the far corner of the room, and got on his cellphone.

"Going back to my question," Crawford said, "assume Ms. Clarke hasn't shown any of those symptoms in the past. What causes them?"

Moulton put his hand on his chin in The Thinker pose.

A nurse turned to Moulton. "What about poison?"

Crais started nodding. "Yeah, you're right, the symptoms are similar."

"Plus," the nurse said, "when we found her, she said she was really nauseous, her vision was blurry, her lips were all dried out—"

"When did she eat last?" Crawford asked.

"Oh, like four hours ago," the nurse said.

"So, it probably wasn't from something she ate?" Crawford asked.

"Doesn't seem likely," Moulton said.

"Did she have any visitors in the last, say, three hours?" Crawford asked the nurse.

"Not that I'm aware of," the nurse said, "but I haven't been around the whole time."

"Could you ask around?"

The nurse nodded. "Sure, I can check the front desk, too. Visitors would have to register there."

Crawford nodded. "What about… have you seen anybody either in the room or nearby, like an orderly, or anybody you didn't recognize?"

"No, but again, I'll ask around."

"Why, what are you thinking?" Dr. Crais asked.

"I don't know exactly," Crawford said, as Ott walked back into the room.

Crawford glanced over at Ott. "What did you find out?"

"Dominica said she's always been healthy as a horse," Ott said. "Said Rose told her she's never had anything except a broken arm when she was a kid."

Crawford nodded to Ott. "Turns out her symptoms were like someone who got poisoned."

"Really?" Ott glanced around. His eyes lit on something near Rose. "I read this article recently—" Ott looked at the nurse "—you took her off the IV, right?"

The nurse nodded. "She was thrashing around with these convulsions, so we unhooked it."

"Understand," Ott said, walking over to the drip bag. He examined it, turned to Crawford, and lowered his voice. "Article I read was about this nurse in a hospital in Japan who killed all these people by putting disinfectants in one of those." He pointed at the drip bag, then got his nose right up next to it and examined it closely. "Hey, check this out, Charlie."

Crawford took a few steps closer to the bag. Ott pointed.

"Looks like a needle-sized hole in the top," said Crawford.

26

"**S**on-of-a-bitch," Crawford said so softly only Ott could hear him. "This is like out of a bad movie."

"I know," Ott said. "I wonder if someone did it after reading about that thing?"

"You mean the nurse in Japan?"

Ott nodded. "Copycat," he said. "Think there was a similar case in Germany, too."

Crawford turned to the doctors and nurses and raised his voice. "This is a crime scene. We need to speak to everyone who was either in this room or near it in the last three or four hours. We're going to need to bring in crime-scene technicians to examine that—" he pointed at the IV bag "—and dust for fingerprints. Could you relocate Ms. Clarke to another room?"

Moulton nodded. "Absolutely. Whatever you need us to do."

Crais and the nurses nodded.

"Thank you." Crawford turned to Ott. "Get a couple of uniforms up here to guard her room, will you?"

"Will do."

Crawford turned to Moulton. "It's not going to be a problem to move Ms. Clarke, is it?"

"No, no problem at all," Moulton said.

"Okay," Crawford said, turning to Ott. "Let's go check the reception desk. See what they saw, then come back." He turned back to Dr. Moulton. "If you could gather everyone who may have seen something together, we'll be back in fifteen minutes. We need to talk to them."

"Will do," Moulton said.

Crawford and Ott walked over to the stairway, started down the steps, then Crawford stopped and pulled out his cellphone. "I want to get the techs here."

Ott nodded as Crawford dialed. He got someone in the department, made his request, and they continued down the stairs to the ground floor. Then they went over to the reception desk and identified themselves. "Do you have a sign-in for visitors?" he asked, flashing his badge.

The woman at the desk nodded and pointed to a book at the end of the reception desk.

"How long have you been here today?" Crawford asked.

The receptionist raised her eyebrows, then looked him in the eye. "I came on at eleven."

"Good," said Crawford. "So that means you've seen everyone who's come into the hospital and left since that time?"

"Yes, I have."

Crawford nodded and glanced down at the book. "Good… so it says when they arrived and who they visited."

"Oh, sure. Otherwise, anybody could just wander in."

Ott pointed to a name on the log. *Robert Clarke, brother Rose Clarke.*

Crawford was pretty sure that Rose only had a sister, who lived in New York City. "Robert Clarke, do you remember him?"

"Yes, I do, visiting his sister in four-fifteen. How could I forget him?"

"What do you mean?"

"Well, I remember thinking, it's in the high eighties and he comes in wearing long pants, a long-sleeved shirt, a hat and those sunglasses that cover half your face."

"You mean those big protective glasses... look like a shield almost?"

"Yes, exactly," she said. Then, lowering her voice she added, "You see old people wear 'em a lot."

Crawford nodded again. "So, what about the hat? A baseball cap or what?"

"No, it was a hat with a brim. I think they called them bucket hats."

"So, I guess you couldn't see much of his face or hair."

The receptionist nodded.

"How old was he, if you had to guess?"

"Um, maybe thirty-five to forty."

"And race?" Ott asked.

She thought for a second. "White. Caucasian."

"How about height and weight, approximately?"

"Tall. Six-two at least. Maybe around two hundred pounds."

"Any distinguishing features?"

"Like what?"

"Well, like a mustache or a beard, a scar or a mole on his face. Anything at all like that?"

"No mustache and no beard. Sorry, I just can't remember anything else. I mean, he was only here for like fifteen seconds or so."

"Okay, well, thank you," Crawford said, turning to leave. "Oh... did you notice if he was carrying anything?"

"Yes, he had a nice orchid in a vase."

Ott shook his head and exhaled heavily. "What a sweetheart."

"What?" the woman asked.

Ott smiled. "Nothing."

"Well, thanks again," Crawford said, heading toward the stairway.

"You don't believe in elevators anymore?" Ott asked.

"Not in hospitals. They take forever."

Ott shrugged and followed.

"You know that kind of hat? A bucket hat?" Crawford asked, going up the steps.

"Yeah, I call 'em dork hats."

"What?"

"Dorks wear 'em."

Crawford laughed. "But not spiffy dudes like you."

"Never."

"Remind me we need to check all the cameras in the lobby and fourth floor," Crawford said.

Ott nodded.

They got up to the fourth floor and walked to the room Rose had been in. She had already been moved. There were about ten people in the room, including Dr. Moulton, Dr. Crais, and the two nurses from before.

Moulton looked over at Crawford. "As you requested, these are all the people who worked in or near Ms. Clarke's room." He pointed to a short man in an orderly uniform. "Donnie here saw a man walk in this room. I'll let Donnie tell it."

Donnie nodded and took a step forward. "Yeah, so he was a man in long pants, long-sleeved shirt, and a hat."

"A bucket hat, right?" Crawford asked. "And wearing big sunglasses?"

"Yeah, I guess that's what they call it. The hat, I mean. With a brim. But no sunglasses."

Crawford glanced over at a bureau and noticed for the first time an orchid in a long, skinny vase sitting on top of it.

"Did you see him put that vase down?" Crawford asked, pointing at it.

"Yeah, I was just mopping the floor outside. It wasn't like I kept an eye on him," the orderly said. "I mean, I was working."

"I understand. But when you saw him, was he near the IV bag?"

"Well, yeah, he was next to the lady—the patient—and, of course, she was connected to it."

Ott chimed in. "Did you see him *do* anything?"

Donnie shook his head. "I just saw him close to her. Couple times he looked out the door. Saw me, I guess."

"So, was it like he was checking to see if you were watching him, maybe?" Ott asked.

"Now that I think about it, it could have been," Donnie said. "I mean, I heard something happened to the IV bag, right?"

"Yeah, we think so," Ott said. "Do you know how long the man was in here?"

"Not long. I'd say maybe just a couple of minutes. I thought maybe he figured she was sleeping and he didn't want to wake her up. Just drop that orchid and go."

"Thank you, Donnie," Crawford said. "We might need you to describe the man to our sketch artist, if that's all right. Give my partner your name and cell number, please."

Donnie nodded and gave Ott the information.

"Anyone else see this man?" Crawford asked.

A nurse spoke up. "He walked past me in the hallway, but I don't remember much. Just that he was pretty tall."

"How tall would you say?" Crawford asked.

"About your height," she said. "Maybe even an inch or two taller. But he had a hat on so it was hard to be sure."

"So, somewhere between six-three and six-five?" Crawford asked. He was six-three.

"Yes, I'd say that's about right."

"Anybody else get a look at this man?" Ott asked.

The assembled group looked around at each other and shrugged.

"We were all just going about our business," Dr. Moulton said, almost apologetically.

"No worries, we understand," Crawford said. "Can we go see Ms. Clarke, please?"

"Sure, follow me," Dr. Moulton said.

They walked down the hallway and Crawford saw two uniform cops already guarding the door of one of the rooms. One was Ken Bullard, a guy Crawford had worked with before. Crawford recognized the other uniform but didn't know his name. He thought he was pretty new.

"Hey, Ken," he said, then to the other uniform, "Charlie Crawford. Don't think we've met before."

"Andy Lamm," the cop said. "Good to meet you."

Ott said hello, and he and Crawford followed Moulton into the room. A nurse was there.

"How's she doing?" Moulton asked the nurse.

"Good. Her pulse is down, breathing is regular."

"This is Detective Crawford and Detective Ott," Moulton said. "Nurse Larson."

They nodded a greeting.

"She hasn't regained consciousness?" Crawford asked.

"Not yet," the nurse said, "but I expect her to at any moment."

"That's good," Crawford said, then turned to Moulton. "Okay, doc, I guess we've done all we can here. The crime-scene techs should be here shortly. If you could, give them whatever help you can."

"Will do," Moulton said. "I normally get off at six, but I'm happy to stick around."

"Thanks," Crawford said. "We appreciate that."

He walked over to Rose's bed, squeezed her hand softly, and didn't care who saw it.

27

Crawford and Ott spent over an hour checking the hospital cameras for a tall man in a bucket hat with a vase in his hand. They found nothing. Ott conjectured that the man had probably gone out of his was to avoid being detected by the cameras. After that, Crawford dropped Ott at the station.

Then Crawford made a quick stop at his favorite Italian take-out restaurant and went back to Good Samaritan Hospital. Bullard and Lamm were guarding Rose's room.

"How's she doing now?" Crawford asked Bullard.

"She's conscious. Seems all right to me," Bullard said. "Dominica McCarthy was here to see her. Just left a few minutes ago."

"Was McCarthy on duty?" Crawford asked.

"No, Stallings and Goldie are the techs on it. Came right after you left. Dusted for prints, took that drip bag with 'em." Bullard lowered his voice. "Seemed to think it had some bad shit in it."

"Oh yeah, I guarantee you it did," Crawford said. "Did they dust the vase that orchid was in?"

Bullard nodded. "Yes, definitely."

Crawford patted him on the shoulder. "Thanks, man," he said and walked into Rose's room, putting the bag he was carrying behind his back.

Rose looked up and smiled. "I thought I heard you."

He walked over and kissed her on the cheek. "You look a little pale. How you feeling?"

"Like someone tried to poison me," Rose said. "Jesus, Charlie, that was scary."

"Yeah, but don't worry, we're gonna get the guy," Crawford said, taking the bag out from behind his back.

"What's that?" Rose asked.

"Well, after what happened I figured you might not trust hospital food, so I stopped by Renato's—"

"Don't tell me…"

He nodded.

"*Insalata caprese?* Yes!"

"You guessed it." He put the bag on her table and opened the large white container it held. "Your favorite salad, complete with buffalo mozzarella, heirloom tomatoes, basil oil, and balsamic vinaigrette."

"You're the best, Charlie," Rose said. "Give me another kiss."

He leaned over, aiming for her cheek again, but she gave him her lips, which were still parched. After giving the door a peek, Rose reached under the covers and pulled out a bottle of Santa Margherita pinot grigio. "From Dominica," she whispered. "Chilled and complete with corkscrew."

Crawford shook his head forcefully. "You can't mix that with all the drugs in your system."

"I know. I'm going to have it later."

Rose fished around under the sheets and pulled out two plastic wine glasses. "Not very elegant, but they'll get the job done."

Crawford lowered his voice. "Talk about extreme violation of hospital policy," he said. "That Dominica, she's a bad influence."

Rose laughed. "I know. That's why I love her."

Crawford just shook his head.

Rose held up the bottle again. "No reason you can't have a little taste."

He shook his head. "I'm on the job."

Rose laughed. "Such a straight arrow." She put the bottle and plastic glasses under her covers, opened the food container, and took a big bite of the Caprese salad. "Ahh, heaven. Thanks again, Charlie."

"Glad you like it."

She smiled. "Just wish I could wash it down with that wine."

"You're just gonna have to wait," he said. "So, you mind if I ask you a few questions?"

Rose smiled and nodded. "The all-business Charlie I know and love."

"Hey, I want to *get* this guy… bad."

She laughed. "And, trust me, I want you to."

"So, talk to me. Couple people who saw him didn't give me much. Just that he's tall, six-three or more. Nobody got a good look at his face 'cause he was wearing a big hat and those sunglasses that cover half your face."

"Wish I could help you, but I was in dreamland."

"I know you were." He stopped to ponder his first question. "So, Rose, let me put it bluntly. This guy really wants you dead. Who could he possibly be?"

"You don't think I've been searching my brain?" Rose said. "I mean, the hit-and-run could've been an accident, a drunk or something, but this…"

Crawford nodded. "So, the question is, what man, at least six-three, have you ever had a serious run-in with? I mean, something really big that would have gotten a guy to… take extreme risks to kill you."

Rose shrugged. "Does that sound like me? I mean I can guarantee you, I've never done anything to anybody to warrant something like this."

"I hear you. I'm thinking this might be a guy with a screw loose, who you probably did nothing at all to. I'm just struggling to get to first base here."

"I know, I understand. The only one I can think of is the guy in that real estate deal I told you about. He's tall, like your height. I'm sorry, but I just can't see it, though. Only other man who's tall and might be pissed off at me is John Muldoon. You know, the guy you called John the shrink."

Crawford flashed back to six months before when he first met Muldoon at a barbeque at Rose's house. It was Dominica, Rose, John the shrink, and him. John was an odd duck who didn't merit a woman of Rose's class, style, and beauty, and Rose had cut him loose shortly after that.

"John the shrink… you think he could do something like this?" Crawford asked.

Rose thought for a second. "No, not really. And, besides, he's got a white car. A Mercedes station wagon. But he was pretty devastated—his word, not mine—when I told him I wanted to end it."

"He said that? That he was 'devastated'?"

"Yeah, a couple of times, actually."

"What did you say?"

"What could I? Just that I was sorry, but it wasn't meant to be," Rose said. "We were at my house and, man, he completely lost it. Started throwing things. I was scared. He grabbed a lamp and threw it halfway across the room."

"Jesus, you never told me that."

"Never told anybody," Rose said, pulling the wine bottle, corkscrew, and a plastic glass out from under the covers. "Be a love and open this. I just want a thimble full."

"Jesus, Rose, you're incorrigible."

"Hey," Rose said with a smile, "I've had a traumatic couple of days."

"You sure have," Crawford said, reluctantly opening the bottle of wine and pouring it.

"Come on, Charlie, that's half a thimble full."

Crawford laughed. "That's enough. Now tell me where I can find a photo of the real estate guy and John the shrink?"

"John's easy," Rose said, downing the wine. "I have a couple of shots of him on my iPhone. And Jack Nestor, that's the home-builder guy who lost out on the sale. He runs ads with his picture in them. Big dufus smile on his face like he just won the lottery."

"Where's your iPhone?" Crawford asked.

"In my purse over there," Rose said, pointing at a leather bag on a chair.

Crawford went over and fished the iPhone out of the bag. He took it over to Rose. She clicked it on and went to Photos. "Here we go," she said. "I'll forward it to you."

"Thanks," Crawford said. He had his iPad out and was searching for Jack Nestor. "Jack Nestor, Nestor Homes, right?"

"That's him."

"Got it right here."

"What are you going to do with the photos?"

"Show 'em to the woman at the reception desk and an orderly who was on duty when the guy came into your room."

"What if it's neither one of them?" Rose asked.

"Then we got a real mystery on our hands." Crawford shrugged. "The problem is, neither of them gave me much of a description anyway, so I'm not all that hopeful. Gotta start somewhere, though…"

Crawford snapped his fingers.

"What?" Rose asked.

"I just thought that maybe a camera in the parking lot caught the guy. Maybe before he put on the hat and the shades."

Rose nodded. "That would help a lot."

"Sure would."

Crawford heard steps off to the side and turned. It was a nurse. The bottle of wine and the plastic glass were on Rose's table next to the half-eaten Caprese salad. The nurse's face hardened into a stern frown. "Ms. Clarke, what in God's name… you can't drink in the hospital. This is outrageous!"

Rose put her hand up to her mouth and summoned up her most remorseful look. "Oops. I'm sorry."

The nurse, her forehead furrowed, turned to Crawford. "Who are you?"

"Name's Detective Crawford."

"A detective," she said, wagging her finger at Crawford. "I can't believe it, a law enforcement officer letting Ms. Clarke drink wine here, in her condition?"

"Sorry, I—I... thought it was the non-alcohol variety."

She clearly wasn't buying it, but what could she do? Give him a lie-detector test?

"Do you happen to know if Donnie the orderly is still on duty?" Crawford asked the nurse, eager to change the subject.

"Yes, I just saw him a few minutes ago at the end of the hall."

"Thanks," Crawford said, then turned to Rose. "And, thank you, Ms. Clarke, for the valuable information. But, as the nurse said, you really shouldn't be drinking alcoholic beverages."

The nurse nodded enthusiastically, then turned and walked out. Rose was smiling ear-to-ear.

"Nice, Charlie," Rose said with a laugh. "Throw me under the bus."

Crawford put up his hands. "Sorry, but the woman scared me... dead ringer for Nurse Ratched."

28

Donnie the orderly, unfortunately, was not the most observant man around. When Crawford showed him the photo of the builder, Jack Nestor, he said, "Yeah, that could be the guy." That got Crawford psyched until he showed him the photo of John the shrink. "Yeah, that could be the guy, too." Fact was, they didn't look that much alike. Nestor had a dark complexion, John had a light one. Nestor had a pudgy face and crooked teeth, while John had prominent cheekbones and a perfect, white set of chompers.

Next, Crawford went to the receptionist desk. The woman he'd met before was preparing to leave for the day and clearly didn't want to hang around looking at photos of tall men. Still, she took a look and said apologetically, "I really don't know. I just got a quick look at him, and his face and head were pretty much covered up."

Crawford thanked her and was directed to an administrator who showed him where the footage for the parking lot security cameras was stored. He spent an hour and a half going through the footage but couldn't find anything. He concluded that the perp must have parked on the street or somewhere other than the hospital parking lots, then walked in such a way to avoid the exterior cameras.

It was eight o'clock and Crawford was eager to question John the shrink and Jack Nestor, but it would have to wait until the morning. He dialed the hospital from his car and was quickly put through to Rose's room.

"I'm still chuckling about you throwing me under the bus," Rose answered with a laugh.

"Hey, last thing I wanted was a lecture. Where is John the shrink's office? Thought I'd pay him a visit tomorrow."

"It'll cost you. Three hundred bucks for forty minutes."

"No discount for being a friend of yours?"

"Probably charge you double. It's 1501 Presidential Way in West Palm."

Crawford knew the area. It was near his dentist.

"Let me know what happens," Rose said. "And thanks again."

"No prob, Rose."

BEFORE HE CALLED IT A NIGHT, Crawford left a message on the answering machine of Dr. John Muldoon. Rose had shared his number and, much like John himself, the message on the machine came off as odd. "I am not in my office tending to tortured souls at the moment but will return shortly. Please leave a message."

Crawford did so, leaving his cell number. As he drove over the bridge to West Palm, Crawford shook his head at Muldoon's voicemail greeting. How was a patient of his, one who happened to call his number, supposed to react to being referred to as a "tortured soul"? And what if, in fact, that patient didn't have a tortured soul at all, just needed to work out a few kinks in his or her relationship with their spouse? Or was dealing with a bout of low-grade depression? Or felt so lonely that they desperately needed someone to talk things out with?

Crawford was glad Rose had ended things quickly with John Muldoon. He was also glad Muldoon wasn't his shrink. Actually, he didn't have a shrink, but he had gone to one a couple times back in New York when his marriage got shaky. As it happened, those sessions hadn't done much to right their marital ship, which had been taking on water up to the gunnels.

He went to bed and had a dream about a mysterious man in a bucket hat spiking Rose's IV.

29

Crawford called Muldoon again at eight the next morning, having no idea what his schedule was. His sense was that shrinks started late and ended late. But no telling with John the shrink. He got the "tortured soul" voicemail announcement again and asked him to call back. Having heard nothing by 10:30 that morning, he decided to pay a visit to Muldoon's office at 1503 Presidential Way in West Palm. It was in a strip mall but a relatively nice one. Heretofore, Crawford hadn't realized there could be such a thing as a nice strip mall. He'd never seen a parking lot so verdantly landscaped, and the two-story building was sheathed in what looked to be antique, gray barnwood, found more often in Vermont than West Palm Beach. Crawford wondered how the strip mall's owner could charge enough rent in this barely average location to make a profit.

Muldoon's office was on the ground floor and there was a large, yellow Post-It note in the middle of the door that said: *GONE FISHING*. Then, below it: *Just kidding, I have a touch of the flu and won't be in for a day or two. Medical emergencies call-561-349-6222.* Crawford hadn't picked up on just how lame Muldoon's sense of humor was at the barbeque at Rose's house, nor did he have a medical emergency, but he called the number on the Post-It note anyway. Once more, Muldoon didn't answer but his announcement directed callers to dial 911 if they had an emergency.

Sick of the runaround, Crawford called Rose in her hospital room.

"Hello, Charlie," she answered.

"Hey, how ya feeling today?"

"Much better, thanks. I'm trying to get the doctor to let me out of this dump, but you know how they are. Always want to keep you around longer than they need to."

"I hear you. Hey, question. Where does John the shrink live?"

"Somewhere down on Hypoluxo Island. Not sure exactly where."

"Wait. You never went there? Didn't you go out with the guy for a couple of months?"

"Yes, but he always came to my house."

"But that time he got really drunk at your barbeque, Dominica and I took him to some place in El Cid." A section of West Palm Beach.

"Yeah, he said that was a friend's house where he'd crash when he had too much to drink and didn't want to drive all the way to Hypoluxo."

Made sense, Crawford thought. "All right, thanks. I'm trying to track him down. Then I'm going to go talk to Nestor."

"Good luck. Let me know what you find out. Meanwhile, I might have to break out of this place."

"What are you gonna do, tie a bunch of sheets together and shinny down 'em?"

"Yeah, something like that."

He found the address of Dr. John R. Muldoon at 182 Pilson Road and decided to head straight there.

On his way, he flashed back to the Crabb case and had a pang of guilt that he had essentially dumped it on Ott. Ott was good, but with all the suspects that were still out there he'd need to work twenty-four hours a day to make up for Crawford's sabbatical. Crawford knew his partner was putting in probably sixteen to eighteen now and his guilty feelings intensified. Not that that did Ott any good.

It was about a fifteen-minute drive down 95, onto East Ocean Drive, then onto the island of Manalapan. He parked in the large circular driveway of the white two-story Spanish-style house, got out of his car, and pushed the doorbell. A few moments later, a woman came to the door. She looked to be in her early thirties and was medium height, attractive, and had a nice smile.

"Hi, my name is Detective Crawford, Palm Beach Police. I'm looking for Dr. John Muldoon."

A frown zig-zagged across her face. "He doesn't live here anymore," she said simply.

"He did, though, at one point, right?"

"Yes, up until two months ago, when I found out he was having a raging affair. Had a little love nest up by you," she said. "I'm his soon-to-be-ex-wife, Wendy. What's this all about, Detective?"

So, John the shrink was right up there with Wayne Crabb in the dirtbag department.

"I need to ask him some questions."

"Well, I can tell you where I forward his mail to, if that helps," she said, rubbing her forehead like she wanted to erase her frown. "He moved there about a month ago."

"Thanks, that would be very helpful."

She nodded. "It's inside," she said, turning. "It's on Sherwood Street in Delray, but I forget the number. Wait a sec. I'll get it."

No wonder Rose had never been to his house. The jerk's wife had been in residence there. Crawford knew there were a lot of guys in Florida who cheated. A lot of guys everywhere, for that matter. He had read somewhere that two-thirds of the guys on Match.com were married.

Wendy-soon-to-be-John-the-shrink's-ex-wife reappeared with a piece of paper in her hand. "One-forty-seven Sherwood Court," she said.

"Thank you," Crawford said. "I appreciate it."

"You're very welcome," Wendy said. "Do me a favor?"

"What's that?"

Her smile brimmed with restrained fury. "Would you please ask that deadbeat to be so kind as to pay some of the bills I've forwarded to him?"

30

John Muldoon's house in Delray was about fifteen minutes away. Crawford figured it was a rental. As palatial as Wendy Muldoon's house seemed, John's was modest. A one-story yellow ranch on a decent but far from prestigious block. Crawford pushed the doorbell, heard footsteps, then the door opened. Muldoon was dressed in khakis, a cardigan sweater with a geometric pattern on it, and flip-flops with a Nike swoosh. He was handsome in a square jaw, high-cheekbones, big, luminous blue-eyes kind of way, but Crawford had pegged him as a man with a fatal flaw the one and only time he'd met him: he drank way too much, to the point of slurring, getting really loud, and doing everything but tumble into Rose's barbeque pit. That might be okay when you're eighteen, but not in your thirties.

Muldoon didn't seem to recognize him.

"Hey, John, Charlie Crawford, long time no see," he said.

Muldoon snapped his fingers. "I'll be damned. What are you up to, Charlie? Got your message and I was going to call you back," he said.

"I need to ask you a few questions."

"Oh, yeah," he said nervously. "You're a detective. I forgot."

Crawford didn't believe that for a moment. "Did you hear about what happened to Rose Clarke?"

"No," Muldoon said. "As you probably know, Rose and I don't go out anymore. What happened to her?"

"Can I come inside, John? This might take a while."

Muldoon blinked a few times but didn't budge. "It's a real mess inside. Bachelor pad, you know."

Crawford brushed past him, thinking he might be trying to hide something.

Muldoon quickly caught up. "Let's go into the den. It's a little neater."

They went through the living room, which had an open newspaper and a mug on a coffee table. Was that Muldoon's idea of a mess? He quickly ushered Crawford into the den on the far side. "Have a seat," he said, gesturing to a brown chair. Crawford sat and Muldoon chose a chair facing him.

"So, tell me what happened. To Rose, I mean?" he asked, scratching his face.

Jittery, Crawford thought, like maybe he didn't really want to hear the answer to the question.

"Night before last, she got hit by a car. The next day, someone injected her IV bag at Good Sam hospital with some kind of poison, and she had violent convulsions and seizures and nearly a heart attack."

Muldoon put his hand up to his mouth the way a soap opera star might. "Oh my God, that's horrible. Any idea who—" then he shook his head slowly. "Wait a minute, you're not thinking—"

"I talk to a lot of people in the course of an investigation—" standard answer number five "—and I ask them where they were when the crime occurred."

"So, you're asking *me* that? Jesus, Charlie, I loved that woman. Why in God's name would you ever think—?"

"Wednesday night at around seven-forty-five and yesterday at two-thirty, where were you, John?"

"Yesterday at two-thirty, right here. Thought I had the flu and didn't want to give it to my patients. Wednesday night, seeing patients. Want to see my appointment book? I got it right here."

"Yes, I would."

Muldoon stood up and went over to the mahogany desk. He picked up a dark green book sitting on top of the desk and opened it. He brought it over and handed it to Crawford.

It said *7:30 – Wallace Hamrick.* Then *8:15— Penny Schuster.*

Crawford nodded. "You always work that late?"

"Just on Wednesdays and Thursdays. For people who work during the day and can't get away."

Crawford looked again at the names and handed the book back to Muldoon.

"Is Rose okay now?" the shrink asked.

"From what happened in the hospital, yes. From the hit-and-run, no. She's got a broken hip and three broken ribs, plus internal bleeding."

"Oh Jesus, I'm so sorry to hear that. She in the hospital for a long time?"

"She's trying to get out as soon as possible. She's not one to lie around."

Muldoon nodded. "I bet she's itching to get out and do a real estate deal," he said. "Why in God's name would you ever suspect me?"

Crawford decided to answer the question with a question. "How angry were you when she broke up with you?"

"Jesus, you still suspect me, even though I just gave you an iron-clad alibi?"

"People hire other people to do their dirty work all the time."

"I don't know what you want to hear from me. I would never lay a hand on Rose… or hire someone to. How do you even find someone like that?"

"How angry were you when she broke up with you?"

"Angry. Hurt. Sad. I won't lie. I thought we had something really good."

Zinger time. "To this day Rose has no idea you were married. How did you think that was going to fly?"

"I was going to tell her," Muldoon said, back to scratching his face like his fingers were a rake.

"And she was supposed to say, 'Oh, no problem, that's cool'?"

Muldoon shrugged. "Turned out I never found out the answer."

"You mean, 'cause she pulled the plug."

"Yeah, exactly, and I still don't know why she did."

'Cause you have a sketchy sense of humor and get drunk, obnoxious, and totally incoherent? Cause you call your patients 'tortured souls'? 'Cause you wear nerdy cardigan sweaters... And, he was quite sure Rose had a dozen more.

But as far as a suspect went, Muldoon wasn't quite adding up. After all, as Rose had told him, Muldoon drove a white Mercedes station wagon, not a dark sedan, and the man had what appeared to be a solid alibi for both incidents.

Crawford could only hope he'd have better luck with Jack Nestor, because Rose's case was taking considerable time away from the Crabb homicide.

Crawford stood. "Okay, John, I guess that does it. Thank you for the time and hope you get rid of that flu."

"Thanks," Muldoon said, getting to his feet.

Muldoon led Crawford out of the den, then sped up through the living room, like he was rushing Crawford through the space.

Crawford happened to glance to his right and saw the reason why he was doing that.

31

On his way out, Crawford caught a glimpse of the bottom two rows of a wide bookcase in Muldoon's living room. The shelves held a collection of framed photos. On one row were people he didn't know, but on the row above were photos of Rose Clarke. Lots of them. It was almost a shrine. The guy had clearly *not* put Rose in the rearview mirror. It flashed through Crawford's mind to ask Muldoon why he had photos of a woman who had broken up with him three months before, but he decided instead to stow it away in his unfinished-business file. Circle back later if he came up dry on other suspects.

CRAWFORD HAD A HUNCH.

And since he was south of Palm Beach, he decided to see if his hunch went anywhere.

He drove up to the condo at 3524 Ocean Boulevard, where Dominica had gotten the grainy photo of the couple launching the drone from the security camera.

When he got to the building, he saw where the photo had been taken. It was a far back corner of the 3524 parking lot, next to a dune off to the right.

Another condo building loomed up just to the north of it.

He drove back out onto Ocean Boulevard and took an immediate right into the entrance of the building next door to 3524. He saw a sign with the building name and its address: 3528 Ocean Boulevard.

Then he saw what he was looking for—security cameras. Six of them, to be exact, mounted about ten feet up on the building, pointing in all directions. One was pointed in the direction of the building to the south.

He went into the reception area of the building, introduced himself, and asked for the manager.

As Dominica had done two days before, Crawford spent a long time going over the footage of the camera facing south.

Finally, he found something that he hoped might just crack the case.

He dialed Ott's cell phone.

"What's up, Chuck?"

"I'm down at the building just north of where the drone took off," Crawford said. "Just went through security cam footage from a camera facing south—"

"Don't keep me in suspense."

"—I'm looking at the drone couple, still unrecognizable, but the footage shows them getting out of a car—"

"And you can see the license plate?"

"No such luck, but it's a big car—like in the Mercedes, BMW family—and it looks like it's two-toned."

"That helps," Ott said. "But the couple, you're seeing them from a different angle, is there anything else you can make out?"

"No, 'fraid not. Just more grainy footage from pretty far away."

"So you gonna take the footage with you?"

"Yeah, thought I'd get one of the techs to try to enhance it."

"Good idea… so we're making progress."

"Yeah, but too damn slowly."

Next, Crawford called Dominica to see if she could try to enhance the footage. She said she'd give it a shot, then asked, "Why didn't I think of that?"

"What?"

"To go to the building next door."

"Hey, don't kick yourself, you set the whole process in motion."

CRAWFORD'S GUILT about dumping the entire Crabb case on Ott was somewhat assuaged. He still was looking forward to when he could jump back on Crabb full-time.

Next, he drove west to I-95 and forty-five minutes later reached the office of Nestor Homes in Jupiter. Jack Nestor had called him right after he left Muldoon's house. When Crawford told him why he was calling, Nestor tried to dissuade him from coming up. But Crawford insisted on seeing him in person since Nestor was his only other suspect at the moment.

To Crawford's disappointment, Nestor had alibis that seemed even better than Muldoon's. He was speaker at a Rotary Club dinner on Wednesday night from six-thirty to nine and gave Crawford five names and numbers of people who had attended. The next day he was at his son's baseball game up in Vero Beach, which he proved by showing Crawford receipts for lunch at Sonny's BBQ in Vero and from a gas station in Port St. Lucie. Not to mention, Nestor made a convincing show of outrage over Crawford even suspecting him of doing harm to Rose.

Nestor was shaking his head, almost violently. "Come on, man. Yeah, I was pissed off at her 'cause I wanted to get that deal. But, hey, you can't get 'em all. Not only that, Rose is the best broker around. I really didn't want to end up on the wrong side of the woman."

Crawford nodded and wrote in his notebook. *Not my guy.*

"Did she really think I might have had something to do with what happened to her?" Nestor asked, cocking his head.

"No, I asked her about bad blood in the recent past, and she told me about that deal that went sideways. It was my idea to come talk to you."

"Which means you don't have any good suspects yet."

Crawford shrugged and stood. "Thanks for your time." He shook Nestor's hand and walked back out to his car.

CRAWFORD GOT BACK to the station at two that afternoon. Bettina—don't-call-me-Betty—at the reception desk said that Norm Rutledge was looking for him, which was never a good thing. He thanked her and went back to his office. Three minutes later he heard the thudding steps of Rutledge's lead-footed gait.

And then, there he was… in a red, short-sleeved shirt and a white tie with tiny blue polka dots. Not only was the man sartorially splendid but patriotic as well.

"Hey, Norm, little early for the Fourth of July."

It was June,

"Funny," Rutledge said. "What have you been doing all day?"

Crawford had suspected that's what this was about.

Crawford put his feet up on his desk as Rutledge plunked his plentiful ass down in Ott's customary chair. "Had a couple of interviews. Why?"

"What case?"

He wasn't going to lie. "Rose Clarke. You heard the latest, right?"

Rutledge nodded grimly. "Yeah, how's she doin'?"

"She's had a pretty tough go of it."

"Well, give her my best" —*boy, would that make her day!*— "but what about Crabb? I mean, what's goin' on there?"

He had previously brought Rutledge up to speed on the footage Dominica had found.

"I told you about the couple and the drone."

"Yeah, but you couldn't see shit."

Crawford nodded. "So I found some more footage from another camera from a different vantage point. It shows the couple getting out of a big car. Car looks kind of two-toned."

Rutledge raised his hands and his eyes narrowed. "That's it? Could be a two-toned car?" he said. "Shit, man, I saw fifteen two-toned cars on my way to work today."

"You counted?"

"Come on, Crawford. That's a clue?"

"It was a big car. A big luxury car."

Rutledge shook his head. "What's Ott doing?"

"He's been working his ass off on Crabb."

Just then he heard the unmistakable footsteps of Ott. Heavier than Rutledge's but quicker paced.

He looked up and saw Ott stop abruptly, clearly hoping Rutledge hadn't seen him so he could tiptoe back out.

But Rutledge had seen him. "Get your ass in here, Ott."

Ott walked in looking cranky all of a sudden. "You do know that's my chair, Norm."

"I didn't see a 'reserved' sign on it."

Ott sat next to Rutledge and shot Crawford a quick eyeroll that Rutledge couldn't see.

"The subject is Crabb," Rutledge said to Ott. "Whatcha got?"

"We've probably interviewed fifteen possibles. We're getting closer."

Crawford nodded.

"Meaning you ain't got shit."

"No," Crawford said. "Meaning we're going about Crabb the same way we go about every other case."

"Yeah, but you still ain't got shit," Rutledge said to Crawford. "Here's the thing: you spent all day and probably most of yesterday on Rose Clarke. Now, I know she's a good friend of yours, but she ain't dead. It ain't a homicide."

"Why you say 'ain't' so much, Norm?" Ott asked, pure deadpan, as Crawford stifled a laugh. "It's not good English."

"Fuck off."

"Neither is that," Ott added.

"Look, Norm," Crawford said, "as I know I don't need to remind you, we got a pretty good record so far."

"Eleven for eleven," Ott chimed in.

"Thank you, Mort," Crawford continued. "We're just not first-forty-eight guys, you know that—" meaning solving cases in the first forty-eight hours "—but we always get there."

"I'm well aware of your track record, since Ott reminds me about it every two days—"

"I could make it every day."

Rutledge ignored Ott. "The thing is, this one's gone national on us."

"Yeah, I know. *New York Times.*"

"*New York Times, Washington Post, Boston Globe.* Having a drone hitter turned out to be pretty newsworthy."

Ott tapped the edge of Crawford's desk. "I got a new round of interviews lined up. We're on it, man."

Rutledge nodded. Semi-appeased, it seemed. "Hey, you need new recruits, I got 'em. I know you guys like to keep cases to yourselves, but I got plenty of manpower." He glanced over at Ott and stood up. "Here's your seat back."

"Gee, thanks."

"Get it wrapped up by the end of the week, will ya, fellas?"

"Uh, Norm," Ott said. "It's Friday."

"I know," Rutledge said, with a smile. "So, you got the rest of the day."

He walked out the door with a big, fat smile. He didn't usually get the last word.

Crawford lowered his voice. "So, tell me about this 'new round of interviews' you've got lined up."

"Well, I might've exaggerated a little. I just have one."

"With who?"

"Preston and Gina Platt."

Crawford frowned. "Why them?"

"Well, one, they're a couple. And two, Preston Platt has a BMW seven series."

"Two-tone?"

"That I don't know."

Crawford thought for a few moments. "I don't know, Mort, seems a little thin."

"Yeah, well, so's everything else we got," Ott said. "Gina Platt kind of looks like the woman in that photo."

Crawford slowly shook his head. "You mean, because she has long hair?"

"Come on, Charlie, we never ruled those two out."

Crawford shrugged. "Okay, what do we have to lose?"

"Only other couples involved that we know about are the car dealer husband and golfer wife, and Arthur and Lauren Doe, right?"

"I was thinking maybe that guy Zheng and one of the girls from the massage parlor…"

Ott nodded. "Did you ever think that if Zheng's the guy, he could be a lot harder to find the second time?"

"Yeah, I did. Or could've even gone back to China."

"Maybe."

"When do we have the Platts?"

Ott looked at his watch. It was 9:35. "Ten o'clock at his office at Phillips Point."

Crawford's cell phone rang. He looked down. It was Bob Shepley, a uniform cop.

"Hey, Shep. What's up?"

"I just heard something on the PBSO scanner"—Palm Beach Sheriff's Office—"you might want to know about."

"What's that?"

"Airport security arrested two Chinese guys at PBI who appeared to be gang members. They were getting into it with some dude, a Latino gangbanger, supposedly."

"At PBI?" Crawford stared at Ott in disbelief. Palm Beach International Airport was one of the most lily-white airports you'd find anywhere. A lot of old people—slow-moving traffic in madras shorts and black knee socks—half of them shuffling along behind respirator carts. It was hard for Crawford to get his head around a gang duke-out, or really any kind of fight, at PBI.

"The Chinese guys," Crawford asked, "were they coming or going?"

"Going back to the Apple," Shepley said.

"You know when they got down here?" Crawford asked.

"Sorry, that's all I know."

"And they're all in custody?"

"No, they let the Hispanic guy go. Chinese guys are cuffed and in the custody of a couple of uniforms and a TSA guy."

"Tell them we're on our way. Be there in fifteen."

Crawford clicked off. He could see Ott was dying of curiosity.

"What's up?" Ott asked.

"Two Chinese guys had a little disagreement with a Hispanic guy at PBI, got 'emselves arrested."

Ott's eyes got big. "You gotta be kidding," he said, shaking his head. "That's kinda like having a shootout in the middle of Worth Avenue."

"Yeah, I know," Crawford said. "Let's go. You're gonna have to call the Platts and push back our interview."

"I'm on it," Ott said, pulling out his iPhone as they headed for the elevator.

32

The two uniforms and, by now, three TSA officers, were in a small room to the right side of where the car rental agencies were located. Crawford and Ott were directed in by a fourth TSA official, who muttered on the way in, "You ain't gonna believe these fuckin' Chinamen."

Now Crawford could see why airport security assumed the men in custody were gang members. Crawford had seen plenty of gang tats in New York, where he'd worked for sixteen years. Ditto Ott in Cleveland. But he'd never seen anything like these two.

A cop named Murphy, who Crawford had worked with before, made the introductions. "Dude sitting over there," Murphy said, pointing, "goes by the name of Yuen Ko. Short guy standing is Phillip Biao."

Ko had almost every square inch of his face inked up. On his forehead in big red letters was the word, *Gucci*, stretching from one side to the other. Below his left eye were three tear drops, and below the right one, a fierce-looking dragon. From his neck up to his nose was what appeared to be an abstract green, orange, and black mural of God-knows-what. The other guy, Phillip Biao, had the tattooed words

Speak No Evil in an oval, circling his upper lip. Beneath his left eye, his first name was spelled out in a script that looked close to Times New Roman. And across his forehead was a cartoon pig face wearing sunglasses, a cigar butt clenched in the side of his mouth, and a round red splotch on its plump, porcine cheek.

Ott shook his head, bemused. "Nice to meet you, boys," he said, checking out Biao's pig tattoo. "What's the little oinker supposed to signify?"

Biao stared back. "What?"

"Your little piggy."

Biao's expression didn't change. "Peppa Pig."

Ott glanced at Crawford and shrugged. "Peppa Pig?"

Crawford shrugged back. "Can't say I'm familiar with Peppa," he said. "So, where you boys from?"

"Brooklyn, New York," Ko said.

"Whereabouts? Sunset Park?" He knew that to be a traditionally Chinese-American neighborhood.

Looking surprised, Ko nodded.

"I'm from the city," Crawford said. "And how long you been down here?"

"Since last week," Ko said.

"What day?"

"Wednesday."

That was the day before Wayne Crabb was killed. "So, what did you come down for? And don't tell me Disney World."

Ko shifted in his chair and shot Crawford a sober look. "If we were going to Disney World, we would have flown to Orlando."

"So, Lion Country Safari then?" It was Ott's little joke.

"Matter of fact, we did go there," said Biao.

Crawford looked impatient. "Okay, boys, we need to cut to the chase. What were you doing down here?" He addressed Biao.

"My sister's kid got christened on Sunday," Biao said, flicking his head at Ko. "He's never been to the Sunshine State. We wanted to check it out."

Crawford remembered a religion course from long ago at Dartmouth. "Thought you guys were all either atheists or Buddhists."

"No, we got some Christians. Hell, man, even a few Jews."

Ott didn't look entirely sold. "So, you came down on a Wednesday for a Sunday christening. What did you do the rest of the time?"

"Like I said," Biao said, "Went to Lion Country Safari one day."

"What about last Thursday?"

"Drove up to the Everglades and went on one of those hydrofoil things."

"Alligator farm after that," Ko said.

"Oh, yeah," Biao said. "We'd never seen one of those before."

"No gators in China."

"Not that I know of," Ko said.

"All right," Crawford said. "So, your story is you were just doing the tourist thing. Ever hear the name Yu Jintao before?"

They both shook their heads.

"What about Wayne Crabb?"

Ditto.

"Ever flown a drone before?" Crawford asked.

Ko burst out laughing. "What kind of a question is that?"

"Have you?" Ott pressed.

"No," Ko said.

"What was the fight with—" Crawford looked over at Murphy for help "—who'd they have the fight with?"

"Guy from Sureños, we think," Murphy said, referring to a Hispanic gang.

"Yo, bro," Ko said, "if you call that a fight it must be pretty sleepy around here. Dude shoved me, I shoved him back."

"And I didn't do shit," Biao said, holding up his hands.

Murphy shook his head. "There was a lot more to it than just that."

But Crawford could see they didn't have much to work with. "All right. Give the officer here," he pointed to Murphy, "a full schedule of where you went every day, plus your sister's name, her phone number, and the church where the christening took place. Also, your names and phone numbers."

"Already got those, Charlie," Murphy said.

"Okay, good. What's the name of your gang up in Brooklyn, by the way?"

"Gang?" Ko said. "What gang? I got no clue what you're talking about."

"I can find out easily enough."

"Well, knock yourself out, bro. I'm a waiter and he's in the insurance business."

Crawford simply nodded, wondering what customer would take out a homeowner's policy with a guy who had *Speak No Evil* circling his upper lip and a tat of Peppa Pig smoking a stogie on his forehead.

33

"I can't get that guy's face out of my mind," Ott said, as they made the short drive from Palm Beach Airport to Preston Platt's office at Phillips Point.

"Which one? Gucci or Peppa?"

"Gucci," Ott said.

"I hear you," Crawford said. "It's not a look you see around these parts a lot."

Ott chuckled. "The understatement of the year."

Ten minutes later they were sitting in Preston Platt's conference room having parked their Crown Vic at the west garage.

Crawford thanked Platt and his wife for agreeing to meet.

Platt shrugged. "Anything we can do to help law enforcement, right, hon?" he said with a twinge of sarcasm.

"Yes, I guess," said Gina, less than enthusiastically.

Crawford's cell phone rang. He looked down at it and hit the mute button.

He was not optimistic that the interview would go anywhere, primarily because he didn't think Gina and Preston Platt were the perps. In part, he was humoring Ott, but, in part, it was because they were stalled on both cases and he had no better suggestion.

He glanced at Ott. "Okay, then, you want to lead it off, Mort?"

Ott was used to being the follow-up man. He looked caught off-guard.

"Ah, sure," he said. "Might as well just get right to it." He slipped two glossies out of a manila envelope and slid them across the table. "These two people in this photo, they bear a certain resemblance to you two?"

Preston Platt picked up the photo and held it between him and his wife. "You mean because one's a woman and one's a man. I mean, come on, Detective," Platt said. "And where were these taken, from the goddamn moon?"

Gina snickered.

"Are they or are they not you? And your car?" Ott asked.

"They are not," Platt answered.

"No way," Gina said. "What would we be doing out in the middle of nowhere with a—I guess that's a drone, right?"

"Yes," Ott said. "It's a drone and we believe the one used to kill Wayne Crabb."

"Look fellas, I don't know what it's gonna take to convince you, but we had absolutely nothing to do with Wayne's murder. I have never flown a drone in my life and, just for the record, have never even seen one except in a photo." He turned to his wife. "How about you, you ever seen a drone before?"

"On TV, I think. That one the Iranians shot down a while back," Gina said. "Besides, the one thing you don't seem to be understanding is this: Wayne was a friend of ours. He had been to our house and we had been to his. Yes, he and Preston had their differences, but we even had dinner with him and Betsy a couple of months ago."

Crawford's cell phone vibrated in his pocket again. He clicked it off.

"You have a BMW 7 series, right?" Ott-the-dogged asked.

"Yes," Platt said, pointing at the photo, "Is that what you're saying this is? Funny, 'cause it looks like it could be a Lincoln, a Cadillac, a Lexus, a Mercedes, a..." He gave an exaggerated shrug.

Exactly what Crawford had pointed out.

Ott fingered the photo again. "So you're saying, categorically, that this is not you and that's not your BMW?"

Platt groaned theatrically. "That's exactly what we're saying. Plus, this car looks kind of two-tone; ours is solid black."

Ott turned to Crawford. "Anything else, Charlie?"

Crawford had to ask something. He couldn't just leave Ott high and dry.

"Mrs. Platt, we never asked you this, but where were you between the hours of eleven and twelve on June the eighth?"

She sighed impatiently. "I had just gotten home when you two came by right after Wayne was killed," Gina said. "I had been playing croquet at the National Center out on Florida Mango. There was a tournament there. Plenty of eyewitnesses there can confirm that."

Ott had gone from interrogator to notetaker; he scribbled something down in his old notebook.

Once again, Crawford's cell phone vibrated and he clicked it off.

Platt's gaze went from Ott's eyes to Crawford's. "Is that it? 'Cause if not, I've got work to do."

Crawford shrugged. "I think that'll do it. Thanks for your time."

They all shook hands and Crawford and Ott walked out of the conference room, then through the reception area and out into the long corridor.

Ott stopped and turned to Crawford as if he had something momentous to say.

"Well," he said, then after a pause, "that went well."

34

Crawford checked his phone messages as they headed back to the station. They were all from the same number, one he didn't recognize. But only one voicemail had been left.

"This is Mimosa. I was beaten by Wang Zheng. One of the girls told him I told you about him."

That was all she said. Crawford quickly dialed her back.

"Hello…?" she said tentatively.

"Are you all right, Mimosa? It's Detective Crawford. Where are you?"

"In my car. I am going to the emergency room at Stuart Hospital."

"What did Wang Zheng do to you?"

"He beat me on my back and my shoulders. It hurts very much. Also, I was fired by Meifeng, the owner of Heaven."

"You're kidding. Why?"

"I think because Wang Zheng told her to."

"Are you going to be able to get to the hospital by yourself?"

"Yes, I'm almost there. But after that I have nowhere to go."

"Do you have any money?"

"About forty dollars."

It crossed Crawford's mind to let her sleep on the couch at his condo. But the bigger issue was that she'd run out of money in no time at all. Then he had another idea. He started to ask her if she had medical insurance, but he already knew the answer.

"I want you to call me after you've been examined at the hospital and let me know how you are, okay?" he said. "I'll come see you."

"Okay, Detective Crawford. Thank you."

"Call me Charlie."

"Okay, Charlie."

CRAWFORD TOLD Ott about his conversation with Mimosa. In the course of discussing it, the detectives had widely diverging ideas about how to proceed with her situation. After further discussion, they decided to go with the plan Ott had come up with, which involved purchasing a certain item. The problem was, neither one of them knew where it was sold. With Ott at the wheel, Crawford summoned up Google and found that what they were looking for was sold at Walmart. Not a big surprise, since the big-box chain sold most everything.

Ott took a U-turn on South County and headed to the Walmart on 45th Street in West Palm Beach. Ott pulled up in front of the store fifteen minutes later, and Crawford went in and shelled out $6.88 plus tax for the item they needed. While he was in line, he also picked up a copy of *Golf* magazine with Ricky Fowler on the cover.

"You get it?" Ott asked as Crawford opened the door.

"Yup," he said, and he flashed him the magazine. "This, too."

"Jesus, Charlie, *Golf?*" Ott said, irritably. "You could've at least gotten a *Playboy* or something."

"Got bad news for you, Mort. Walmart is a wholesome, family-oriented, god-fearing kind of store. They don't sell *Playboy*."

"Okay." Ott dead-panned. "Well, how 'bout *Penthouse?*"

THEY PULLED into the Squirrelwood strip mall in Stuart half an hour later, and Ott drove around to the back.

Crawford pointed. "That's the back door of the place. You stay here and I'll go in. If he's here, he'll probably exit there."

Ott nodded. "I'll trip the guy on his way out," Ott said, smiling, then had an afterthought. "Or maybe just shoot the fucker."

"No, man, save him for the fun we talked about."

Ott nodded as Crawford got out of the car and walked around to the front of Heaven.

Crawford found the same woman at the front desk as last time. He guessed she was Meifeng, the owner, and probably the person who'd tipped Wang Zheng. This time she shouted one word loudly as Crawford glanced at Mimosa's empty chair. Much like before, he heard running footsteps in the back room. He hurried back and saw Wang Zheng exit the back door, followed by what sounded like a cry of pain. He got to the door and saw Ott standing over Wang Zheng, who was prone with his hands behind his back and being cuffed.

"What did you do?" Crawford asked.

"Just like I said: I stuck out my foot," Ott said. "Dumb bastard did a perfect chin slide."

Crawford glanced down at Wang Zheng, now cuffed. "We got some unfinished business."

"I don't know what you're talking about."

"You say that a lot," Crawford said. "See no evil, hear no evil… it's getting old. So I'm gonna tell you exactly what we're talking about—one is a man named Yu Jintao, who you claim not to know. The other's name is Mimosa, who I *know* you know."

Wang Zheng turned his head to the right so his left cheek was on the ground. Blood was streaming from his chin. "That girl was fired," he gritted through his teeth. "I had nothing to do with it."

"That girl is in the hospital now and you had everything to do with *that*," Crawford said. "Now get the hell up."

"Yeah," Ott said, giving him a kick in the side. "We've got a delicate operation to conduct."

Slowly, Wang Zheng got to his feet. "What are you saying?"

"You'll find out," Ott said.

Wang Zheng's expression changed to a look of fear, the fear of not knowing what was going to happen next.

Ott put a hand on Zheng's shoulder, led him over to the rear right door of the Vic, opened it, shoved his head down, and pushed him inside. "We're gonna take a little ride," he said. "From Heaven… to hell."

Ott went around to the driver's side and got in, while Crawford slid into the passenger seat.

Ott started the car and exited the parking lot.

"We thought we'd go some place where nobody can hear you," Crawford said.

"What do you mean, 'hear me'?"

"You know," Ott said, "when you start to cry."

"And scream," Crawford added.

35

As Ott drove away from the strip mall, Crawford glanced back at Wang Zheng in the rearview mirror. The massage parlor enforcer now had a look of abject fear on his face. They'd gotten into his head.

"Where are you taking me?" he asked in an urgent tone.

Neither Crawford nor Ott answered this time as Ott took a right onto a pot-holed street. They ended up in a section of Stuart called Krueger Creek, where they found a dirt road that cut through marshland with not a house in sight.

"Not likely to find any eyewitnesses in this neck of the woods," Crawford said.

"Unless you count gators and cottonmouths," said Ott.

"I was thinking," Crawford said, "we don't want to get any blood on the back seat."

"Got you covered," Ott said. "I threw a drop cloth in the trunk."

"Good thinking. Plastic?"

"Yeah. Or nylon, maybe. More like a tarp, I guess. No blood's gonna get through it."

Crawford glanced back at Zheng in the rearview mirror. Beads of sweat dotted his forehead, even though Ott had the A/C cranked. His chin abrasion had stopped bleeding, but it looked pretty painful.

"You can pull over anywhere," Crawford said. "We're far enough off the road where we won't get seen if anyone comes along."

Ott nodded and applied the brakes. "You got something to gag him with?"

"Yeah, roll of duct tape in back."

Crawford turned back to Zheng. "You know, I was reading about great Chinese inventions once and the list is pretty impressive. I mean, paper, the compass, gunpowder—"

"What about the drone? They come up with that?"

"No, I checked. Believe it or not, it was the inventor Nicola Tesla. Or, at least, he had something to do with it back in the early 1900s. Another invention from China—you probably know all about this one, Wang—" he turned around in his seat "— is death by a thousand cuts."

"Ah, yes," Ott said. "Good old *lingchi*."

Crawford put his hand in the bag from Walmart and pulled out two disposable scalpels. One had a pointed end to it, the other more rounded.

Ott glanced over. "Jesus, those suckers look sharp as hell."

Sweat was rolling down Zheng's cheeks now.

"So, what we're going to do, Wang—you don't mind if I call you Wang, do you—" he didn't wait for an answer "— is nick you up a little with this little beauty. Maybe it'll kill you, maybe not. Point is to get some answers out of you."

"You can't do that. You're cops!" Zheng cried, his voice carrying the shrill tone of panic.

"Jesus," Ott said. "You've got a good set of lungs on you, bro. Better tape him up, Charlie."

"I will," Crawford said, then to Zheng. "And, to answer you: yeah, we're cops, and because we are, we can do any damn thing we please."

Crawford got out of the car and went around to the back as Ott hit the trunk opener. Crawford reached in and got the roll of duct tape. There was no drop cloth back there. Ott had made that up. He walked around and opened the back door. Ott opened the other door, the razor-sharp blade in hand.

"Don't fight the man, Wang," Crawford said, brandishing the duct tape, "or he'll slice open your femoral artery and be done quick."

Zheng's eyes were bulging at the sight of Ott's scalpel. He didn't move as Crawford used his teeth to tear off a piece of duct tape, and put it over Zheng's mouth.

Crawford bent down and yanked off one of Zheng's slip-on black shoes. Then he took off Zheng's sock as panic welled in the man's eyes. He tried to yell but it came out muffled.

"We heard from our *lingchi* expert that a good place to start is a toe. You won't miss one of those little ones." Crawford looked up at Ott on the other side of Zheng. "You want to do the honors?"

"How 'bout we both do one?" Ott said.

"Sounds like a plan," Crawford said. "But before I do, I'm going to ask you a question, Wang. And if you answer it truthfully, maybe we only cut off one."

"Aw, come on, man. I want to do one, too," Ott said.

"Don't worry, you can go first," Crawford said. "So, the question is —one more time—do you know Yu Jintao? Yes or no. A simple nod will do."

Zheng shook his head violently, from side to side.

"Okay, I'll take that as a 'no,'" Crawford said, then glanced at Ott. "You believe him, Mort?"

"I don't know," Ott said. "The guy's pretty shifty looking."

Crawford nodded. "I'm thinking that's just his look." Then, turning to Zheng, he said, "And you don't know anything about a drone with a gun attached to it, right?"

Again, the violent headshake.

"But you *do* know about beating that woman, Mimosa," Ott said. "Don't you?"

Ott peeled off a corner of the duct tape covering Zheng's mouth as Crawford took a voice-activated pocket recorder out of his pocket.

Ott held the Walmart blade inches from Zheng's eye. "I'll ask you again… you beat that woman, Mimosa, didn't you?"

"Hang on, Mort, we forgot something," Crawford said. It was something Crawford had memorized a long time ago. "You have the right to remain silent. Anything you say can and will be used against you in a court of law. You have the right to an attorney. If you cannot afford an attorney, one will be provided for you. Do you understand the right I have just read to you? With these rights in mind, do you wish to speak to me?"

Zheng was silent.

"Well, do you?" Ott snapped.

Zheng, looking terrified, nodded.

"In words," Ott said.

"Yes," Zheng said.

Crawford switched on the recorder.

"Tell us what you did to Mimosa."

"I beat her."

"Who?"

"Mimosa."

"Okay now put it all together in a sentence."

"I beat the woman, Mimosa."

"And put her in the hospital," Crawford said.

"I don't know about that."

"Trust me," said Crawford. "You did. Say it."

"I beat the woman Mimosa and put her in the hospital."

"And add to that, 'This was not a coerced confession. I am admitting this because I had a… guilty conscience.'"

"This was not a coerced…"

"'Confession. I am admitting this because I had a guilty conscience.' Say the whole thing like you mean it."

"This was not a coerced… confession. I am admitting this because I had a guilty conscience.'"

"Very good," Crawford said.

Ott gave Zheng a thumbs-up. "You just saved a few tootsies there, bro."

36

Before they took Wang Zheng to the Stuart police station on M.L.K Boulevard, Crawford slipped Zheng's wallet out of the man's back pocket. He had a little over $200 in cash in it. Crawford left him a dollar.

"The rest of this is going to Mimosa," he said to Zheng. "It hardly makes up for what you did to her, but it's a start. Doing some hard time for assault will help, too."

They dropped him off and told the deputy chief there what Zheng had done, then played him the confession and said the victim was at Stuart Hospital, where they could take her testimony. That's when Zheng suddenly changed his tune, denying everything and telling the deputy chief that Crawford had threatened to cut off his toes with a scalpel if he didn't confess.

"That's a new one," the deputy chief, whose name was Mike Falco, said to Crawford and Ott. "What's this guy talking about?"

Ott had tossed the scalpel, its packaging, and the roll of duct tape into a dumpster several blocks from the police station after bringing Zheng in.

"No clue," Crawford said with a shrug. "We don't make a habit of going around and cutting off perps' toes."

"Yeah," Ott said. "Check our car if you want. See if you find any toes from past vics lying around."

One trait Crawford and Ott shared was they could play dumb very convincingly when the situation called for it.

Falco nodded and glanced over at a Stuart uniform cop who was in the room. "Okay, Mr. Zheng, we're going to give you the full benefit of the law to see if your story stands up. Marty, go check every square inch of their car... see if you find a scalpel."

Falco glanced over at Crawford with a bemused look. "I've never had a perp confess because his conscience got the better of him."

"Yeah, I know," Crawford said. "That was a first for us, too."

Long story short, no scalpel was found and Wang Zheng was dispatched to a jail cell.

Crawford and Ott headed back down to Palm Beach, got to the station, and went their separate ways. Shortly after Crawford got to his office, Dominica came by.

"I just wanted to see if that new photo of yours—the couple with the car—went anywhere."

Crawford recounted their meeting with Gina and Preston Platt and how nothing had come of it, but he said there were a few more couples he wanted to confront with the photo. Then he told her about Mimosa and that he planned to stop by Stuart Hospital and visit her later.

"You're spending a lot of time in hospitals these days," she said.

He nodded. "I know. But I don't think this poor woman has any family or anything. Not to mention a roof over her head. She said she has forty bucks to her name."

Dominica thought for a second. "I could help with that. Put her up for a while, I mean." Dominica had a second bedroom in her condo.

"You sure you want to do that? You okay with a perfect stranger coming and going?"

"Not forever, but for a while. I can also check my nail place and see if they're hiring. I've seen she does good work," Dominica said with a downward glance at Crawford's hidden green toenails.

"Really good work… woman can paint like nobody's business."

Dominica got to her feet. "Well, I've got to take care of a few things. When do you think you'll head up there?"

"After I return a few calls. Say, in an hour or so. Wanna drop by and see Rose first?"

"Sounds good. But I got the word… No. More. Wine."

"GLAD TO SEE you didn't tie those sheets together," Crawford said to Rose, who was propped up in her hospital bed, reading a paperback.

He noticed the room's side table was covered with vases full of flowers.

"I got a stern lecture from Doctor Moulton about mixing wine with morphine." Rose smiled at Dominica. "You're a bad influence."

Dominica laughed. "You seemed pretty happy when I showed up with it."

'So, Rose," Crawford said, "we need to talk shop. I interviewed both Muldoon and Nestor and they both have solid alibis. Well, actually, I'm still checking Muldoon's." He had put calls into Muldoon's two Wednesday night patients but hadn't yet heard back from either. "I know I keep asking the same question, but is there anyone else you can think of?"

Rose shook her head. "I've gone back as far as high school and nothing. Except maybe my date at senior prom who I didn't put out for."

"No other businesspeople? Nobody at all?"

Rose shook her head. "Most of my real estate deals have good endings."

Crawford nodded, frustrated. Usually, as in the Crabb case, he had to sift his way through a multitude of suspects. Rose's hit-and-run seemed to involve so few.

"When are you getting out?" Dominica asked.

"Couple days, I hope. I'm gonna be hobbling around on crutches for a while," Rose said.

"Well, if you need anything in the meantime, just let me know," Dominica said. "I'm happy to get whatever you want."

Rose smiled. "You're a pal."

"All right," Crawford said. "Since you're no help, it's time to go see our next patient."

Rose raised her eyebrows in question, so Crawford gave her a quick rundown of the Mimosa case. Then he and Dominica left.

Forty-five minutes later, they were in another hospital room, one quite different from Rose's. It was bare bones and had only a modicum of decor. As for Mimosa, she looked pretty bad. Her face was purpled with bruises, and she had two black eyes. Her lips and one cheekbone had been lacerated pretty badly. But, fortunately, nothing was broken, and Mimosa stoically assured Crawford that she looked worse than she felt.

Crawford gave her the expurgated version of their arrest of Wang Zheng, leaving out the scalpel and simply saying that Zheng had confessed.

"Oh, also," Crawford said, reaching into his pocket and taking out a wad of twenties, "this is from Zheng."

He handed it to Mimosa, but she was wary.

"Take it," he said. "It's the least he could do."

It was Dominica's turn. "Mimosa, you don't know me, but I work with the police, like Charlie here. When you get out of here, I'd like to have you come stay at my condo in West Palm Beach. I have an extra bed and bathroom nobody ever uses."

Mimosa mustered a pained smile. "That is so kind of you." She held up the money Crawford had just given her. "I can pay you."

Dominica laughed. "That's not necessary. Also, I go to a place called Avalon Nails in West Palm. They might be able to use you."

She smiled again. "Thank you so much. I need to work."

"And if not there," Dominica said, leaning over and patting her arm, "there are lots of other places."

"I so much appreciate it."

Dominica winked. "You can give me a freebie on my nails every once in a while."

Mimosa nodded. "Every day if you want." She managed another painful grin. "On the house."

37

From day one, Crawford had been going over Wayne Crabb's emails and texts. It was slow, painstaking work because the man was a prodigious emailer and didn't seem to believe in brevity. If something could be said in a sentence, Crawford found, the man would write a long, rambling paragraph. His emails were a mix of business and pleasure—the latter being to and from girlfriends. Usually those messages involved setting up trysts with women at one of the houses he owned or on his yacht. In one week, Crawford found that Crabb visited a different woman every single day. He wondered how in God's name Crabb could keep all the women's names straight, then realized that their names hadn't been of much consequence to Crabb.

He hadn't found anything helpful to the case in the first three years of emails and texts and was now looking at those from four years ago.

As he skimmed the emails, he found one from Preston Platt to Crabb that immediately caught his attention. "Buying Gina things is one thing, taking her out for dinner is another, but now you've crossed the line and you're going to pay."

Wow, Crawford thought. This one seemed like a possible game

changer. He read it over again. There was no other way to interpret the message: it was a threat.

So, the immediate question was, what did 'you're going to pay' mean? Was Platt talking about money or something way more costly? And, second, had this been resolved four years ago or only a few days ago? If Platt did mean Crabb's life and he was the killer, then it sure had taken him a long time to get around to it. Whatever the case, it required another conversation with Preston Platt, this time without Gina. He could already hear Platt: *Come on, not again, how many times are you guys gonna hassle me?*

But first, Crawford wanted to confirm that John Muldoon had met with patients last Wednesday night. He called Wallace Hamrick again, got the same recording as before, and asked him to call back right away. Then he called Penny Schuster and a woman answered. He knew he might be tip-toeing over the line between patient-doctor confidentiality, but he didn't know any other way of getting the facts he needed.

"Ms. Schuster?"

"Yes, who's this?"

"My name is Detective Crawford, Palm Beach Police."

"Oh, yes, I was going to call you back. What's this about?"

"I have just one question for you, ma'am. I know you were scheduled to meet Dr. John Muldoon this past Wednesday. I just wanted to confirm that you did in fact meet with him at that time?"

"No, he canceled it."

Crawford pressed the phone to his ear. "He canceled it. So, you… you never met him Wednesday night."

"No, he said he had the flu and couldn't see me."

"Thank you very much, Ms. Schuster. I really appreciate it."

"You're welcome."

He clicked off and thought for a few minutes, pondering his next move. The first problem was that John Muldoon drove a white Mercedes station wagon, not a black car. He could have rented a black car, of course. Or…

Crawford dialed a number.

"Hello?"

"Mrs. Muldoon?"

"Yes."

"It's Detective Crawford, Palm Beach Police. What kind of car does your ex-husband drive?"

"Well, he's not my ex-husband yet, unfortunately, but he traded in his Mercedes for one of those electric cars."

Electric cars… as in cars whose engines were silent. No wonder Rose never heard it coming. Nor did Anna at the Pilates place.

"And it's black, right?"

"Yup. Sure is."

"Is it a Tesla, do you know?"

"Yes, that's exactly what it is. I couldn't remember the name."

"Thanks, Ms. Muldoon, that's all I need to know." He clicked off and slapped his desk with his open hand. "Yes!"

Two minutes later, Crawford was in the Crown Vic, headed to John Muldoon's house in Hypoluxo Island.

He dialed Ott on his cellphone.

"Yeah, Charlie?"

"One down, one to go,"

"What do you mean?"

Crawford skipped all the background details. "John Muldoon's driving a black Tesla these days, not a white Mercedes, and his alibi for Wednesday night was bogus."

"No shit. Where are you?"

"On my way to his house in Hypoluxo."

"You need me?"

"No, go crack the Crabb case. Got something for you that might help make that happen." Crawford filled Ott in on the threatening email from Preston Platt to Crabb. Aside from saying, "no shit" over and over, Ott thanked him and said, "I never liked that little gerbil, Platt, in the first place."

It occurred to Crawford halfway to Hypoluxo that Muldoon knew it was only a matter of time before Crawford found out his alibi didn't hold up. Or, on the other hand, maybe Muldoon figured Crawford would never check it.

He got to Muldoon's house at 10:45 that morning and the first thing he saw was a bad sign—a blue plastic-bagged newspaper in the driveway. Shit, he thought, the guy's in the wind, took off yesterday some time. Crawford parked, got out of his car, walked up to the front door, and pressed the doorbell. Muldoon didn't answer. Crawford hoped maybe he was at his office or on his way there. But, if he was, why wouldn't he have picked up the newspaper and taken it with him?

Crawford walked around the house and tried the back door, but it was locked. He was hoping to get in and see if there was any sign of Muldoon having fled. He walked around the other side and pressed his nose up against a large picture window. He recognized the space beyond as the living room and glanced to the bottom row of the bookshelf, where all the photos of Rose had been. They weren't there anymore. He walked back toward the rear of the house and looked through another window. It was clearly the master. Looking through it, he could see a light on in a walk-in closet that looked like it had been emptied out. A rumpled shirt and what looked like a pair of khakis lay on the floor.

No doubt about it now. The guy was definitely in the wind.

Crawford ran to his car and headed north to Muldoon's office on Presidential Street but found no black Tesla in the parking lot and no John Muldoon inside. He called Wendy Muldoon.

"Mrs. Muldoon, it's Detective Crawford again. Your husband is wanted for questioning and it's critical that I find him. Do you have any idea where he may have gone?"

"Gone? What makes you think he's gone anywhere?"

"I have a strong suspicion he knows I want to question him, and I believe he may have committed a crime."

"What kind of crime?"

"Attempted murder."

"Oh my God, you're kidding. Who?"

"Her name is Rose Clarke and she's in the hospital now with extensive injuries from a hit-and-run. So, since you know him probably better than anyone, where would he go to hide? To not be found?"

Wendy Muldoon sighed deeply and fell silent for a few moments. "This whole thing's just so inconceivable to me. I mean… I just can't picture him, you know, on the run… a fugitive."

Crawford repeated the question. "Where do you think he'd go, Mrs. Muldoon?"

"I really don't know. He's got a sister who lives in Ponte Vedra, outside of Jacksonville."

"What's her name and phone number, if you have it?"

She gave him the name and number.

"Thank you. Anyone else he might go stay with?"

"He's visited a friend from college up near Savannah a few times. I think that's about a six-hour drive." Then she gave him the name and number.

"Thank you. And what about… do you and your husband have another house anywhere else?"

"Yes, but it's on the market now."

Crawford perked up. "But it hasn't been sold?"

"Correct."

"So, it's empty," Crawford said, patting the wheel anxiously.

"Yes."

"Where is it?"

"Cashiers. Up in the mountains, in North Carolina."

"About how long a drive is that?"

"Takes about eleven hours. Just off Highway 64. 111 Wildwood Road is the address."

Crawford scribbled the information. "Thank you. If you think of anything else that might be helpful, I'd appreciate a call." He had her write down his number. "And if you happen to speak to him, we never had this conversation."

"I won't be speaking to him, I promise you. We only speak through lawyers."

Crawford felt a twinge of familiarity, remembering how it got to that point between his ex-wife and him.

"Thanks again for your help," he said and clicked off.

He first called Muldoon's sister, who told him that she hadn't heard from her brother in months and implied that they weren't close. Then she went on to volunteer that he hadn't yet paid for his half of their mother's funeral six months ago and started in on how doctors, and especially psychiatrists, had a certain arrogance about mundane things like paying bills. It was TMI and Crawford concluded that this was a woman who either had too much spare time on her hands or who needed a friend to unload her grievances onto.

Cutting her short, he dialed Muldoon's friend in Savannah. No one answered there and he left a message on the answering machine.

Then he Googled the police department in Cashiers, North Carolina, and found there wasn't one. The nearest one seemed to be in a town called Highlands. He dialed its number and worked his way up to a sergeant.

"My name is Charlie Crawford," he said. "I'm a detective with the Palm Beach Police Department in Palm Beach, Florida."

"Hey, Detective. Ray Cooley here. How can I help?"

"First question I have, Ray, is do you guys cover the town of Cashiers?"

"Sure do. They're too small to have their own department."

"That's what I thought. So, if I can ask you a favor: a person of interest down here has a house in Cashiers and might have fled to that location."

"So, you want us to check if he's there?"

"Yes, as discreetly as possible. Just see if there's a car in the driveway. Lights on in the house, whatever."

"No problem. Happy to check it out myself."

"Thanks, man. How far is it from you?"

"A twenty-minute drive is all. I can get on it in an hour or so. What's the address?"

"111 Wildwood Road."

"I know where that is."

"Hey, I really appreciate it. You like grapefruit, Sarge?"

"Sure. Who doesn't? Why?"

That was Crawford's way of thanking people who helped on a case. He had cleared it with Norm Rutledge, who thought thirty bucks or so was a reasonable price to pay for a favor.

"Because I've got a big bag of 'em coming your way. What's your address?"

Cooley thanked him, gave him his address, and said he'd get back to him a little later.

Next Crawford called a judge he had a good relationship with to try to get a warrant to search John Muldoon's house. He got the judge's answering machine. "Hi, Judge, it's Charlie Crawford. Yes. I know it's Saturday and you have better things to do than talk to me, but I need a search warrant. Please give me a call."

He knew it was unlikely that he'd find a smoking gun at Muldoon's Hypoluxo house, but it was certainly worth a look. He thought about the photos of Rose that had once been there and now had disappeared along with the good doctor. Muldoon was a shrink, and one of a shrink's main objectives was to put themselves in the heads of their patients. Crawford surmised that if Muldoon thought he had seen the photos during his visit, then Crawford might assume that Muldoon was still... what was the best way to put it?... hung up on, infatuated with, obsessed with Rose? Why else would someone have what looked like ten photos—maybe more—of a woman who had broken up with him three months before?

There was no telling what else might be found in Muldoon's house. One thing was certain; he'd never find a hypodermic needle half-filled with poison.

38

An hour and a half later, Crawford got a call back from Sergeant Ray Cooley in Highlands. "Hey, Charlie, I got a silver Tesla in the driveway of the Muldoon Place."

Crawford perked up. "A *silver* Tesla?"

"Yup, with Florida plates."

"The guy I'm after has a black Tesla."

"I don't know what to tell you, this one was definitely silver."

"Okay, thanks Ray. I really appreciate it."

"No problem. You have anything else you need, just give me a call back."

"Will do."

Crawford clicked off, leaned back in his chair, and stared out the window. Five minutes later he stood up, walked out to his car, and drove toward the Tesla dealership up in Riviera Beach.

When he got there, he went straight to the service department and introduced himself to the guy at the desk. "Did a man named John Muldoon drop his car off for some repair work in the last few days?"

"Sure did," said the man. "He had a dent on the bumper and a little ding on the hood."

"So, I'm guessing he left it here and you gave him a loaner."

"Exactly."

"A silver model, right?"

"Right."

"Have you done the work on his car yet?"

"No. I think the guys were gonna get on it later this afternoon."

Crawford held up a hand. "Hold off, will you? I want to get a tech over here from my department. Check it out and take some photos."

"Uh, sure, Detective. We can hold off. Will somebody definitely be here this afternoon?"

Crawford nodded. "Definitely."

He thanked the man and hurried back to his car.

It was time for a road trip.

AT FIRST, he thought about calling Ray Cooley back and asking him if the Highland Police Department could spare a man to watch John Muldoon to make sure he didn't bolt from his house on Wildwood. But he decided that could backfire if Muldoon spotted the surveillance. If he did, he'd be on the run again, watching his back at all times. And from everything he'd heard about Teslas—zero to sixty in 3.2 seconds, he seemed to recall—Muldoon had a damn good chance of getting away. So, he decided not to call Cooley. A half-hour later, he had a full tank and was on I-95 headed to the Blue Ridge Mountains in North Carolina.

He called Ott to catch him up. They spent a half-hour on the phone. Ott said he was trying to track down Preston Platt to question him about the threatening four-year-old email from him to Crabb, but so far the man had proved elusive. Crawford caught Ott up on his pursuit of John Muldoon and explained how, with a little luck, he might soon be able to arrest the man and bring him back to Palm Beach. He said he was eager to get back on the Crabb case; they needed to wrap it up. They agreed they'd keep each other up to speed and talk regularly.

Before leaving, Crawford had gone down to the crime-scene evidence unit to see who was on duty. It was Robin Gold. He asked her to investigate the damage to John Muldoon's Tesla. His hope was that she might find a trace of something Rose Clarke was wearing the night she was hit.

If she did, it would be almost as good as a smoking gun.

39

There were two ways to get to Cashiers, North Carolina: The first was to take the Florida turnpike to I-75, which bisected the state of Florida and skirted Atlanta before the final stretch up to Cashiers. It was 733 miles. The second way was up the coast of Florida via I-95, getting off at Savannah and then jogging west. According to MapQuest, that way was 732 miles. Crawford had once driven up on I-95 and hit stop-and-go traffic caused by an accident that created an hour-and-a-half delay, so he chose the Florida turnpike to I-75.

Just after he crossed the Florida border into Georgia, he got a called from Robin Gold.

"Hey, Goldie, find out anything?"

"I think I got something solid. Do you know what Rose Clarke was wearing when she got hit?"

"Matter-of-fact I do—a red-skirt and a silver top."

"Bingo," Robin said. "I just took a red thread off the Tesla logo on the car."

Crawford pumped his fist. "You da man, Goldie! I, uh, didn't mean that literally. Nice work. What's the logo look like, anyway?"

"It's like this funky-looking 'T'."

"Gotcha. Anything else?"

"Yeah, I got a tiny piece of leather, too. I'm thinking from a belt maybe. It's alligator, I'm pretty sure."

"That I don't know about, but the red thread might be enough to put this guy away."

"Where are you? I can show you the stuff."

"Not gonna happen. I'm in a town called Valdosta, Georgia, in pursuit of my person of interest."

"All right. Well, hope you catch him. See you when you get back."

"Yup, later. Good job, Goldie," Crawford said. "Oh, hey, do me a favor. Call Ott and update him on everything you got."

"I will," she said and clicked off.

Six hours later, after some stop-and-go traffic around Atlanta, he was on Route 23, the final leg to Cashiers.

His cell phone rang. He looked down at the number. It was Ott.

"Hey, Mort, what's up?"

"The mad droner strikes again," Ott said. "So I called Preston Platt. He answers and it's like the fucker's on speed."

"What do you mean?"

"Tells me he and the wife were out by their pool and they heard this noise, then looked up and all of a sudden this drone was bearing down on them with bullets flying."

"Jesus, are they all right?"

"Yeah, they're fine, but clearly it scared the piss out of 'em."

"And did the thing blow up or anything? Like with Crabb?"

"No, he said it just kept going. I just came from their house."

"You got any crime-scene techs on it?"

"Yeah, Goldie's there now."

"Girl's had a busy day."

"You mean first Muldoon, now this?"

"Yeah," Crawford said. "Did you bring up that email thing? Him threatening Crabb."

"Sure did. He played it down. Like that sort of thing happened every day between them. Just words, he said."

Crawford thought for a second. "I don't know if I buy that. That was the only one I found that sounded so—"

"Threatening?"

"Yeah."

"I don't know, you should probably talk to him," Ott said. "So you expect to be bringing Muldoon back tonight?"

"Assuming I find him. I'll need to get a big jug of coffee for the ride back. It's a long haul."

"Yeah, but in the middle of the night you won't have much traffic."

"Wish I had you at the wheel."

"I volunteered to go."

"I know. Just go find the drone pilot, will ya?"

"Yeah, I'm about to go canvass the neighborhood around Platt's house. See what they saw or heard."

"All right, man, let me know what you find out."

"Will do. What's your next move?" Ott asked.

"Go show up on Muldoon's doorstep."

"I'm sure he'll be happy to see you," Ott said. "Where are you now?"

"I'm winding my way up the Blue Ridge Mountains. Pretty good views up this high."

"Hell of a lot cooler, I bet."

"Yeah, definitely."

"Well, bring that sumbitch back."

IT WAS a little past eight when Crawford motored into Cashiers. It looked like a prosperous little town with signs for private golf clubs, antique shops, and art galleries. He GPS'd his way to Wildwood Road, which was lined with tall pine trees and evergreens and slalomed between boulders and large rock outcroppings. As he counted the address numbers, he climbed up a hill, got to the top, and went steeply downhill. At the bottom, he saw number 111 and, immediately to its right, a dirt driveway. He turned onto it and felt for the Sig Sauer P-28 pistol on his hip. He figured the odds of having a shootout with John Muldoon were slim, but you never knew about a fugitive facing an attempted-murder charge. He slowly drove a hundred yards and saw an imposing two-story, dark-wood house with a porte-cochere up ahead. Under the porte-cochere was a silver Tesla and off to one side a black Honda CR-V. He backed up so he could not be seen from the house and pulled over. He got out, unholstered his Sig and started walking toward the house. As he approached it, he could hear music which, as best he could tell, was coming from the back of the house. It sounded like Dire Straits. Crawford found himself surprised that John Muldoon had decent taste in music.

As he walked around the near side of the house, the song "Sultans of Swing" grew louder. He turned the corner of the house and glanced around to the back. There, on a huge stone terrace with a beautiful view of a vast valley far below, John Muldoon was slow-dancing with a blonde woman in tight white pants and a puce-colored halter top. The woman spotted Crawford—Sig in hand—and her mouth dropped open wide. Muldoon felt her reaction and swung toward Crawford as the song ended.

"Hello, John," Crawford said. "From the looks of it, you've got a girl in every port." He took out his handcuffs. "I'm placing you under arrest for the attempted murder of Rose Clarke."

Then, as Mark Knopfler and the band kicked into their next song, he read John Muldoon his Miranda rights.

40

The woman who had been dancing with Muldoon had a look of pure terror on her face. Like she'd never had a gun pointed anywhere near her direction before. Muldoon was scowling, as if Crawford's sudden appearance was just one big royal pain in the ass. Not to mention, queering his action. The shrink put up a hand. "Before you handcuff me, Detective, how about letting me and my friend have dinner?" He pointed to an elaborate barbeque grill that had smoke wafting up from it. "It would be a shame to waste these succulent steaks."

Who, in real life, ever used the word *succulent*, Crawford wondered?

The woman had other ideas, anyway. "Ah, I think I'm gonna leave now, John."

The idea of having dinner under the vigilant eyes of a detective with a nasty-looking gun apparently had little appeal to her.

Muldoon looked irritated. "See that? You're driving my guest away."

"Bye, John," the woman said, quickly turning to go. She added, "Good luck."

"Goodbye, Gwen." Muldoon walked over and kissed her on the cheek. "I'll give you a call after I take care of this little matter."

She nodded warily and walked away.

When she was out of earshot, Crawford said, "That's gonna be a long time from now."

"Oh, I don't know about that."

"I do," Crawford said. "I can pretty much guarantee that you're gonna be in the joint for the foreseeable future."

Muldoon shrugged. "How about some steak and corn? It's a really good Japanese ribeye."

What the hell? Crawford thought. He hadn't eaten since morning. He shrugged. "Sure. We got a long ride ahead of us."

It was one of the best steaks he had had in a long time. Then again, he was more of an Outback Steakhouse kind of guy.

HE CALLED Rose from the porch of Muldoon's house after he had the man cuffed—and just for good measure—shackled in the back seat of his Crown Vic.

Rose was shocked. Crawford had never heard a tone of pure and total incredulity before.

"I just can't even begin to comprehend it, Charlie. Why in God's name...?" Her voice trailed off.

"I don't know," he said, pacing. "I think the guy is really sick." He shared his theory about what he'd seen before—how certain people get when they realize they can't possess someone or something they used to have.

He could picture Rose shaking her head. "I just can't wrap my simple little mind around that."

"I know what you mean, but there's no question about it. It was him."

Then Crawford told her about Muldoon having been married the whole time they'd been dating.

"Jesus, this bad movie just gets worse and worse," Rose said. "I always wondered why a prosperous doctor would be living in that dump in El Cid. That was his love shack, I guess?"

"Yeah, I guess. He claimed it was a friend's place."

"I was probably just one of many," Rose said, her voice lowered. "You know, Mary on Monday, Sally on Tuesday, Rose on Wednesday…."

Crawford flashed back to the woman Muldoon was having dinner with and figured Rose might be on to something. John the shrink and Wayne Crabb seemed to have a few things in common.

"You know," Rose said, "I've gone through a gamut of emotions in the last ten minutes. First and foremost, detesting the guy for what he did. Then thinking somehow, in some way, I must have been partly responsible. Even feeling a little sorry for him. But now I'm back to loathing the son of a bitch."

"I think that's how you *should* feel."

"God, Charlie… how could I have fallen for the guy in the first place?"

Crawford didn't have the answer. "I don't know, he's handsome?"

Rose sighed. "If that's what it was, that sure as hell doesn't say much about me…but he could be kind and generous. Brought me flowers and stuff—"

"Yeah, like when he showed up with that orchid, you mean?"

"Goddamnit," she said with venom. "What a sap I was."

"Don't beat yourself up, it's just a waste of time. So, when are you getting out of there?"

"Day after tomorrow, I hope. I'm bored out of my mind."

"I bet. How's the hip?"

"Getting better. I'm going to be on crutches for a while, though."

"Well, listen, you need anything, you let me know, okay?"

"I will."

"I gotta hit it."

"How you coming on the Crabb murder?"

Crawford thought how to answer that best. "Let's just say that Wayne Crabb had a hell of a lot more enemies than you did."

41

Robin Gold called right after he started his descent down the mountain from Cashiers.

"Hey, Goldie. It's late. You still working?"

"Hey, Charlie. Ott got the warrant you requested and I got into Muldoon's house."

"That's good. And?"

"I couldn't find anything at first and was about to leave when I ran across a pack of hypodermic needles in the bottom drawer in his bathroom. One of them was missing."

"Well, what do you know," Crawford glanced over at Muldoon. "Just so happens, I'm with Mr. Muldoon as we speak."

"You got him? Nice goin'," Gold said, amped up. "There's a cell on South County that's got his name on it."

"I know. Thanks, Goldie. See you when I get back."

Turned out John the shrink was a chatterbox. They talked sports and politics on the way back, everything but why Muldoon was in handcuffs in the back of Crawford's Crown Vic. Finally, Crawford felt like it was time.

"So, why'd you do it, John?"

Muldoon didn't answer at first. "Do you have any evidence at all?"

"You mean beside the fact that threads from Rose's clothes were found on your Tesla at the dealership, a box of hypodermic needles with one missing was located in your bathroom, and you took off because you had a shitty alibi? Aside from that, no."

Muldoon didn't say anything for a while.

Ten minutes later: "You know, I thought she was going to be the one," he said with a sigh. "After three bad marriages, I thought I had found the perfect woman."

"You were half right."

"What do you mean?"

"You did find the perfect woman, you just didn't deserve her."

"But we got along so well."

"For a while."

"Four months."

Crawford shook his head. "Then Rose started to see some cracks. But she never saw the biggest one."

"That I was married, you mean?"

Crawford nodded. "That's what I mean," he said. "You're a shrink, John. You probably come across obsessive people pretty often in your line of work?"

"Of course. There are lots of 'em out there."

"Yeah, including you," Crawford said. "I had a friend from college. He inherited some money when he turned twenty-one, quite a lot of money. So, he bought this little inn up in New Hampshire, near some ski slopes. His girlfriend dropped out of college in New York and went up there and they started living together. Moved a bunch of her stuff up there."

Muldoon cocked his head. "Why are you telling me this?"

"Hang on, you'll see," Crawford said. "One of the things she brought along was this really nice oil painting of her done by her mother, who was a well-known painter. I remember seeing it—it was full-length and really nice."

"I'm falling asleep back here."

Crawford forged ahead. "So, after a while, the girlfriend got bored with running a little inn in the middle of nowhere, New Hampshire, and told my friend she was going back to college. Then, she went out to ski the next day and he started to drink. He got really drunk, went down to the kitchen and got a knife—"

"Uh-oh."

"No, not what you think... he took the knife and slashed a big X across that beautiful portrait of his girlfriend."

"What an asshole."

Crawford nodded. "There are men—women, too, I'm sure—who feel that if they can't have someone, then no one can." He glanced back in the rearview mirror and saw he had Muldoon's full attention. "My friend expressed that in a... let's just say *less violent way* than you did."

Muldoon let out a long sigh. "That's pretty melodramatic."

"Maybe, but accurate."

Five minutes later, Crawford got a call from Ott.

"Got him?"

"In the back of the Vic."

"Attaboy. Where are you?"

"Somewhere between Atlanta and Jacksonville—oh, wait—coming up on the state line as we speak, about to make my return to the Sunshine State."

"Your triumphant return."

"Why, thank you, Mort. Anything on the drone?"

"That's why I called. I talked to a lot of people in Platt's neighborhood and nobody heard or saw a drone. But a couple of people did hear gunshots—or as people always say, firecrackers—so I don't quite know what to make of it."

Crawford thought for a second. "One thing you should do is ask Dominica if her friend at the airport can come up with something."

"Already done. Called her up just before you."

"Good man," Crawford said. "You got any theories? You've had more time to think about it?"

"Matter of fact, I do. I was thinking Platt knows we haven't ruled him out as a suspect in Crabb's murder, so—"

"I'm with you. So, maybe he faked the whole thing? So it'd look like Crabb's killer came after him, too?"

"Yeah, exactly. Maybe fired off a couple of shots from a pistol or something, so his story would seem credible."

"I like it, Mort," Crawford said. "So, have you heard anything from Goldie? I'm guessing she was still the tech on duty and she covered it, right?"

"Yes and yes. She found a slug at the bottom of the pool. No ID on what kind it was yet."

"There you go. So, Platt fired a couple rounds at his pool?"

"Pretty big target."

Crawford laughed. "Yeah, couldn't miss. All right, well, I'll be getting in around seven in the morning. Making a deposit in the basement—" where the jail cells were located "—so I might as well stay up."

"You're gonna be one tired hombre."

"Yeah, me and Goldie both. Sure we'll both crash hard tomorrow night."

42

It was 7:35, Sunday morning. John Muldoon was in the basement cell of the Palm Beach Police Department at 345 South County Road. Crawford was in his office, having just polished off his go-to Dunkin' Donuts breakfast. And, for good measure, he was on his second mug of jet-black office rotgut. The coffee tasted like mud but gave him the caffeine blast he needed.

As eager as he was to speak to Preston Platt, he had decided to wait an hour, until 8 a.m. to call. It was Sunday, after all. In the meantime, he called Dominica, who he knew was an early riser.

"Good morning, Charlie," she answered.

"Just thought you'd want to know, I got John the shrink in the cell down below. He's the one who tried to kill Rose."

"Jesus, you're kidding."

"No, I've got more evidence than I need."

"Why in God's name—"

Crawford cut her off and gave her his theory. Except he used a different example from the one about the friend who'd slashed and burned the portrait of his girlfriend. He told her a story he'd read about a seventy-seven-year-old man in Maine who had killed a homeless woman he was trying—unsuccessfully—to have a relationship with. She rejected him and said she was moving away to another town. As he testified, he made the spur-of-the-moment decision that if he couldn't have her, nobody could, and then stabbed her twenty-six times with a Swiss Army Knife. The story got grislier, because, forty years earlier, he had done the same thing to his then wife when she, too, threatened to leave him.

He'd been convicted for that murder and ultimately let out of prison at seventy-five, when he was deemed too old to be capable of committing a violent crime. Turned out that had been a bad call.

Dominica sighed. "Jeez, I feel a little responsible."

"What are you talking about?"

"Well, 'cause after that night John was really drunk and we had to drive him home, Rose asked me what I thought of him. I tried not to be too negative—I mean guys get drunk—but I think she knew how I really felt."

"Yeah, she asked me, too."

"What did you say?"

"I kind of beat around the bush. I mean, I met the guy once, I didn't really get to know him."

"How could you? He was shitfaced."

Crawford laughed. "Well, yeah, there was that."

"So, I'm going to pick up your pedicurist tomorrow afternoon."

"Oh, good, so she's getting released from the hospital?"

"Yup. And I got her an interview with my nails place."

"An interview, huh? With like a resumé and everything?"

"Ha-ha. Hey, maybe you should go in with her, show 'em your toes as a reference."

Crawford laughed. "They're pretty faded. I'm due for another paint job."

"Well, hopefully she'll get a job there."

"Hey, speaking of hospitals, I told Rose."

"Yeah, and how'd she take it?"

"She couldn't believe it. Think she was pretty relieved he couldn't try it a third time, though."

"Yeah, no kidding.

Crawford looked at his watch: 8:02. "Okay, I gotta hop. Another bad guy to round up."

"Good luck. Hey, do you ever take a day off?"

"When I do, I want to take it with you."

"I'm gonna hold you to that."

"Please do," he said. "Later."

"But not too much later."

He looked up Preston Platt's phone number and dialed it.

A woman's voice answered.

"Mrs. Platt?"

"Yes, who's this?"

"Detective Crawford. I'd like to come talk to you and your husband about that drone attack."

"Preston's not even up yet."

"How about nine?"

She paused. "Okay. Have you had breakfast yet?"

"Yes, I have. Thanks, though."

"You're welcome. See you at nine."

At just after nine, Crawford pulled into Platt's driveway on Emerald and pressed the doorbell.

Gina Platt opened the door. Her blonde hair was going in all directions, the dark roots more noticeable than the last time he saw her, but she had clearly spent some time with her makeup kit. Eye shadow, bronzer, and white lip gloss were on full display. "Good morning, Charlie, nice to see you again. It is okay if I call you Charlie?" she said flirtatiously.

"Sure, that's fine," he said, sniffing bacon in the air. One of his favorite smells.

"We just started breakfast. You sure you won't join us?"

"Well, maybe one piece of bacon."

"How 'bout two?"

"Okay, thanks."

She led him into a family room off of the kitchen where Preston Platt was hunkered down behind a plateful of scrambled eggs, bacon, and a biscuit.

"Detective," he said with a nod. "I'm not going to get up and shake your hand, because, as you can see, I've got my hands full."

"No problem."

Platt motioned to a chair. "Have a seat."

Crawford did, and Gina Platt brought him a plate with three pieces of bacon and a biscuit.

"Growing boy," she said.

"Thanks a lot. Biscuit looks really good."

Platt nodded. "Trust me."

Crawford picked up a piece of crisp bacon and killed it in two bites. "So, tell me about the drone. I'm glad it didn't do any damage."

"Thank you," Preston said. "Well, as I told your partner, first we heard this noise—"

"—kind of like a loud bee," Gina said.

"And then I looked up and saw it coming over the neighbor's roof."

"On which side?"

"The neighbor to the west."

"So, it was going toward the ocean."

Platt nodded. "It was scary because I could see it getting lower. Then, pow, pow, pow, bullets all over the place, one in the pool."

"But the drone didn't explode? It kept going?"

"Yeah. I know that's different from how it happened with Crabb. Maybe whoever did it didn't want to keep blowing up perfectly good drones."

"How long was it between when you first heard it and when it started firing at you?"

Preston thought for a moment. "Uh, maybe about two minutes or so."

"That long?"

"Yeah, I'd say so. It was going pretty slow."

"And where were you when you saw it? Sitting or standing?"

"We were sitting around the table out back, having a cocktail. I can show you exactly where after we're finished here."

Crawford nodded and took another bite of bacon. "Do you have a weapon in the house, Mr. Platt?"

Platt reacted like he had been accused of something serious. His head jerked back almost imperceptibly, but Crawford caught it.

"A what?"

"A weapon. A pistol."

Platt shook his head. "Nope. Got a shotgun, though."

"But no pistol?"

Preston frowned. "Uh, like I said, no."

Crawford put the half-eaten strip of bacon down on his plate. "So, if I were to get a bunch of my people to go through your house—" he glanced at Gina Platt for her reaction "—and go over every square inch of it, I wouldn't find a pistol?"

Preston sighed and shook his head. "And we were having such a nice breakfast. Until you went and ruined it. For the third time, I *don't own a pistol*, nor is there one anywhere in this house."

Crawford nodded and glanced back at Gina Platt. "You can confirm that, right, Mrs. Platt?"

"Yes, yes, absolutely," she said nervously. "Why in God's name would we have a pistol here?"

Crawford smiled at her. "Oh, I don't know, to defend yourself against a drone attack maybe."

"Is that a joke?" Preston asked.

"Not at all," Crawford said. "Did it occur to you to get your shotgun? I mean, two minutes is a lot of time?"

"No. I mean, I didn't immediately make the connection that this was how Wayne got killed. Not like all drones have machine guns, or whatever, mounted on them."

Crawford nodded, then looked over at Platt's plate. It was empty.

"You mind showing me where you were sitting when you first heard the drone?"

"No," Platt said, standing up. "Come on."

Crawford stood up. "Well, Mrs. Platt, thanks for breakfast."

"You're welcome, but you didn't eat your biscuit."

Crawford reached down, picked up the biscuit and wrapped a napkin around it. "A roadie."

She smiled and nodded as Crawford followed Platt out to the back of the house.

There were two expensive-looking, teak, chaise lounges on the poolside patio, along with four chairs around a glass-topped table under a large white-and-blue umbrella.

"We were sitting in those," Platt said, pointing to the chaise lounges.

Crawford nodded. "But they're facing east, toward the ocean. Opposite direction from where the drone was coming from."

Platt groaned. "You ever hear of turning your head, Detective?"

Crawford nodded. "I have, but I'd like to see you turn your head a hundred eighty degrees."

Platt shook his head and glared at Crawford. "What is it you're trying to prove, exactly?"

Crawford shrugged. "I'm just asking questions, making observations."

"'Cause it seems like you think I'm making this whole thing up."

"I don't know why you'd come to that conclusion."

"Just a cop doing his job, right?"

"Exactly. Well, I guess that's about all I need to know," Crawford said, turning to go, then turning back. "Oh, I forgot one thing—your email to Wayne Crabb."

"What email?"

"Back about four years ago you said something like, *buying Gina stuff is one thing, buying her dinner is another, but you just crossed the line and now you're gonna pay.*"

"Oh, Christ, that again. Your partner brought that up," Platt said, shaking his head. "Four years ago, huh?—" he ladled on the sarcasm. "And when I was a kid, forty years ago, I threatened another kid in the park. I mean, come on, Detective, you got any more ancient history you want to toss out there?"

Crawford had to admit, maybe there wasn't much to it. And it had looked so promising a few days before. "Okay, Mr. Platt, thanks for letting me come over."

"You're very welcome… I think."

Crawford walked alongside Platt's house, got in his car, and left.

As soon as he got back to the station, he planned to look up whether Platt had a handgun or a rifle permit. Something didn't sit right with the man Ott had called a "gerbil."

43

Crawford got a call from Norm Rutledge on his way back to the station.

"You got that guy dead to rights, huh?" Rutledge said.

"No 'hi, Charlie' or 'good work?'" Crawford said. "You're referring to John Muldoon, I assume."

"Yeah, the guy in the cell."

"Let's just say that the prosecutor would have to be totally incompetent not to put him away for a long, long time."

"That's good. So, this frees you up to devote all your time to Crabb, right?"

"Yes, it does, but I'd like to point out something."

"I'm listening."

"Busting John Muldoon was done on the weekend. On my time. All it cost you and the city was a little gas money and ten bucks worth of Denny's swill." He left out the bag of grapefruits for the North Carolina police sergeant.

"What's swill?"

"Stuff you feed pigs."

"I like Denny's."

"So do I. Anyway, Norm, it's Sunday. I'm not getting paid and I'm workin' Crabb as we speak."

"Duly noted," Rutledge said and clicked off.

Once a dick always a dick, Crawford thought.

His phone rang again as he pulled into the parking lot behind the police station.

It was his brother, Cam. He hadn't spoken to him in more than a month. It was a pleasant surprise.

"Hey, Cam, how ya doing?"

"Great, man."

"So, everything good? What's new in your life? Catch me up."

"Well, for one thing, I'm in a plane at Teterboro coming down to see you. It's been too damned long."

"I agree, but… you're on your way… now?"

"Yeah. Sorry, I didn't give you any notice."

Crawford thought for a few moments as he left his vehicle and walked into the station. "Here's the thing, I'm right in the middle of a murder."

"No big deal. I'll stay out of your way. Just need a change of scenery and wanted to catch up with my big bro."

"Is everything really okay?" Crawford asked

"Yeah, sure, hunky-dory."

"Why are you at Teterboro?"

"Guess I didn't tell you. I got a Netjets share on a G5."

"So, it's just *you* on the plane?" The environmentalist in Crawford was thinking that was a lot of gas to fly just one guy from New Jersey to Florida.

"Just me, two pilots, and a flight attendant."

Crawford couldn't even begin to relate to that. "Well, come on down, I'd love to see you."

"Looking forward to seeing you, too. I got a room at the Breakers for three nights. I don't want to overstay my welcome."

"You could never do that. Let me know when you're here."

"I will."

Crawford clicked off, plopped down behind his desk, and started doing the math. Private metal with two pilots and a flight attendant, five hundred a night at the Breakers, plus Cam would probably rent the top-of-the-line car at Hertz or Avis… It wasn't that Cam was ostentatious about how he lived, it was just that, as a highly-compensated hedge-fund manager, he'd become accustomed to a certain style of living. He liked to spend his money, but, on the flip side, Cam gave a good portion of it to charity. Crawford knew that because Cam's first wife had once groused about it to him. Something subtle, like, "Your brother gives away too much money instead of spending it on me."

Crawford put Cam out of his mind and plowed even deeper into Wayne Crabb's emails, hoping for one that might shed light on his killer. Maybe a new name along with a motive to add to the mix of possible suspects. He didn't find anything that he considered incriminating but found two that required further follow-up. Both based on emails sent to Crabb.

The first one was from the car dealer in Kansas City, the golfer's husband, Merle Bolling. It was cryptic: "To follow up my phone call, if I hear any more rumors about you pursuing Jan, I'm going to come there and make you regret you ever laid eyes on her." He couldn't find any email from Crabb in response to what Bolling had written.

The second email was from Lauren Doe, Crabb's daughter, and it was much longer: "Hi Dad, At the risk of sounding like a broken record, I would really like it if you could see it in your heart to bestow some generosity on me and Arthur that you so freely bestow on others."

Was she referring to his various girlfriends? If so, Crawford didn't find it to be the most effective way of asking for money.

"As you know," Lauren went on, "Arthur is struggling with his practice and sometimes it is hard for us to put food on the table." That sounded like a massive exaggeration to Crawford and one that Wayne Crabb had probably rolled his eyes at upon reading.

Lauren's email continued: "As your only heir, I just don't

understand why you can't give me money now, as opposed to when you pass on."

Oof. Another clumsy suggestion. What sixty-two-year-old man wants to hear about dying? Or that his daughter is maybe hoping that day will come sooner than later?

"In any case, I will respect your decision in whatever you decide, as I always have."

What alternative did she have?

"Your loving daughter, Lauren."

Oh, please.

It hadn't seemed, at least from Crawford's interview with Arthur Doe, that Crabb had at some point transferred a large amount of money into his daughter and son-in-law's checking account. Crawford flashed to the photo of the indistinguishable image of the couple with the drone and decided to interview the Does together the next day, Monday.

He thought some more about Merle Bolling and Jan Silvestre. Flying out to Kansas City was something he would do if necessary, but not something he was eager to do. Especially with the added complication of Cam arriving in town. He decided that first he'd go meet with Jan Silvestre and called the number Ott had given him.

She answered after the first ring. "This is Jan."

"Hello, Ms. Silvestre, this is Detective Charlie Crawford. You spoke to my partner, Detective Ott. I'd like to come ask you a few questions tomorrow, if possible."

"I'm in Oregon playing in a golf tournament."

Damn. She couldn't have gone much farther away from home.

"In that case, can I ask you a few questions right now?"

"Sure, but I have to go to the range in half an hour."

"It won't take that long. So, my first question is, when your husband was in Florida, did he ever go see Wayne Crabb?"

"I went over that with Detective Ott. No, he did not. He came here to see me, not Wayne Crabb."

"But you weren't with him every minute he was here. I mean, I presume you went and played golf or practiced?"

"Well, yeah, it is my job," Silvestre said. "But I would have known if Merle saw Wayne."

"How?"

"He would have told me."

"What if he didn't want you to know?"

"Look, Detective, I never had anything to do with Wayne beyond a business relationship. As I told Detective Ott, he fronted me money to play on the tour. It's very expensive. End of story."

"What contact *did* your husband have with Wayne Crabb?"

"I don't know that they had any."

His opening. "I have an email from your husband to Wayne. It says, 'To follow up my phone call, if I hear any more rumors about you pursuing Jan, I'm going to come there and make you regret you ever laid eyes on her.'"

"Okay," Silvestre said. "Merle could get a little possessive. Maybe like any man whose wife works thousands of miles away."

"Well, I would call that email more than 'possessive'. 'Threatening' comes to mind."

"Call it what you want, Merle never laid a hand on Wayne. Or, I guess in this case, a drone."

"When will you get back to Palm Beach, Ms. Silvestre?"

"After this tournament, I'm playing in Arizona next week, then I come home."

That was all the questions Crawford had. "Okay, then, thank you for your help. Good luck in the tournament there."

"Thanks," she said with a sigh. "I'm gonna need it. I'm nine strokes back."

CRAWFORD and his brother had just arrived at Pistache, a French restaurant in West Palm Beach. It was Cam's choice. Crawford—

despite having never been there before—deemed it too fancy (read, *expensive*) for the likes of him. He had heard Rose talk about the place once, raving about selections like 'duck foie gras' and 'charcuterie' this and 'moules mariniere' that. It was way over his culinary head, but Cam had read about the place and wanted to try it. Plus, Cam had never let Crawford grab a check, even when he tried really hard.

Cam had always had issues with alcohol and depression. Which, actually, was putting it mildly. In fact, the year before he had spent a month at a place called Clairmount drying out and, as Cam put it, "Getting my shit together." Before meeting Cam at Pistache, Crawford had gone to the Clairmount website to review what the rehab facility professed to do for its patients. He had visited Cam there once and been impressed with the place, both physically and how effective it seemed to be at treating his brother. They had a program specifically designed for, as the website said, "executives and professionals who struggle with substance abuse or psychiatric issues, and have reached a moment of crisis." Crawford's initial reaction was that it sounded a little rarified—*executives and professionals, huh? What about cops and detectives and the rest of us lowly schlubs?*

The long and the short was that Cam left Clairmount after a month, having had a setback or two, but dedicated to never touching another drop of alcohol and feeling as though he had made great strides in defeating his demons. Now, in person, Crawford felt encouraged by the newfound shininess in his handsome brother's eyes, by an optimistic, less cynical outlook, and by the fact that he had married a woman named Christie, who was the daughter of a Clairmount patient and who seemed perfect for him.

But then the waiter came to the table and Cam, without even hesitating, ordered a double scotch.

44

Crawford, trying hard not to react like big brothers do, asked the waiter for a glass of red wine.

When the waiter walked away, Crawford eyed his brother and shrugged. "So, you're drinking again?"

"In moderation."

"Hey, Cam, I know you and, no offense, you don't know the meaning of the word."

"Christ, Charlie, we're together five minutes and already you're giving me a lecture."

Crawford put his hand on Cam's arm. "It's not a lecture. I just—"

"Telling me I don't know how to drink in moderation. I'm a drunk."

"Okay. Well, you *were* a drunk. By your own admission."

Cam nodded grudgingly. "I have a couple of drinks with dinner now. I can handle that."

"So, let me ask you this: how does Christie feel about it?"

A long pause. "I won't lie. She's not too crazy about it."

"Do you hide it from her?"

Cam shrugged. "Hey, I'm not going to flaunt it."

"So that's a yes."

"Christ, man."

The waiter showed up with their drinks.

"Now I feel like chugging this in one gulp," Cam said with a smile. Crawford didn't smile back.

"That was a joke, Charlie," Cam said, picking up the menu. "Hey, let's order something. I'm starved."

"I hear the duck foie gras is exceptional," Crawford said.

Cam laughed. "You wouldn't know a duck foie gras if it bit you on the ass."

"Or you might want to try les moules mariniere."

Cam laughed again. "Where the hell'd you get this? You haven't even looked at the menu?"

Crawford shrugged. "It just looks like a duck foie gras, moules mariniere kind of place."

THEY WERE HALFWAY through their dinners. Thus far, Cam had indeed been moderate in his drinking—one scotch and one glass of red wine. But Crawford was still curious.

"So—and this is not a lecture, just a question—when did you start drinking again?"

Cam frowned. "Gotta tell ya, Charlie, it sounds judgmental."

"I promise you it's not. I just wondered whether something had triggered it."

Cam put his fork down. "No. Just thought I could handle it. Missed it a little bit, too."

Crawford only nodded.

"What's going through that brilliant, deductive mind of yours?"

"Nothing."

"I can see the cogs churning."

Crawford put his hand on Cam's. "Don't overthink it. It was just a question."

"Okay, and I answered it. Let's talk politics or sports or your sex life."

Crawford laughed. "Politics and sports, yes. Sex life, assuming I have one, off-limits."

"You're no fun," Cam said. "Well, then, catch me up on the case you're working on."

"Oh, Christ it's a long story." But for the next twenty minutes he filled his brother in on Crabb. All his suspects, all his theories, all his questions.

"Guy sounds like a real sweetheart," Cam said. "Wanna know what I think?"

Crawford smiled. "Of course." His brother had an intuitive mind and surprisingly accurate insights about people. He could size someone up in no time flat.

"Mary Beth's the key. She knows more than she's letting on."

Crawford nodded. He had that sense, too.

"I mean she worked for the guy forever, right?"

"Long time. Thirty-odd years."

"So she knows him backwards and forwards. His girlfriends, his enemies, everything."

"I just don't know what I can find out about her that I don't already know. Ott and I've spent a couple hours with her."

Cam shrugged. "Just sayin', she's the key."

"You might be right." Crawford smiled at his brother. "All right, let's get out of here. I've got a long day tomorrow."

Ten minutes later, Crawford was in his car en route to his condo and Cam was headed back to the Breakers in Palm Beach.

Cam decided to have a nightcap in the Breakers bar, even though it was only 9:30.

He ended up having a lot more than one.

45

Cam Crawford lost track of how many drinks he'd had, though he hadn't really been counting. Suffice it to say, it was enough to get him thrown into the drunk tank at the sheriff's office jail in West Palm Beach. Cam woke up in the cold, gamy cell, feeling as though a handful of daggers had been thrust into his throbbing head and an elephant was spread-eagled on top of him. He had a vague recollection of driving from the Breakers to a place on Clematis Street in West Palm, then another place, then a third, which he closed down, then back to the Breakers. But he only got halfway back. He had reached the middle bridge in his rented Jaguar when not one but two of West Palm Beach's finest pulled him over, lights flashing with the low whine of sirens.

Next thing he knew, two Maglite flashlights were thrust into his bloodshot eyes.

"You don't look so good, partner," one of the cops said.

"I'm fine, I'm just heading back to my hotel," Cam slurred.

"Not anymore you're not," the other one said. "I can smell you from here."

So, he blew .338 on the breathalyzer machine and they threw him in the tank despite his repeated protestations that he was "just fine."

It occurred to him at one point to tell them that his brother was a detective in Palm Beach, but a little voice told him to bite his tongue.

As he opened his eyes and took in the cell around him, he saw that he had roommates. There was a big black guy who never said a word but farted constantly and a tat-covered Hispanic man who kept asking him if he was that Simon guy on the TV show.

"No," Cameron answered without elaboration. No clue who "that Simon guy" was.

"Yeah, you are," the Hispanic guy insisted. "You know that one, *America's Got Talent*."

Cam had vaguely heard of the show. He shook his head. "Ain't me, man."

The big black guy cut another long and loud one as Cam looked over at the fourth man in the tank. He was wearing a Hawaiian shirt and a rumpled blue blazer. Their eyes met.

"How ya doin'?" Cam asked.

"How the fuck you think I'm doin'? I'm here, aren't I?"

"Yeah, you sure are. What did you do?"

"Partied a little too hearty. You?"

"Same. Shoulda called an Uber, but I figured my GPS would guide me right into bed."

"Last thing I remember was being on a boat. A bunch of fine ladies on board."

"Then the dream ended and here you were, right?"

The man laughed. "Something like that."

"Hey, how the hell do we get out of here?" Cam asked.

The Hawaiian-shirt guy didn't seem to have the answer, but the tat man did. "They arraign you and you pay a fine."

"But they got my wallet." And his cell phone.

Hawaiian-shirt man shrugged. "They must give it back to you."

The black guy nodded and cut another fart in what seemed like confirmation.

At just before ten, Cam got a cab back to the Breakers. His rental car had been impounded but he got his wallet and cellphone back.

He had four messages on his phone. One from his wife, Christie, and three from Crawford. Christie said she missed him. Crawford's first voicemail asked if he wanted to have breakfast; the second asked him where he was, and the third asked him *where the hell he was* and added, "I'm worried."

He called Christie first and said he'd had a nice dinner with Charlie. He and Charlie talked about a million things, Cam said, and had a really good catch-up. Then he called Crawford. He wasn't going to tell him what happened at first, but he knew his brother had an infallible knack for sniffing out the truth, telling when someone was either lying or holding back. He figured he'd better just give him the plain, unvarnished truth.

Crawford answered his cell right away. "Where are you, man?"

Cam eked out a groan and blurted it out. "At the Breakers. I drank too much and got a DUI."

He waited for his brother's response with dread akin to that which he'd felt when he told their father he'd been booted out of boarding school.

"Yeah, I know," Crawford said. "When you didn't call back, I made a few calls. How was your cot in the West Palm jail?"

Cam let out a full-throated groan. "Met a couple awesome guys there."

"Yeah, I'll bet. But you're okay?"

"I'm okay. A little poorer. Plus, they suspended my license."

"Oh, shit. Guess I need to drive you around *and* babysit you."

"Nope. I already got a car and driver lined up for the rest of my stay."

"Well, I gotta work. Then we can have dinner," Crawford said. "I'm buying."

"And I'm drinking ginger ale."

"Wise decision."

TURNED out that Crawford had taken a nice, long nap to catch up on the lack of sleep he'd accumulated while driving John Muldoon back from Cashiers, North Carolina. Not normally a napper, Crawford closed the door to his office and nodded off in his Herman Miller Aeron chair, the one splurge that Norm Rutledge had authorized after Crawford and Ott's fourth straight murder conviction.

"Can't say I don't treat my boys like kings," Rutledge had said at the time.

Ott, who had been standing next to Crawford at the time, just rolled his eyes the way he did at most things Rutledge said.

46

Crawford and his brother went to an Italian restaurant called Lynora's on Clematis Street for dinner. Cam ordered a ginger ale and Crawford…brother in solidarity, a Diet Coke.

"I got to be kind of an expert on this stuff during my thirteen months of sobriety," Cam said, raising his glass of ginger ale, "and, just for the record, Vernor's is the best."

"Ginger ale?"

Cam nodded.

"Not Canada Dry?"

"Oh, God, no. Vernor's by far." Cam leaned in close and said, "It comes from Michigan," like he was revealing Coke's secret formula.

"I'll remember that," Crawford said. "So, how's work going? You haven't said a word about it."

Cam was the star investment advisor and managing director of a New York hedge fund. He took a sip of his ginger ale. "I had a bumpy patch a while back."

Crawford shrugged. "What happened?"

"A few bad trades. A hundred-million-dollar hit."

That might explain something, Crawford thought, but he let his brother keep talking.

"We can absorb it. We'll be fine. But I guess maybe it proved I'm not bulletproof. I was beginning to believe all the hype."

At twenty-eight, Cam had been named a hedge-fund wonder boy in a *Financial Times* article and, immediately thereafter, became a sought-after guest of Jim Cramer on CNBC.

"I see your brain whirring," Cam said. "You're thinking, 'Okay, I get it, that's why you're drinking. Suffered a little adversity and needed to go see your old friend, Johnnie Walker.'"

Crawford didn't say anything.

"Well, you're not altogether wrong, but my marriage had a little to do with it, too."

"How so?"

"I don't know, a bunch of things." Cam drew a long, deep sigh. "Well, that's not really true. I guess, the reality is, the only thing wrong with the marriage was my drinking."

"Has Christie gotten on you about it?"

"Yeah, she has. But if I'm being completely honest about it, I don't blame her. I mean, her old man was an alkie. Her grandfather, who killed himself by the way, was too. It wouldn't be hard for her to think, 'Christ, here we go again.'"

"I hear you," Crawford said. "So, it's simple."

Cam laughed, knowing what his brother was saying.

"You mean, quit again—" he snapped his fingers "—just like that."

Crawford shrugged. "You did it once. For quite a long time. Do it again."

Their food arrived and neither said anything for a while. Crawford took a bite of his cannelloni, a sip of his Diet Coke, and put his fork down. "Tell you what. How 'bout we do the buddy system. I'll quit if you quit." This wasn't something he had given even five minutes of thought to before this moment. Could he really do it? His thinking was that Cam had always followed him and emulated him. If he knew that his big brother was abandoning an old friend that had been with him—what, over twenty years?—then he could do it, too.

"What do you want to do that for?" Cam asked. "You don't have a problem."

"Maybe not. But would I be better off if I didn't have three drinks a day? Absolutely."

Cam thought for a second. "I don't know. I don't think I'm ready to quit at this moment."

"No time like the present," Crawford pressed.

Cam shook his head. "Not right now."

"Come on, man, I'll buy you a case of Vernor's ginger ale. From Michigan."

"No," Cam said firmly. "I'm not ready yet."

47

As he was waiting for the check, Crawford asked Cam if he wanted to play a speed nine the next day.

Cam nodded exuberantly. "Hell yeah, I'll kick your ass. I'm down to an eight-handicap. I can rent clubs there, right?"

"Or you can use mine."

"The way I remember it, yours are like twenty years old. Made out of wood or something. You still got that Sasquatch driver?"

It was a big gaudy yellow driver made by Nike.

"Yeah, why?"

"'Cause its heyday was back in the '90s. I remember some places were trying to ban it because of the noise it makes."

"What do you mean?"

"It's like a *'plink'*. Real tinny-sounding."

"Yeah well, whatever, it still launches drives three hundred yards out there."

Cam laughed. "In your dreams. So what are we playing for?"

"Five bucks a hole," Crawford said.

"Hey, big spender," said Cam.

"Well, the last time I played, I lost to Dominica."

"That's nothing to be ashamed of. She's a damned good athlete."

"And she cheats."

Cam smiled from ear to ear. "I gotta admit, I'm really looking forward to beatin' your ass since you were the big jock when we were kids. I used to brag to my buddies about big brother getting seven letters in lacrosse and football. Now, poor bastard... you're a mere shadow of yourself."

"Just six."

"What?

"Six letters."

"Still pretty impressive."

Crawford told Cam he was going to have a long day, so they planned it for seven the next night. It would only take them an hour to get around, so Cam made plans to meet an investor of his for an 8:30 dinner.

Cam got back to the Breakers at 8:45 and, despite not having had anything stronger than ginger ale with his brother, decided to have one drink at the Breakers bar, which was called HMF.

"So, I've been trying to figure it out," Cam said to the bartender as he sat down. "What's HMF stands for?"

"Henry Morrison Flagler. Railroad man, developer of Florida, and notorious robber baron."

Cam nodded. He had been to the Flagler Museum, just down the road, on his last visit to see Charlie and had learned the rags-to-riches story of Flagler, the son of a humble Presbyterian minister from New Jersey.

"He built this place, too, right?" Cam said, meaning the Breakers.

"Sure did. Along with the first railroad here, a college somewhere up north, his fifty-five-room house, you name it."

Two women came and sat down next to Cam. One turned to him and smiled. She looked to be in her mid-thirties and was showing a lot of leg along with a porch-full of well-tanned bosom.

"Hel-lo," Cam said.

"Hello," she said. "Haven't seen you around."

"I live in New York."

The other woman looked over and raised her glass. "Me too. Where?"

"SoHo," Cam said.

"I live in the West Village," the second one said. "West Fourth Street."

She looked to be in her early thirties, a blonde with Mick Jagger lips and ice-blue, wolf-like eyes. He detected a slight Russian accent.

Cam nodded. "So, what are you doing down here?"

"A shoot in Miami."

"You're models?"

They both nodded.

Cam raised his glass. "Well, I'm buying the next round."

Then came a next-next round, and another one after that.

Halfway through her latest martini, the woman next to him leaned closer. "Feel like a little bump?"

Cam missed cocaine. It had been more than a year and a half since he'd even looked at a line of blow. As a matter of fact, the last time had been the night before he admitted himself to Clairmount.

"Sure," he said. "We can go out to my car. Take a little ride, maybe."

She nodded, turned, and whispered to her friend. They finished their drinks and stood. "Let's go, lover boy," the second model said.

They walked out to Cam's limo. It was a black Mercedes, modest by limo standards, but Cam hadn't hired it to impress.

The driver opened the back door for them. "Thanks, Bobby," Cam said.

Bobby nodded. "Where to, boss?"

"Why don't you just drive south along the ocean?"

"You got it."

When they were seated, the first model lowered her voice. "Bobby looks kinda like a narc."

Cam whispered, "Nah, just a good ol' boy."

She took a small, dark bottle out of her purse. She opened it and took a snort with a tiny spoon. Then she handed the bottle to her friend and smiled at Cam. "Ladies first."

The second one took a snort, smiled, then handed it to Cam. Cam stuck the spoon in, filled it, then snorted it. "Oh, yeah," he said with a big grin. "It's been a while."

"This is good stuff," the first one said.

"I can tell," Cam said.

After their drive along the beach and a few more bumps of coke, the second model suggested they go dancing. Cam Googled places that had live music on his iPhone, and they ended up at a place called Blue Martini. The three danced together for about five dances, with the occasional male straying in and out of their orbit. Then the first model said she'd heard of another good place not far from where they were, and they went there. It was called Respectable Street which, it turned out, was a gay club. Cam quickly found his dance moves were not up to Respectable Street standards. But not all was lost: it seemed the two women had gotten into a competition for Cam's affections, and what man in his right—or wrong—mind wouldn't be flattered by that?

"Come on, Cam," the second one said, grabbing his arm. "We had a little tete-a-tete in the ladies' room and decided to share you."

Cam held up his hands. "Whoa. Whoa. Maybe I forgot to mention something."

"What's that?" said the first one.

"I'm married."

"So?" said the second one.

"So, I can drink and dance and do blow with you all night long, but… that's it."

The first one looked at the second one, then back at Cam. "Are you fucking kidding?"

Cam smiled and shook his head.

The second model didn't seem to think he was serious. "So, are you telling us you're going to pass up two of the best-looking women in Palm Beach and… go back to the Breakers… alone?"

Cam nodded. "Yeah. Hey, I never said I was sane."

The second one, shaking her head, glanced over at the first one. "This is a night to remember."

"Yeah, we end up with the only man in the universe who didn't forget he had a wife."

"You know, Cam," said the second woman, looking around the room, "maybe you're at the right place."

"What do you mean?"

"Well, you're obviously gay."

The two walked out and didn't look back.

48

C rawford had put two calls in to Arthur Doe, DDS, and had not heard back from him. It was funny how that worked. Over the years, Crawford had noticed a trend: the innocent ones usually tended to call back pretty quick, the guilty ones took their time and often never called back at all. There was a third category of people in his callback theory—the rich and powerful. Their MO was to have an underling call back or simply never bother. When Crawford showed up on their doorsteps, they'd come up with a lame apology and say how they were just *so damn busy*.

He put in a call to Cam at nine. Clearly, he'd woken up his brother.

"I remember when you'd get up at 5:30 and do a five-mile run."

"I still do," Cam said, "but I'm on vacay now. By the way, I love hearing those waves crashing below."

Crawford laughed. "I wouldn't know. At my place, all I hear is cars honking in the Publix parking lot."

Cam laughed. "So, before you grill me, I'm gonna confess. I met a couple of hotties last night and we ended up cutting a rug at some of West Palm's finer establishments. Last one turned out to be a gay bar."

"Oh, Jesus, so you got back into the booze again?"

Cam sighed. "Yeah, I did."

"Anything else?"

"Anything else what?"

"You know. Yayo or something?"

Cam laughed. "I'm impressed you're up on the slang."

"That's pretty old."

"Whatever," Cam said, "so at one point I thought about calling you, making it a foursome…"

"Thanks for not."

"You've turned into such a straight arrow."

"Hey, man, I'm a cop."

"You saying no cop's ever done blow before?"

"Doing blow in a gay bar with strange women, that'd look good on my resume."

Cam laughed like it was a painful act.

"So, what are you doing before golf?"

"Having lunch with an old college friend at the Palmetto Club, then I don't know. Get Christie something on Worth Avenue, I was thinking."

"All right, well, get up and go do your run."

"Yeah, yeah, and puke my brains out."

ARTHUR DOE finally called back and Crawford made an appointment to go to his dental office at five. Doe, of course, asked what it was about, and he, of course, said he just had a few more routine questions. Doe sounded like he wasn't looking forward to it.

Crawford saw that he had gotten a call from Dominica while he was on the phone with Doe and dialed her number.

"Hey, Charlie," she said. "I just wanted to let you know that we came up empty on the ASR, the airport surveillance radar. No sign of a drone over Palm Beach or anywhere near Preston Platt's house on Emerald at the hour in question."

He thought for a moment. "Thanks. I'm thinking he might have made that whole thing up."

"Why would he do that?"

"Because he knows he's still a suspect in Crabb and wants it to seem like Crabb's killer tried to take him out, too."

"That's kind of convoluted."

"Yeah, but I'm not putting it past him."

"So you're thinking… he just took a pot shot at his pool?"

"That's my guess. What other evidence would he have that the attack took place?" Crawford said. "Hey, what are you doing later?"

"No plans."

"Good. How about another speed nine? I want to get revenge for that humiliation last week. I also got my brother in town; he's gonna play, too."

"Oh, great, I'd love to see him. What time?"

"Balls on the tees at seven."

"I'll be there."

As he was picturing Dominica swinging a golf club, Ott came charging into his office.

"Hey, we gotta go see the chief."

"Oh, Christ," said Crawford. "What's Norm's problem now?"

"Not that chief. Leroy Mack," Ott said, not bothering to sit.

"Why? What did you find out?"

"Get this: Mack just called me—he sounded pretty amped up—and said Yu Jintao, the Chinese guy who came here a month ago, showed up at his house. He had a translator with him and—long story short—said he wanted his money back."

"What money back? I thought he was one of the plaintiffs in the Sabal House lawsuit. That EB program or whatever."

"EB-5," Ott said, shaking his head. "Poor bastard's a two-time loser. Also invested in Wayne Crabb's casino. The one Crabb was going to do first with Leroy Mack, then Ricky Slashpine."

"Jesus, Mort, you need a playbook for all this shit."

"No kidding. So Yu Jintao, I'm guessing, came back hoping to salvage something."

"How much money did he have in the casino deal?"

"Two hundred fifty."

"And refresh my memory, where'd that money go?"

"Well, unofficially, to lawyers, accountants, and consultants to get the project off the ground. But, in reality, to bribe town officials, building inspectors, and other pols who had influence over the process."

"Christ, this is one hell of a tangled mess."

"You can say that again. So let's go see Mack. He's waiting for us."

"All right, I just gotta be up in Jupiter at five to meet with Dr. Doe."

"We got plenty of time."

Ott drove and they showed up at Leroy Mack's luxury trailer forty minutes later. Mack was outside with his dog, a Siberian Husky. Ott introduced his partner, and the chief welcomed and led them into his living room.

"So, Leroy," Crawford said, "I know you already told my partner what happened, but go through it again, please."

"All right," Leroy said. "This, ah, Chinese gentleman shows up here with this other guy, who turns out to be his translator. He was Chinese, too. He tells me Mr. Jintao, that's his name, was an investor in the casino deal that never happened. You know, with Wayne Crabb—"

Crawford nodded "—and that Mr. Jintao wants his money back. I tell him I had money in it, too, which I lost and ain't gettin' back. He didn't seem to care much about the money I lost and said he'd be back tomorrow and maybe I'd come up with the money by then."

"Or what?" Crawford asked.

"He didn't say."

"Was it a threat?"

"Not exactly… but not exactly *not*."

"So, what's gonna happen?" Crawford asked. "He's gonna come back here tomorrow?"

"That's the way it was left. Said he'd call beforehand. Look, man, even if I wanted to give him 250K, all I got is about five hundred bucks in the bank."

"Tell you what," Crawford said. "One or both of us will be here when he shows up tomorrow. Okay?"

Leroy nodded and smiled. "That's good because otherwise I was going to get the hell out of Dodge."

"Just call us when he calls you. Stall him if necessary so we have time to get here."

"You got it. Thanks for coming out so quickly."

"No problem," Crawford said. "But, just so I'm clear, he never actually threatened you?"

"Well, no, he never did. He just kept saying over and over that he wanted his money."

Ott shook his head. "Now in the pockets of corrupt lawyers and politicians."

BACK AT THE STATION, as Crawford prepared to drive up to Jupiter, he got a call on his cell. It was Arthur Doe.

"Hi, Detective," Doe said. "Listen, I have a medical emergency here. A kid fell off his bike and his teeth are a mess, so I need to cancel."

Crawford knew from earlier that morning that Doe was reluctant to answer any more questions, but what could he say?

"Okay, let's reschedule for the same time tomorrow."

A lengthy pause. "Okay, I guess that works," Doe said in a tone decidedly light on enthusiasm.

CRAWFORD, Dominica, and Cam were standing on the first tee of the par-three golf course in South Palm Beach. Given the extra time he had because of Doe's cancellation, Charlie picked up Cam at the Breakers and drove him to the course.

The round had gotten off to an auspicious start for all three players. They each had driven the green and had putts for birdie. None of them ended up making their putts, but all three carded pars.

On the third hole, Crawford and Dominica had to slow their pace to let Cam catch up with them.

"Come on, Cam, your ass is dragging," Crawford said.

"Yeah, what's the story, you're the youngest," said Dominica.

Cam smiled at Dominica. "Sorry, had kind of a rough one last night."

"Oh, this oughta be good," Dominica said. "Tell me all about it."

Cam glanced at his brother, like 'should I?'

"Go on," Crawford said with a nod. "She's probably heard worse."

"Well," Cam said as they walked down the short fairway, "I was minding my own business at the Henry Morrison Flagler bar at the Breakers when I struck up a conversation with a couple of babes. Models, in fact. Next thing you know, we're at that place Blue Martini dancing and then an hour later at a gay bar… dancing."

"You left out the eleven drinks you had—"

Cam held up his hand. "We don't need to go there, Charlie." He flicked his head at Dominica and said, "Your friend here's a cop."

"All right," Crawford said, walking over to hit his ball. "To be continued after I knock my ball in the hole."

"Fat chance," Dominica said.

Crawford's drive was twenty yards to the right of the hole. He chipped to ten feet from the pin, then Dominica hit her ball to about the same distance from the hole. Cam was already on the green. They all putted out and walked over to the fourth tee.

After Cam drove with a four-iron, Crawford pulled out his trusty Sasquatch driver. The hole was just over two hundred yards long.

Cam looked at the yardage on his scorecard. "Hey, man, it's only two-hundred and eleven yards."

"Yeah, so?"

"You said you could hit that sucker three-hundred yards."

Crawford shrugged. "Yeah, with a sixty-mile an hour wind behind me." He stepped up to the ball and roped his drive over the green into yet another sand trap.

Cam turned to him. "Did you hear that?"

"What?"

"The *plink*. Sounds like when you pounded a xylophone with a hammer."

Crawford laughed and shrugged. "I like it."

Dominica turned to Cam. "So I have a question about your adventure last night."

"Okay," said Cam, "but I gotta warn you, I don't exactly have total recall."

"Understood," Dominica said. "So my question is, was one of the women a tall blonde with a Russian accent and the other one a cute brunette with those plastic braces?"

Cam nodded. "Yeah, Jesus, you know 'em?"

Dominica chuckled. "I know *of* them." She turned to Crawford. "They're a pair of working girls who hang out at the Breakers and the Lizard Lounge at the Chesterfield."

Crawford shrugged. "Don't know about 'em. But… braces?"

"Yeah, you know, those clear things. Invisi-whatevers."

"Don't you just wear those when you're sleeping?" Crawford asked Dominica.

"Jeez, Charlie," Dominica said with a shrug, "you think I'm an orthodontist or something?"

"Sorry," Crawford said, "but why would any man ever think braces was a good look?"

"Can't tell you," Dominica said. "But maybe she was hoping some rich pedophile would come along. You know, trolling for a couple of fourteen-year-olds."

"That's sick," Crawford said.

Cam put up his hands defensively. "For the record, I didn't do anything with 'em besides dance." Then he added, meekly, "I think they thought I was gay. They left me to fend for myself at the gay bar."

"Which one?"

"Respectable Street, it's called."

"Oh, yeah," said Dominica. "You should feel complimented."

"Oh, yeah, why's that?"

"'Cause some women think that all the really handsome men are gay."

Cam shook his head and smiled. "That's a new one."

"Don't stroke his ego," Crawford said, motioning for his brother to drive his ball. "All right, Cam, it's your honor. Fire away."

Cam chuckled. "I like it when you call me 'Your Honor.'"

Cam hit a drive that hit the pin but bounced fifteen feet away. Then Crawford drove and, finally, Dominica.

As they walked down the ninth fairway, Cam asked, "They really have hookers in Palm Beach? 'Cause they never brought up anything about money."

Dominica pulled a club from her bag. "Probably were just about to when they decided you were gay."

On the ninth green, Cam tallied up the scores. "Okay, Charlie, you won... one hole, we tied two, Dominica won three and me three."

Crawford groaned and reached for his wallet. "A week's salary... hope you two feel bad."

49

Crawford and Cam were driving back from the par-three. Crawford was going to drop his brother at the Breakers, where Cam was having dinner with an investor in his fund.

"So, I've been thinking," Crawford started as he rounded a turn on South Ocean Boulevard.

"Uh-oh. Here we go… Is it possible you think too much, Charlie?"

"You mean, because you know it's going to be about you?"

"Well, yeah. All right, go ahead, give me both barrels."

"No, it's not like that. No lectures. No big-brother bullshit. Just a suggestion."

"I know what you're going to say."

"What?"

"Go back to Clairmount."

Crawford nodded. "Yup."

"It, obviously, has occurred to me."

"Well, it's obvious it could help."

"The problem is work. I mean Grey was okay with it the first time I went—" he was referring to Grey MacLeod, the head of Trajectory

Partners "—but I'm pretty sure he doesn't want me checking in on a regular basis."

"No, just once more. It worked the first time, for a while anyway. I think the second time would solidify it."

"You hope it would."

"I'm pretty sure. I know you *want* it to work. I doubt you want to spend any more time in the West Palm hoosegow."

Cam laughed. "That's for sure. I'm just glad it wasn't your hoosegow," he said as Crawford pulled into the long alley of trees that led to the Breakers Hotel. "Anyway, before I head north I want to help you wrap up your case… so you can go work on your golf game."

Crawford shook his head. "Oh, Christ, this oughta be good. Okay, I'm all ears."

"Like I said before: Mary Beth… whatever her name is."

"Hudson."

Crawford pulled over to the right side of the Breakers, and Cam said. "You gotta put a tail on her, or whatever you call it. Sit her down and give her the first degree."

"Third degree."

"Yeah, that. I'm tellin' you, man, she knew Crabb cold. How could she not? She worked for the guy for thirty years, right?"

Crawford nodded. "Yeah, you might be right. Nothing else is panning out."

"'Course I'm right. Have I ever led you astray?" Cam laughed and held up his hands. "Don't answer that."

He opened the car door, slid out, and got his expensive leather carry-on bag from the back seat. Then he approached Crawford.

Crawford put his arms out. "I'm not big on man hugs," he said, "but for you I'll always make an exception."

Cam put his bag down and hugged his brother. "Just don't kiss me."

～

CRAWFORD WENT BACK to his office, got on his computer, and

navigated to several sites he had used in previous cases. One was called Nexus, a Department of Homeland Security site, which allowed pre-screened travelers expedited processing when entering the United States and Canada. He was trying to get more background on Yu Jintao, who seemed to have been in the country for more than a month, and to ascertain what the man was doing there.

After that he went to another site that was abbreviated FDLE, which stood for the Florida Department of Law Enforcement. It was a division of the Criminal Justice Information Service and served as a central repository of information about crimes committed in Florida. If you were ever convicted of a felony in Florida, you were on it. He entered all of his suspects in the Wayne Crabb murder and none of them popped up. That is, with the exception of Dr. Arthur Doe. Doe had been convicted of counterfeiting two and a half years back. Clearly, pulling teeth was not as lucrative as it was cracked up to be.

At 9:45 p.m., he clicked off his computer, left the office, and headed for Dominica's.

She had told Crawford during their golf round, out of earshot of Cam, "To paraphrase that Motel Six dude, 'I'll leave the light on for you.'"

50

Dominica kept a box of Cracklin' Oat Bran cereal and Nueske's bacon in her kitchen because of Crawford's often-declared fondness for the two. So, he was having both, along with two slices of Arnold's Healthnut toast slathered with strawberry jam. She was wearing panties and his blue long-sleeved shirt; he had on her pink terrycloth bathrobe, which was a little snug on him. They were sitting on barstools at her island, watching the news.

"So, you picked up Rose yesterday?" Crawford asked.

"Yep," Dominica said. "She was pretty excited about getting back to that fancy bed of hers."

The one Crawford had spent many a not-so-restful night in. "Bet she's glad to get back to work."

Dominica nodded and poured another cup of coffee. "She is. Even though she sold a house while she was in her hospital bed."

Crawford shook his head admiringly. "Nothing slows that girl down."

"She told me she once wrapped up a deal on her cell phone when she was in the Galapagos Islands cavorting with tortoises and iguanas."

Crawford chuckled. "She's unbelievable."

Dominica nodded. "What are you doing today?"

"Well, first I've got an Indian chief, at least he claims to be an Indian chief, and a Chinese national. Then, later, a dentist up in Jupiter, Wayne Crabb's son-in-law."

"Sounds like a fun-filled day."

"Yeah, but it's time we wrapped up Crabb. It's getting really stale."

Neither said anything for a few moments. "What about Cam? How's he doing?" Dominica asked.

Crawford told her about Cam's first night, which had landed him in the West Palm Beach jail.

"Oh, God, that's not good," Dominica said.

Crawford nodded. "So, he agreed to go back to that rehab place in Connecticut. At least, I think he agreed."

"Is it one of those private addiction-treatment centers?"

"Yeah, but more than that. They teach you how to get rid of negative thinking and self-destructive stuff. Something called DBT. Don't ask what that stands for, I can never remember."

"Well, I hope he goes. He's such a good guy."

"He'll go. Even if I have to go up there, cuff him, and drag him off to the place." Crawford stood.

"Where you going?"

"Much as I'd like to hang around in this stylish pink robe all day, I gotta work."

Dominica stood up and kissed him. "And I suppose you want your shirt back."

AT A LITTLE PAST ELEVEN, Crawford got a call from Leroy Mack. "The Chinese guy's translator just called and said they'd be at my place in fifteen minutes. I said make it an hour and they said okay."

"All right," Crawford said. "I'll get Ott and we'll be on our way."

Crawford clicked off and went and got Ott. They got in the Vic and his partner drove them west.

"You think this is our guy?" asked Ott.

"I don't know, it just seems a little too easy."

"What do you mean?"

Crawford thought for a moment. "Well, if Yu Jintao was the killer, why wouldn't he have finished the job yesterday instead of dragging it out another day? Giving Mack a chance to run or bring us into it."

"You mean, just demand Mack pay him back his lost money right away and if he didn't, kill him?"

"Yeah, something like that."

"It's a good point. Maybe he thought by waiting he'd actually collect."

Crawford shrugged. "Guess we'll soon find out."

At first, Crawford and Ott considered hiding out in Leroy Mack's trailer and waiting until Yu Jintao and the translator were a threat to Mack. The upside was they could catch them in the act. It was a little dicey, though, because you never knew when a hothead might lose patience and just plug a guy. They finally decided simply to be two cops there to question Yu Jintao about Wayne Crabb's murder.

Yu Jintao was a slight man—a hundred and forty pounds or so—with wire-rimmed glasses and thinning hair. It was a little strange because he greeted Crawford and Ott warmly when they showed him their police IDs. His translator introduced himself as Zhao Zhanshu and appeared ten years younger than Jintao—Crawford guessed no more than thirty years old. It turned out he was Jintao's brother-in-law. Neither of them had the air of men practiced in the arts of mayhem and violence, and both were exceedingly polite.

Crawford had just asked Jintao exactly what his purpose was in coming to see Leroy Mack.

The translator translated the question.

"I assume Mr. Mack told you. I invested money in what I thought was going to be a casino of his, but then the money just... disappeared. I want it back because I need it."

Crawford's eyes flicked from the translator to Yu Jintao. "You need it... Can you be more specific about that?"

Jintao seemed to understand without his brother-in-law's translation. He spoke slowly in English. "I have a sister who lives in Atlanta. She is very sick with cancer. I planned to move to the United States because of the EB-5 program so I could be near her and take care of her. She used to run a small store in a Chinese neighborhood near Atlanta. Chamblee, it is called. But she got so sick, she lost it."

"I'm sorry," Crawford said.

Yu said something in Chinese. This time the translator translated. "She'll die if she doesn't get chemotherapy. When I first came here, I met with Wayne Crabb and told him about my sister. He didn't seem to care and wouldn't give me any money."

Meanwhile, Crabb seemed to have unlimited funds for his gang of mistresses, Crawford reflected.

"When you came here today, Mr. Jintao, what did you expect to happen?"

Zhao didn't translate. Jintao asked in English. "What do you mean?"

"I mean, I know you came here hoping Mr. Mack would give you money, but what were you going to do if he didn't?"

Zhao listened to Jintao's brief answer and translated. "What *could* I do? If he didn't give me the money, that would be the end of it—" Zhao shrugged "—unless you've got another idea."

Crawford turned to Leroy Mack. "Let me talk to you in private—" then to Ott "—Let's, the three of us, step outside for a second."

Mack, Ott, and Crawford went outside.

"I feel really bad for the guy," Mack said. "I mean, poor bastard's a two-time loser. Plus, his sister..."

Crawford nodded. "You said you only got five hundred bucks in the bank, right Leroy?" he asked, his eyes boring into Mack's.

"Yeah, that's about it."

Crawford took a half-step closer to Mack and got in his face. "So you wouldn't mind if we had a forensic accountant look into the books for that casino of yours, would you?"

"Ah—"

"'Cause something tells me we might run across some investor money that found its way into an account of yours. Am I right?"

"Hey, man, like I told you, I lost money on the thing, too."

"All right, so this forensic guy is really good at following the money. You wouldn't have a problem if he spent a few days going through your books, right?"

Mack didn't say anything but seemed suddenly mesmerized by his shoe tops.

Crawford kept going. "Okay, I'll call this guy right after we leave here and—"

Mack held up a hand like a traffic cop. "I guess I could give the Chinaman a couple grand."

"Make it ten, Leroy."

Mack raised his hands. "No way in hell."

Crawford turned to Ott. "You got that accountant's number, Mort?"

"All right, eight, then," Mack said. "That's the best I can do."

Crawford patted Mack on the shoulder. "Well, good. It's for a worthy cause. You'll probably sleep better at night."

Crawford glanced at his partner. "How much you got on you, Mort?"

"A hundred or so."

"Good," Crawford said, digging in his pocket for his wallet. "I'll match your hundred."

He opened his wallet and Ott did the same. He handed Mack five twenties, then Ott handed him a hundred-dollar bill.

"Okay, Leroy, you write the man an eight-thousand-dollar check and give him this cash and we'll all feel as though we did our good deed for the day."

Crawford turned toward the front door, and Mack and Ott followed him back inside.

Crawford sat down facing Yu Jintao. "Mr. Jintao, it's not as much as you were hoping for, but Mr. Mack is able to give you a check for eight-thousand dollars plus another two hundred in cash."

His brother-in-law translated.

Jintao's face lit up and he turned to Mack. It looked for a second like he was going to hug him. "Oh, thank you so much," Jintao said.

"That will help a lot," Zhao added, excitedly.

Tears were streaming down Jintao's face as he spoke again.

Zhao translated. "You are an exceedingly kindhearted man and I can't tell you how much my sister will appreciate your generosity. Thank you, thank you, thank you."

"You're welcome," Mack said. "I'll get my checkbook."

It wasn't the outcome that Crawford and Ott had hoped for: taking down the killer of Wayne Crabb. But a happy ending, nonetheless.

51

Crawford was back in the office. He had accumulated a lot of information about the history of Arthur Doe, and a shaky history it was. The more he looked into it, the wobblier it got.

Before seeing Doe, Crawford decided to shoehorn in a quick drop-by to see Mary Beth Hudson at Wayne Crabb's office. It was partly because of Cam's conviction that she knew more than she was letting on and partly because he thought she might be able to ID the couple or the car in the photos from the South Palm Beach condos. She had mentioned when he and Ott met with her before that it would take her at least two weeks to clean up Crabb's affairs and—sure enough—she was there when Crawford called. He asked if he could stop by in a half hour and she agreed.

She answered the door and let him in. They went into the conference room and sat down facing each other.

The first thing he noticed was that she was wearing a bulky gold necklace she wasn't wearing last time he was there. Dangling from her ears were large emerald studs that looked expensive.

"Pretty earrings," he said.

"Thanks."

He looked around the walls of the conference room at the photos of Wayne Crabb, middle-aged surf fanatic, still on the walls. Blown-up, framed photos of him on big waves, small waves, and gigantic waves. There were cliffs in the background in one, sandy beaches in another, and a black, rocky shore in a third.

Crawford glanced from the photos to Mary Beth Hudson. "Looks like Wayne went a long way to find the perfect wave."

Hudson nodded and smiled. "The man was obsessed. His one true love."

"How long ago did he start?"

"Before I started working for him. Thirty-five years ago or so, I think."

"It looks like a lot of fun."

"It looks really scary to me."

Crawford nodded. "So how much longer are you going to be here, Ms. Hudson?"

"Well," she said with a big smile, "I had planned to just make it a couple of weeks, but Betsy—Mrs. Crabb—generously offered to pay me for the next six months."

"Lucky you," Crawford said. "That was really nice of her."

"I know, she's a first-class lady. So, what is it you wanted to know?"

"Really just one thing," Crawford said, taking a photo out of the envelope in front of him and handing it to her. "Do you have any idea who this couple might be?"

She took it and looked at it. Crawford thought he saw a flash of recognition, but then it was gone.

"Who is it, Ms. Hudson?"

She quickly handed him the photo. "I have no idea. You can't even see their faces."

"But you seemed—"

"I said, I have absolutely no idea."

"Did you… at first… think you recognized them?"

"No."

Crawford shrugged. "Okay, well thank you. That's all I wanted to know." Slowly, he got to his feet, hoping she might volunteer something. She didn't. "If you have any further thoughts on who they might be, please give me a call."

"I sure will, Detective. Thanks for coming by."

He paused to look at a photo of Crabb surfing, still hoping she might burst out with a, *Oh, yeah, now I remember that's...* But no such luck.

The second thing he noticed was when he walked outside. In a parking spot marked *Crabb Development* was a shiny new red Audi. He remembered a white Camry with a dent on the driver's side last time he was there.

HE ARRIVED at Doe's dental office at just past five. He walked into the reception area and pressed the buzzer. A minute later, Doe walked out in his white coat and greeted him. Crawford was glad to see no blood on the coat.

Doe shook his hand. "Sorry I had to cancel last time," he said. "Had a real crisis on my hands."

"No problem," Crawford said. "I'm just going to get straight to the point, doctor. I've done a lot of digging around and know a lot more about you and your practice than the first time I came here."

Doe raked a hand down his cheek but kept silent.

"I know, for example, your previous practice went bankrupt five years ago and that you were charged with malpractice just before that. I know that you had several lawsuits pending at the time of your bankruptcy. I'm guessing that you declared bankruptcy to nullify those lawsuits."

Doe's hand shot up. "Look, I admit it. I had a lot of problems back then. I had an assistant, fresh out of dental school, who botched a couple of things really badly."

"I read about her. Lindsay Harkness, right?"

"Herkness."

"So, are you saying none of it had to do with you? It was all your assistant's incompetence?"

"Yeah, mostly."

"Well, doc, the reality is, it doesn't much matter because the buck stopped with you." Crawford had read enough to know that the malpractice charges had been leveled against Doe himself. Crawford had read on Yelp that Doe Dental averaged one and a half stars. "It was, after all, your practice and your office."

"So, what does any of this have to do with my father-in-law?" Doe asked.

"I also know that two and a half years ago you were convicted of a felony," Crawford said. "Counterfeiting, to be exact. Reading between the lines, it looks like you got off because your father-in-law pulled a few strings."

"Yeah, well, that's because he was worried about how it was going to reflect on him. *Humiliate* him, was the exact word he used. With Wayne, it was always about him. Never Betsy, Lauren, or me. He couldn't give a damn about anyone but himself."

Doe's level of hostility toward his father-in-law had amped up considerably from the last time.

Crawford opened the manila envelope he was carrying. "I've got something here that I'd like you to take a look at." He held up the photo of the couple, the drone above them, and the car off to the side.

Doe pulled it closer and studied the photo. "Holy shit."

"What?"

"That's a two-tone car, right?"

"Looks like it."

Doe's eyes went wide with… something more than surprise but less than shock. "Don't see one like that around much."

"Yeah, I know."

Doe slowly shook his head. "Except in my mother-in-law's garage."

52

"**D**amned if that's not Betsy's Maybach," Doe said, pointing at the photo. "The upper part's silver and the lower panels are blue."

It had come totally out of left field. But it suddenly dawned on Crawford, as far as a motive, that Betsy Crabb had one. In spades. Her husband was a serial cheater, after all. It must have finally reached the breaking point with her...

But then Crawford remembered what he had been told—how Betsy Crabb lived a totally independent life from her husband. What was it... bridge, tennis, garden club...? Then he remembered someone had mentioned Betsy's boy toy. He hadn't thought anything of it at the time.

"This man," Crawford asked Arthur Doe, "any idea who he might be?"

"I have every idea who he might be," Doe said. "His name is Bill Kelly."

"Keep going?"

"He was Wayne's pilot."

"His pilot?"

"Yeah. Wayne had a Citation 10. He used it a lot to go on his surfing trips. Oahu, Australia, New Zealand, Indonesia, you name it. Took his bimbos along on lots of 'em. When Bill wasn't flying Wayne around the world, he was romancing my mother-in-law. Hey, she deserved to have a little fun, 'cause all Wayne ever gave her was headaches."

"Where's he live? Kelly?"

"I don't know."

Crawford's mind was spinning. "You got any more surprises, doc?"

"No, I just figured you knew about Bill by now."

Crawford shook his head. Maybe he should have.

Doe snapped his fingers. "Oh, I just remembered something. Lauren told me Kelly's hobby was flying drones. Figures, right? Him being a pilot and all."

"All right, thanks," Crawford said, bolting for the door.

He figured anyone with a Citation 10 at his disposal was the definition of a flight-risk.

He got in his car and called Ott on his cell.

"Hey, Charlie."

"Go to Betsy Crabb's house and arrest her for the murder of her husband."

He heard Ott exhale, low and slow. "You're shittin' me."

"No. She and her boyfriend, who was Crabb's pilot. Name's Bill Kelly. I'm trying to track him down."

"*Jesus*, Charlie. Sweet, demure Betsy?"

"I know."

He clicked off. Then his mind jumped to Mary Beth Hudson, and it dawned on him that she had recognized Betsy Crabb and Bill Kelly in the photo earlier and had probably warned Betsy that Crawford would be showing the photo to others. He took it further and wondered if Mary Beth had suspected Betsy all along. Then had maybe hit her up for some *keep quiet* money. Hence, the new red Audi and green emerald studs.

He hit redial for Ott.

"What'd you forget?"

"I'm going straight to Signature," Crawford said, referring to the private airport just south of Palm Beach International Airport.

"Sounds like Lil Fonseca all over again," Ott said.

"Never thought of that."

Ott was referring to their first case together, in which they arrested a former girlfriend of Crawford's named Lil Fonseca as she was making her getaway at Signature.

Crawford stepped on the gas. It was a straight shot on I-95 to Signature, which he figured he could do in twenty minutes. He flashed back to Lil. They'd had a brief, shining fling that ended well before Ott and he arrested her at the airport. She was sentenced to five years in a North Carolina prison for a massive art-fraud scheme. Crawford had gone up there to visit her but she refused to see him, which was understandable since he was the one who had arrested her and read her her rights.

His phone rang a few minutes later. It was Ott.

"Yeah, Mort?"

"She's gone," Ott said. "Her maid said she packed some clothes and left in a hurry."

"How long ago?"

"Ten to fifteen minutes."

"Okay, meet me at Signature as fast as you can get there. I'll call them now and try to stop their plane."

"Want the number?"

"Yeah, you got it?"

"Right here." Ott read him the number.

"Thanks."

"All right, I'm on my way," Ott said, and as if to emphasize it, Crawford heard the screech of burning rubber. Ott loved any excuse to drive fast.

Crawford dialed the number for Signature.

"Hello, Signature," a woman's voice answered.

"Hi, my name is Detective Crawford, Palm Beach Police. Has Wayne Crabb's plane taken off?"

"No, sir, but his pilot's in it now."

"But not Mrs. Crabb?"

"No, sir, I haven't seen her."

"Okay, I need you to stop the plane from leaving."

There was a pause.

He dialed up his *extremely forceful* tone. "This is a police matter and they need to be prevented from taking off at all costs."

"Okay, sir, I just don't know how to do that."

Crawford scrambled for a legit-sounding reason to delay its takeoff. "Tell the pilot that you have a situation. A plane's got to make an emergency landing and all planes are temporarily grounded."

"Okay," the woman said, tentatively. "Oh, I see Mrs. Crabb's car driving out onto the tarmac now."

"Okay, radio Kelly right away and tell him what I just told you. Tell him no other planes are allowed to take off or land until the situation I described is resolved."

"Yes, sir," the woman said, a little less tentative but a long way from forceful.

Crawford clicked off. He wondered whether she could sell it. She had to tell Kelly in such a way that it sounded like a genuine crisis. He wasn't confident she could manage that, though, and he feared Kelly would see through it.

He hit speed dial.

"Yup?" Ott answered.

"How far away are you?"

"Ten minutes."

"Me too."

A few minutes later, he called Signature back.

The same woman answered.

"This is Detective Crawford again. How'd it go with Kelly?"

"Um, not so well. He sounded kind of suspicious."

"But he hasn't started taxiing or anything, right?"

"Not yet."

"What's his flight plan?"

"After you called, I looked that up. He's flying to Bosnia."

"Bosnia?"

"Yes."

"Do you know how far that is?"

"Sorry, I don't. A long way, though."

Yeah, no shit. "Thanks." He clicked off.

He pushed a button on his dashboard. "Siri, I have three questions: One, how far is Bosnia from West Palm Beach, Florida? Two, how far can a Citation 10 fly on a tank of gas? And three, does Bosnia have an extradition treaty with the United States?"

Siri took a while. "Hi, Charlie, Bosnia is five thousand three hundred and fifteen miles from West Palm Beach. I have two answers to your second question. One source says that a Citation 10 can fly six thousand seven hundred fifty miles on a tank of gas and another source says seven thousand seven hundred and sixty-seven. In response to your third question, Bosnia currently has no extradition treaty with the United States of America."

He figured as much. "Thank you."

"You're welcome, Charlie."

"Oh, wait. I have another question."

Siri didn't respond.

"*Siri,*" he said loudly. She pinged in response. "How high is the fuselage of a Citation 10 off the ground?"

Siri took her sweet time on that query. "The fuselage of a Citation 10 is ten feet off of the ground."

Crawford thought for a second. If Betsy Crabb and Bill Kelly took off, there was every likelihood that they'd be gone for good. He thought a little more, then dialed Ott with a plan.

After talking to him, he called the woman at Signature and made sure that Ott and he had access to the tarmac. The woman gave them directions and explained how to drive onto the runway. He asked her where the Citation was parked and what distinguishing features it had. She said it had a red surfboard on its tail.

Of course.

He called Ott back and quickly gave him the layout and entry point. "Where are you now?"

"Approaching the gate."

"I'm a minute away. Hold up." He told Ott the location of the Citation and about the red surfboard and kept the phone line open.

A minute later Crawford saw Ott idling at a gate open to the tarmac. "All right, man," he said. "Let's do it."

Ott laid down a thirty-foot patch of rubber and sped out onto the tarmac, Crawford twenty feet behind him. He saw the plane a hundred yards away. Ott got it up to about seventy, raced across the tarmac, then slammed on his brakes. He came to a skidding stop a foot from the front tires of the Citation, then hopped out and drew his Glock. Seconds later, Crawford skidded to a stop several feet behind the front tires. He jumped out, yanked out his Sig Sauer, and aimed it up at the cockpit window, through which he saw a man's face.

Clearly, the man was not happy to see them. The expression *shock and awe* came to Crawford's mind.

53

Crawford and Ott split Betsy Crabb and Bill Kelly up immediately. This was pretty much Detective 101—don't give suspects any chance to talk between themselves and cock up some bogus story. Crawford took Betsy to the Palm Beach police station in his car, and Ott drove Bill Kelly in his. Then they led them into separate interview rooms, Crawford with Betsy Crabb in one and Ott and Bill Kelly in another.

To his surprise, Betsy did not clam up or demand a lawyer. It was almost as if she'd wanted to get things off her chest. The first thing she blurted out was that the whole thing was Kelly's idea. She said how he had first suggested it more than a year ago and kept pounding it into her head, eventually wearing her down. Crawford was a little surprised: the widow couldn't give up the poor pilot fast enough. Finally, she explained how Kelly boasted about having attached a tracking device to the bumper of her husband's car so he'd know where he was at all times. How proud he was about it being so *cloak and dagger*.

Crawford could play good cop or bad cop equally effectively, but he figured with Betsy he'd play *gentle cop*, slowly cajoling the full story out of her. Or at least her version of it.

After implicating Kelly in great detail, Betsy unloaded on her late husband.

"The whole world knew about his cheating. I mean, I caught him with a prostitute on our honeymoon. Came back early from shopping in Rome and…"

Crawford got the picture. Couldn't get much lower than that.

"But the crowning blow was when he told me he was going to divorce me and marry that tramp on his boat," she said with a deep sigh.

"Really?" Crawford said. "But wouldn't that kind of solve all your problems? He'd be out of your life and you could… have a relationship with Bill Kelly."

She twirled a strand of hair behind her ear and nodded. "So you'd think. But I signed a terrible pre-nup—" she came close to a smile "—I think it was the first one in recorded history. Thirty-eight years ago, to be exact. Long before Wayne made his money. I think it said I'd get half of everything he had *at that time*. We had a fifty-thousand-dollar house and about three thousand dollars in the bank."

"And there was no adjustment to present day?"

"No. What did I know? I'd had one year of college and—"

"And when Wayne said he was going to marry the other woman, he didn't volunteer to make your divorce… equitable?"

She shook her head emphatically. "Wayne? Not in a million years. He just said things like, 'The law's the law' and 'We signed that agreement.' I know," she said, gauging Crawford's reaction. "You never met the man." Then she unloaded a little more. "I realize that everyone thinks I just looked the other way, lived my own life, and it was all right. Well, no, goddammit, it wasn't alright at all. It was totally humiliating." She sighed. "My friends… I could imagine what they were saying. 'Oh, poor Betsy, so nice and sweet and cultured… has to put up with that lowlife philanderer.' Well, over time, that humiliation grew and turned into an enormous hatred for the man."

Crawford nodded in sympathy. "Mrs. Crabb, I'm curious about something."

A knock came at the door. Crawford looked up and saw Norm Rutledge's face in the porthole window. Crawford got up, walked over to the door, and opened it. He tried not to let his face betray what he was thinking: *What the hell do* you *want?* Or his fear: *I got this. Don't go screwing it up.*

"Hey, Charlie," Rutledge said, then looked past him to Betsy Crabb. "Hello, Mrs. Crabb. I'm Norm Rutledge, the chief here. I trust my detective is treating you well."

Rutledge was an interminable suck-up to rich people, or, in this case, what he thought was a rich person. Didn't much matter whether they were murderers or not.

"Yes, the detective has been a complete gentleman," she said, then winged off in another direction: "I had nothing to do with the death of my husband, you know. It was all Bill Kelly. He came up with the idea."

Rutledge weighed in. "But my understanding was that you and he... had a relationship and that was why—"

"Bill wanted Wayne's money, plain and simple."

Rutledge nodded and cocked his head. "Well, maybe you want to speak to a lawyer. Just in case."

Jesus. Crawford wanted to rear back and deck Rutledge. Why volunteer it if she hadn't asked? He'd read Betsy her rights, after all. The law didn't require that you offer concierge service or sage advice to suspects.

Betsy Crabb thought for a moment. "You know what? Maybe I should."

∾

NOT UNEXPECTEDLY, Bill Kelly told a quite different version of events.

He told Ott that Betsy Crabb had repeatedly urged him to kill her husband. One time she'd suggested he make it seem like one of

Crabb's irate mistresses was behind Crabb's death. Another time she went so far as to urge Kelly to eject himself from the Citation and parachute to safety while flying Crabb on one of his surfing safaris. But never did he admit that he had been behind the drone attack on Crabb and, after about five minutes, he lawyered up.

Crawford and Ott were in his office, comparing notes.

"What's your best guess on what's gonna happen?" Crawford asked Ott.

"I don't know, but I bet there's going to be a lot of sympathy for Betsy with all the #metoo stuff in the news," he said. "I'd say she does fifteen, he does twenty. No way either one gets a lethal injection or Old Sparky."

Old Sparky was the nickname for the electric chair.

"I thought they got rid of Old Sparky."

"Nah, you can choose either one. In fact, this one guy chose the chair back in 2016."

Crawford nodded

"While we're on a subject I know something about, take a guess how many convicted murderers are in line for the death penalty in Florida?"

"I don't know, five… ten?"

"You're way off. Try three hundred forty-one."

"Come on, really?"

Ott nodded.

"How do you know so much about this?" Crawford asked, putting his feet up on his desk.

"Hey, it's our business. Don't you want to know everything you can about your trade?"

"Yeah, but, I don't exactly think of execution as part of the job."

"Sure it is," Ott said. "It's the last part."

Crawford chuckled. "I guess you're right."

Ott nodded. "You know what it is, Charlie… you just put it out of your mind. We put killers in jail and that's the end of it for you."

"Well, no, that's not true. There's the trial."

"Yeah, but you hate that part."

"Yeah, I do. 'Cause we just sit around and drink coffee. It's boring as shit."

"Agreed," Ott said. "But you know how it is. All jobs have parts that are boring. We, on the other hand, get to shoot guns, chase people in our muscle cars, put bad dudes in jail, interview strippers and hookers… what am I forgetting?"

"Get to drink at cop bars."

"Damn straight." Ott got to his feet. "Let's go."

54

It was Saturday, and Crawford and Dominica were sitting on the beach at the north end of Palm Beach. They were watching three surfers—two men and a woman—and getting their courage up.

Dominica turned to Crawford. "What made you think of doing this?"

"Lust."

"What?"

"I wanted to see you in a skimpy bathing suit again. But instead you wore that one-piece."

She looked pretty damned good in it, though. It was white and contrasted nicely with her dark skin and showed off her curves and incredible legs to perfection.

"No, really, how'd you come up with this?" Dominica asked, squinting into the sun.

"Well, for one thing, I suck at golf and was beginning to get a complex 'cause you beat me all the time. That's number one. Number two is Wayne Crabb had these cool pictures of him surfing in different places around the world. It was like, 'Wow, that looks like fun.'"

Dominica got to her feet. "Okay, come on, let's give it a shot." She leaned down and picked up a bright yellow surfboard while Crawford picked up his neon-green board. They had rented them from a surf shop in West Palm.

"I wish these things had training wheels or something."

Crawford had emailed his brother, Cam, that morning. "Bad guys in the slammer, all quiet in PB, gone surfin' with Dominica."

A few hours later, Cam had emailed him back. "Headed back to Camp Dry-Out with case of Vernor's in trunk. Hang Ten!"

Dominica, board under her right arm, looked out at the waves. "These waves aren't exactly the Banzai Pipeline."

"What's that?"

"I did a little research," she said. "It's in Oahu. Huge waves crash right next to a reef."

"Sounds perfect for surfers with death wishes."

"Yeah, we're not quite ready for that."

They got up to the water's edge and stuck their toes in.

"I'm not even sure I'm ready for these little waves yet," Crawford said.

"Come on, Charlie, a big college athlete like you?" Then, more firmly: "This *was* your idea."

They watched a female surfer catch a small wave and take it for a good ride.

"See how easy it is?" she said, watching.

Dominica walked out a little deeper, then got on her board and started paddling. Reluctantly, Crawford followed her. Staying on the board was easier than he'd figured it would be, but moving away from shore was serious work. Finally, they reached an area where two men were waiting for waves.

"How ya doin'?" one of them shouted.

"Hey," Crawford said back. "I'm kind of a jake, but, don't worry, I'll stay out of your way."

Dominica turned to Crawford. "A jake?"

"Yeah, I did a little research, too. It's surf lingo for a beginner. You know, like a hodad or a Quimby."

Dominica chuckled. "I have no idea what you're talking about."

"Don't worry, I'll translate as we go," Crawford said, paddling a little closer to the other surfers, who had now been joined by the woman. "You guys seen any men in gray suits out here?"

One surfer glanced at the one next to him and chuckled. "Ah, no. Never seen one yet."

Crawford turned to Dominica. "Men in gray suits are sharks."

Dominica nodded. "Better not be *any*."

Crawford turned to the other surfers. "Not a lot of nugs, huh?"

One surfer nodded.

Crawford smiled at the female surfer. "Mostly mushburgers, right?"

She nodded back and suppressed a chuckle.

Crawford turned to Dominica. "A nug is a good wave. Mushburgers are bad waves."

"Jesus, Charlie, more surfing, less lingo." With that, Dominica began paddling furiously and—miracle of miracles—caught a wave.

Wobbling a little, she got to her feet and rode the wave for about fifteen feet, then bailed out to her right. She surfaced and smiled back at Crawford.

He gave her a thumbs-up. "Epic!" he shouted.

The other surfers clapped.

Now, Crawford felt challenged. Would this be a replay of their golf competitions? Or would he discover he was a natural-born surfer dude?

A quasi-mushburger came along and he paddled hard into it. Shakily, he tried to get up, but didn't, so he flattened back onto the board and rode it toward shore, finally sliding off in knee-deep water. He turned the board around and paddled out to where Dominica had joined the other surfers. He got to within ten feet of them.

The woman surfer shot Crawford a big grin. "Know what they call what you just did?"

"No, what?" Crawford said.

One of the men laughed in anticipation.

"It's called a dick drag," the woman surfer said.

They all laughed. Especially Dominica.

"Bitchin'," he said, grinning at Dominica.

"Gnarly," she said.

THE END

AUTHOR'S NOTE

I hope you enjoyed Palm Beach Blues.

Since Charlie Crawford's brother, Cam, played a featured role in *Blues*, I've included the first two chapters of my standalone novel, *Broken House*, a novel quite different from the Palm Beach and Charleston mysteries. It's been out for about two years and, frankly, some readers were disappointed with it, even though it may be my favorite book yet. The problem was, I didn't forewarn readers that *Broken House* wasn't about Charlie and Mort solving murders or, depending on the day, Charlie in hot pursuit of Dominica or Rose. For those of you who haven't read it yet, the novel opens with Cam Crawford checking into an exclusive mental-health and chemical-dependency facility in Connecticut. He's battling the twin demons of alcohol and depression and—so far—losing. If it sounds like a downer, it's not. There are plenty of laughs, patients bonding, and romance… but a murder mystery *it ain't!*

So don't say I didn't warn you… but as I said, it's definitely a personal favorite of mine.

BROKEN HOUSE

1

Tell you right now, you're not going to like this guy at first. For starters, he's way too handsome—square jaw, piercing avocado-green eyes, thick dirty-blond hair. Too rich, too. Twenty-nine-year-old managing director of a New York hedge fund, pulling down six mil a year. Then there's his car—a shimmering midnight-blue Bentley. And the clincher, his license plate: *RAINMAKER.*

Case closed? Heard enough?

Hold on... half the people you talk to will say Cameron Crawford is big-hearted, sweet, and utterly charming. The other half? Probably something along the lines of superficial and shallow. Fatuous, even.

Maybe he's all the above.

The only thing not in dispute is that Cam is an alcoholic and substance abuser of Herculean proportions—a half bottle of Johnny Walker Blue and a side of pharmaceuticals on his nightly menu.

He works with his older brother Evan, and together they manage a billion-dollar fund. Evan is the brains behind the operation. Or at least that's what he hammers into Cam's head all day long. But besides being an MIT summa and brilliant at currency futures and every known derivative, Evan is beyond socially awkward. Schmoozing billionaire clients in the company box at Giants stadium... *so* not Evan's gig.

That's where Cam steps up. Bottom half of his class at the University of Virginia, but valedictorian of the party-hearty crowd; he's the contact guy with clients. Goes to their charity balls, wines and dines 'em, takes 'em out for eighteen at Shinnecock. Not that he likes it all; he's just a total natural. Cam is also one of those guys who is conversant in a vast spectrum of subjects, though not particularly fluent in any. Except maybe where to find bartenders who go heavy on the pour, light on the chitchat.

One time, Evan told Cam he was the virtual master of the fluffy conversation, spinning it like it was a compliment. Cam, accustomed to Evan rubbing his nose in it, nodded, smiled, and told him to go fuck himself.

One thing you wouldn't expect about Cam is his extraordinary knack for explaining to clients the complex mix of investments his brother puts their money into. And yes, he understands it all. If they listened to Evan, they'd stall out on his first sentence, the one where he monotones on about "systematic/qualitative" versus "quantitative directional" investing or the snore-inducing Dodd-Frank Act. That's where Cam steps in and breaks it all down. Simple. Clear. Concise.

So, the question is this: with good looks, the aforementioned charm, and enough intelligence to get by, why is Cam pedal to the metal on the self-destruction highway? The answer is not entirely clear at the moment, but at least he's finally realized he'd better do something quick, before he pitches off a barstool while they administer last rites to his liver.

～

WEAVING TOWARD CLAIRMOUNT HOSPITAL in the pastoral hills of Connecticut, Cam was singing along to a Mumford & Sons CD to stay awake. It was five in the morning, and he was slumped down in the driver's seat of his *look-at-me* wheels, formerly owned by his boss. What happened was, six months before, Trey MacLeod handed Cam the keys to the Bentley when he saw Cam pull into the company garage in a banged-up three-year-old Prius.

"That shit-box has gotta go. Not exactly the image we're tryin' to project," MacLeod had said with a monster scowl.

When Cam had started in on how good the gas mileage was, MacLeod cut him off. "Who gives a shit? Jesus, Cam, you some kind of tree hugger or something?"

Macleod, whose net worth was half a billion dollars and could give away a $150,000 automobile like it was a ten-dollar tip, didn't want to hear it when Cam said he wasn't much into cars. As for the lame license plate, Cam kept putting off going down to the DMV and waiting in line for hours to change it.

Clairmount Hospital, according to its website, specialized in "the treatment of psychiatric and addictive disorders" and was a "unique and extraordinary place that helps people find the path back to mental health and wellness."

At the moment, Cam was just trying to find the path to the admissions office.

Check-in time at Clairmount was nine o'clock Friday morning, so he figured he had one last blowout in him on Thursday night. So, after closing up Eugenia's on Gansevoort Street at four in the morning, Cam stumbled back to his car and aimed it in the general direction of Connecticut. Straying off course more than once, he almost took out a wild turkey on a winding back road in New Canaan. But finally, he GPS'd his way into Clairmount, spotted the red *Admissions* sign, and pulled into the parking lot. He still had two and a half hours to kill.

Parking his car in the handicapped spot—where else?—he reached over, pushed a button, and opened the burled walnut glove compartment of the Bentley. He grabbed a small dark-tinted bottle, twisted off the cap, and shook out a crooked line of white powder on his Black Amex card. He snorted half the bulky line, then switched to his other nostril and polished it off.

Reaching into the console, he pulled out the bottle of Johnny Blue that had been three-quarters full when he started his little misadventure seven hours before. Taking a long, heroic pull, he winced and shook his head a couple of times.

"Whoa," he said to his steering wheel, shoving the bottle back in the console.

Then, pushing open the weighty Bentley door, he tried to get out to take a leak. But as he slid to his left, he went too far and thumped down onto the asphalt parking lot, his left elbow and butt absorbing the fall.

"Shit," he muttered, searching his addled brain for the best way to achieve verticality. Pushing up from the pocked pavement, he staggered over to a nearby tree, hugged it like he was in the middle of a Cat 5 hurricane, and relieved himself.

Next thing he remembered was waking up in his car to a tapping sound. A woodpecker? Rain? He wondered how he could have nodded off with all the coke coursing through his veins. Cam looked up and saw a small, older woman in a nurse's uniform knocking on his windshield, a frown etched deeply into her forehead.

She put her hands up to her mouth and bellowed at Cam. "Will you pleeease get out of your automobile, sir?"

His head racked with hellish pain, he hit the button, and his window descended noiselessly. The woman walked around to the driver's side.

He smiled up at her and couldn't resist. "Yes, please. Two Egg McMuffins, hash browns, and a coupla Bud tall boys."

She just sighed and shook her head. "Follow me," she commanded, as if to a misbehaving twelve-year-old.

Cam did as he was told. She reminded him of his grandmother— triple-chinned and mad-dog mean. Used to grab him by the ear and haul him off to the woodshed whenever he pulled one of his adolescent shenanigans.

He saw the woman's eyes zoom in on his jacket lapel. He glanced down and saw a slick pool of drool. She just shook her head, realizing she had a major-league fuck-up on her hands.

He followed her into the big open sitting room in Admissions. Martha Stewart's fingerprints were all over the place: lots of chintz, all warm and cheery, with three vases of fresh-cut flowers on tables surrounded with bright-colored club chairs and couches. On one wall hung a large watercolor of a sailboat in the ocean, its blood-red spinnaker ballooning out. The upscale homey look was spoiled, though, by a shiny defibrillator mounted on a rustic hand-hewed beam and a straitjacket hanging next to a raincoat in a half-open closet.

A woman at the desk gave Cam a clipboard with several pages of forms on it and asked him to fill them out.

Cam looked over at a man in his fifties with his head in his hands. He sat in a straight-back chair next to a woman who had the sad gray eyes of a long-suffering wife. When the man moved his hands, Cam caught a glimpse of his face—tortoiseshell glasses and a sickly pallor. He looked massively depressed.

"You going to be okay, honey?" the wife asked, as Cam struggled to fill out the form with head-scratchers like 'age' and 'home address.'

"I don't know," the man mumbled without looking up. "Don't know *anything* anymore."

Cam felt sorry… for *her*. The man sounded like he was ready to swan dive off the GW Bridge. Dude needed to suck it up a little.

After a few minutes, the outside door opened and a woman with sunglasses strolled in and sat down next to Cam. She shot him a glance, as if trying to sniff out his affliction. He smiled at her, then went back to the questionnaire, his right leg bouncing up and down as if to some driving hip-hop beat.

Cam looked over again at the man. His head had slumped farther forward. The wife patted him on the knee.

"It's going to be okay, Ted," she whispered.

Cam envied Ted. No way Cam's wife, Charlotte, would ever be so supportive. She had volunteered to come home a day early from her quarterly tune-up at the Canyon Ranch in Arizona and drive him to Clairmount. But when he said he could manage it alone, she didn't push it. He wondered if maybe she had rendezvoused with her boyfriend out there. The boyfriend he wasn't supposed to know about.

He could tell Ted's wife had insisted on coming, probably arranged the whole thing. Ted didn't look capable of much on his own.

Meanwhile, Ted's head had dropped another six inches, just above waist level now. Like it was a twenty-pound medicine ball. His glasses had slid down to the tip of his nose. Cam started to say something to Ted's wife, but her eyes were locked in a thousand-yard stare, focused on something far, far away. Remembering better days, Cam guessed.

Without warning, Ted pitched off the chair and his head bounced off the beige Berber rug. His glasses snapped and went flying. His wife dropped down on all fours next to him.

"Teddy! Teddy!" she cried out, cradling his head in her lap. "Oh my God, are you all right?"

Cam slid out of his chair and crouched on the other side of the fallen man.

A muffled chuckle from Ted rumbled into a full-scale laugh. "I don't know what happened," he said at last.

His wife patted his head sweetly, smiled, and kissed his forehead. "That's the first time I've heard you laugh in years."

Ted looked over at Cam, embarrassed a little. "How'd you like my little Nagasaki nosedive?"

"A perfect ten." Cam picked up half of Ted's glasses. "Gonna need a little Krazy Glue here. I'm Cam, by the way."

"Ted," Ted said, getting to his feet.

After Cam had climbed back into his chair, he looked over at the woman in dark glasses next to him. "You know, you remind me of someone," he said.

"You remind me of someone, too," she said, deep into her *Vanity Fair*.

"Oh yeah? Who?"

"A guy who hangs out in gin mills too much."

Cam laughed. "Opium dens, too."

She raked him with scorn. "I believe it."

Cam dropped his voice. "Could I tempt you with a cocktail? Out in my car?" he asked, momentarily forgetting he had killed the Johnny Blue.

She turned and glared through the thick dark glasses. She had beautiful skin, jutting cheekbones, and a major-league scowl.

Cam held up his hands. "Hey, we're not officially inmates yet."

She shook her head with withering disdain.

Turning to Ted, Cam asked, "How 'bout you?"

"How 'bout me what?" Ted asked.

Cam shielded his mouth and stage-whispered, "A pop... out in my car?"

Ted's eyes brightened. "I wouldn't mind a beer if you got one."

Ted's wife looked up. "Okay, you two, you're all done with that."

"Sorry," Cam said, chastened yet again.

"I usually have a couple beers a day," Ted said.

"A couple?" his wife said. She turned to Cam. "The doctor said alcohol makes his depression much worse."

Ted nodded. "It's true. A black cloud literally hangs over me."

A male attendant walked up to Cam. "Mr. Crawford, if you're ready, I need to get you to the lab," he said. "Take a little blood, then up to Main House."

Cam smiled and rose, his balance wobbly.

"Just a couple things first," the attendant said.

"What?" Cam asked.

"I went through your suitcase. That candy—sorry, you can't have that in your room."

"No?"

The attendant shook his head.

"Well, how 'bout if..." Cam opened his suitcase and pulled out a large bag of M&Ms.

He tore open the bag and offered it to Ted's wife. "Sweet tooth?"

"Thank you," she said and took a handful.

Cam turned to the woman with the sunglasses and held out the bag. She ignored him.

Cam shook the bag.

Seeing he wasn't going away, she asked, "Plain or peanut?"

"Peanut."

She shook her head. "Yuck."

Cam laughed. "But thanks for asking, Cam. That's very kind of you."

Nothing.

Cam turned to Ted. "How 'bout you, Black Cloud?"

"No, thanks," Ted said.

Cam shook out a handful for himself, then handed the bag to the attendant.

"Here you go. All yours, bro."

"Thanks," the attendant said, pointing to Cam's suitcase. "Oh, and that green T-shirt of yours—"

"The Heineken one?"

The attendant nodded.

"Kinda sends the wrong message, huh?" Cam said.

2

Avril pulled up in a black stretch to the Admissions building later that day. Her driver, Lenny, scurried around and opened her door. She stepped out, sucked in a deep breath, and started toward the little house with the red *Admissions* sign on the door. She caught her reflection in the passenger-side mirror and didn't like what she saw. She U-turned back to the car and told Lenny to cool his heels while she worked on her face. The face that the boy director had just told her looked "haggard" on the set of the big budget rom-com they were shooting in Westchester Country. The same face that had graced the cover of *OK!* magazine only a month ago. That was an all-time low, Avril's picture right below the lead story: "Kim Jong Un's Plan To Snatch Jennifer Anniston!" She thought she looked like a hooker who had just crawled out of a Sunset Strip crack house at five in the morning.

The headline screamed, "Avril's On-Set, Off-Color Antics!" It was a bogus headline, designed to get readers to fork over five bucks to paw through the pathetic rag, expecting sin and salaciousness, only to find vague references to Avril being "tortured and tormented."

Well, Christ, she thought, who the hell wasn't?

Avril had been tense and edgy from day one on the rom-com set, having just crash-landed from a manic high. It was brutal playing the perky, high-spirited news anchor as she slogged her way through the thick mud of a full-blown depression. Then there was the whole mess with her co-star, Rankin Hanley.

"Do I look puffy, Larry?" she asked.

She knew she had screwed up his name, but couldn't be bothered.

"You look beautiful, Ms. Ensor," Lenny said as he opened the door again for her.

Bullshit, she thought.

Avril Ensor was about to become Colleen Higgins, her rehab alias so the tabloids wouldn't get wind of her being at Clairmount. Colleen Higgins was actually the name of her seventh-grade drama teacher, the one who had picked her to play Dorothy in *The Wizard of Oz*, her first nibble at applause and adulation.

She wore a black beret pulled low and big wraparounds as she opened the door to the Admissions building and walked up to the desk. Trying to be invisible, she whispered to the woman in charge, "Hi, I'm Colleen—"

"I know," the woman said, her eyes bulging, then she winked at Avril like they were co-conspirators. "There's quite a bit of paperwork so if you're ready, we can get started."

She handed Avril a clipboard with a form on it. Avril handed it right back to her. "Fill it in and I'll sign it."

"Ah, Colleen, I'm afraid that's not how—"

But Avril was halfway across the room.

She sat and looked over at an older man opposite her. Shaking, the man was bent forward, folds of skin dangling from his chin and neck. His eyes were glassy. He looked like he was on the tail end of something. Beside him sat a stern-looking, older woman staring at a dog-eared *Cosmo*. She looked like she'd rather be at a Megadeth concert. Avril's eyes shifted to another woman in her thirties, dead still, like a mannequin. Her eyes had a glint of terror in them, as if she was reeling back through a scene of some dark, personal hell.

Avril looked at another woman in a turtleneck. Something was a little off. Then it occurred to her. Well, yeah, no shit, everyone at this place was going to be at least a *little* off. Whether it was drugs or alcohol, drugs *and* alcohol, borderline personality disorder, post-traumatic stress, depression, or God-knows-what, people didn't come to Clairmount for the ambiance.

She pulled her beret lower, stood, and walked around. Antsy.

She saw an ambulance pull up outside. An attendant in a white jumpsuit went around and opened the back door. He stepped up into the back of the ambulance. A minute later, he hopped back down and was followed by a tall, skinny redheaded girl. Late teens, max. Her hair was the color of a Key West sunset and surrounded her pale freckled face like a halo.

Avril saw a six-inch-wide bandage on her left wrist as the girl followed the tech toward Admissions.

Seven sets of eyes zoomed in on her bandage as she walked inside.

"Okay, so what," the girl said loudly, seeing everyone staring. "Tried and failed. What are your lame-ass stories?" Her eyes strafed the room.

A tech put his hand on her shoulder and tried to steer her toward the check-in desk. "Come on, Rachel," the tech said, "let's just get through the process, nice and—"

But there was no stopping her—she was in fifth gear.

"Goddamn roomful of zombies—" she said, zeroing in on a mousey, older man standing nearby.

"I just work here," he said.

"Coulda fooled me," she shot back.

Her eyes flicked to the older woman next to the glassy-eyed man, trembling now like he was on top of an L.A. quake.

"Just a wild guess: pill popper?" Rachel said.

The woman rolled her eyes. "I happen to be a family member."

Rachel nodded.

"You tellin' me you never knocked back a Xanax or two?"

She didn't wait around for an answer.

The social worker was suddenly in her face.

"Okay, miss, you need to stop talking right now," she said, hand on hips. "You're being very disruptive."

Rachel ignored her and looked across the room, spotting Avril for the first time.

"Hey, I really dig those Jackie Os," she said about Avril's sunglasses, "and that funky *chapeau*."

Avril was in no mood. "Listen, you little—"

"That'll be enough," said the social worker, taking a step toward her.

But Avril wasn't done. "You come in here like some loudmouthed drama queen... whatever your problem is, how 'bout keeping it to yourself? Everything was nice and peaceful till you showed up."

The social worker and the tech moved between them like hockey refs. Then the social worker took one of Rachel's arms.

"Let's go, Rachel," he said, guiding her across the room toward a door.

Rachel didn't resist and walked zombie-like to the door. But then suddenly she turned, caught Avril's disapproving eyes, raised her right hand, and extended her long, skinny middle finger.

IS TODAY YOUR LUCKY DAY OR WHAT?

Preview for the next book!

What follows are the opening chapters of the first installment in my new series set in Savannah, Georgia. *The Savannah Madam* features two protagonists, sisters-turned-private investigators. First there's Jackie—how did a woman go from the film business to chasing badass killers? Then there's Ryder, whip-smart and model-beautiful. Some say sassy, some say wise-ass, everyone agrees, brash.

To solve their new case, they dive deep into a murky demimonde of crooked cops, high-class brothels, and low-rent thugs.

Hope you enjoy it!

THE SAVANNAH MADAM SERIES SNEAK PEAK

1

Diana Milton, reporter for the Savannah *Morning-News*, was writing a feature series on women who worked in unusual —read: male-dominated—professions.

She had just asked private investigator, Jackie Farrell, about the Philomena Soames murder case up in New York. Diana had read about it on the Savannah Investigations website, and it was the reason why she had contacted Jackie in the first place.

Jackie, whose full name was Jacqueline Gardiner Farrell, was the founding partner of Savannah Investigations. At five-foot-three, Jackie joked about her parentage, since her father was six-three and her mother five-ten. She was a blonde with striking blue eyes, a dazzling smile, and a gym-trim body. Her clothes tended to run somewhat conservative but watch out because every once in a while, she'd surprise you with a slit skirt eight inches above the knee and a plunging neckline.

"Savannah Investigations' principal, Jackie Farrell," read the firm's website, "was instrumental in cracking the New York murder case of actress Philomena Soames." Immediately below the headline, the site announced: "We specialize in domestic surveillance cases, missing persons, and undercover operations."

The backstory on the Soames murder was that Jackie, twenty-nine at the time, worked for the New York branch of a Hollywood film production company called Montana Films but got such a pathetically anemic paycheck from them that she had taken on a part time job. (A "side-hustle," the millennials called it.) Through a low-level showbiz contact, Jackie got hooked up with the British actress, Philomena Soames, who had worked in a few indie films that had done well at Sundance but not at the box office. Philomena also fancied herself a writer and figured she just might have the great English novel in her but had stalled out halfway through chapter five. So, she put the word out that she needed a "creative muse."

A few years before, Jackie had written a screenplay that seemed terminally stalled in development and before that, while an undergrad at University of North Carolina, had won the Scribner Award for "Best Young Novelist"—even though, technically speaking, it was a novella. So, Jackie applied for the job with Philomena Soames, got it, and the two soon became fast friends.

"So, give me all the details," Diana Milton asked Jackie. "The Soames murder, I mean."

"Well," Jackie said, taking a sip of her coffee. "The murder took place five and a half years ago. I don't know if you remember the story or read about it, but Philomena lived down in Tribeca," Jackie said, explaining that she went to Philomena's apartment three times a week to work on her novel with her, "and was stabbed twenty-seven times there."

Jackie had actually discovered her mutilated body and still had nightmares about it. Three of the four rooms in Philomena's apartment had been splattered with blood. More blood than Jackie thought a human body could contain.

"I remember something about it not turning out to be who the police first suspected, right?" Diana asked.

Jackie nodded.

The police had three suspects. A maintenance man in the building where Philomena lived who had been arrested for rape but had not been convicted. His name was Hector Milagros. The second suspect was a former boyfriend of Philomena's named Dylan Kidd, who was a TV commercial director. The third was Angus Benedict, a businessman, and Philomena's wealthy fiancé.

The detectives who caught the case talked to Benedict first at his West Side brownstone. He was a Managing Director of an English-based hedge fund and was overcome with grief, seemingly incapable of accepting the fact that his future wife had just been brutally murdered. The detectives showed him the least graphic crime-scene photos of his dead fiancée while he sobbed inconsolably. He claimed that Philomena and he had planned to have brunch together the next morning—a Sunday—at a place in the West Village. The detectives thanked him, said that they were sorry for his loss and that they'd be in touch as soon as they had something.

Then they took in Milagros and put heavy pressure on him for seven straight hours in a closet-sized room at the downtown precinct house. He claimed to have been at his apartment in Bensonhurst watching TV when it happened but had nobody who could back up his alibi. The long and the short was they couldn't break him, and their attention shifted quickly when they talked to a few people who knew Dylan Kidd, an ex-boyfriend of Philomena's. Turned out that Kidd, one of those men who was handsome in a three-day-growth, blue-eyed-badass kind of way, had kind of a sketchy reputation. One of his ex-girlfriends volunteered that the main reason she was his ex-girlfriend was that she discovered he had more girlfriends than there were deli's in New York. Also, a friend of Philomena's volunteered that she had heard Kidd had a habit of pulling out S&M paraphernalia after a few tequilas.

After hearing this, the detectives went to Kidd's apartment in Chelsea to talk to him. They hit his apartment buzzer on the building intercom. Kidd answered, they identified themselves as cops and he buzzed them up. Only problem was when they got up to his apartment on the twentieth floor, he wasn't there.

They got the building superintendent to let them in and found the stove on, a piece of uncooked salmon in a pan along with a half-finished Heineken on a granite countertop.

The detectives figured that Kidd had taken the back elevator or the stairway down while they were coming up on the front elevator. They put out an APB and tipped a TV reporter, who went on the eleven p.m. news and said that a "person of interest" in the Philomena Soames murder case had "eluded" the cops and was now the object of an "intensive, city-wide manhunt."

The next day Kidd walked into the precinct house and gave himself up. He explained that he had panicked and run. They put him in a small room, too, and good cop/bad copped him for four straight hours. The real reason he ran, he said, was the fact that he had had dinner with Philomena the night she was killed at a restaurant on the Lower East Side. He figured the detectives had found that out and that's why they were coming after him. He explained that he was trying to talk Philomena into giving their relationship another go, and she had allegedly told him she'd think about it.

No way the cops bought that, though, since she was engaged to Angus Benedict. And because six hours after dinner with Kidd she was found dead. Kidd allowed that the police might reasonably jump to certain conclusions about his guilt.

At that point, the detectives read him his rights and arrested him. The next day the front-page articles in both the *Daily News* and *Post* were about the arrest of Philomena Soames's murderer. To juice up the stories, the papers made not-so-subtle references to handcuffs, leather masks, and other sado-masochistic sex toys found at the apartment of the alleged killer.

To everybody in New York, it looked like the cops had their man.

Everybody except Jackie.

Part of it was Jackie had inside knowledge. For one thing, Philomena had broken off her engagement with Angus Benedict three days before she was killed. The main reason, Philomena explained tearfully to Jackie, was that he was jealous of every man Philomena even looked at. He had actually assaulted an actor who had a sex scene with her in a movie that was never released. Five hours after he beat the guy up, Angus called the actor and offered him twenty-five thousand dollars to pretend it never happened. That was more than the actor made for any part he'd ever played. He took the money and kept his mouth shut.

There also was the fact that Angus sometimes carried a pistol with him. When Philomena told Jackie that, Jackie said, "Are you kidding? That's so totally un-British."

Philomena laughed and said, "British? The man's as American as you are."

Turned out that Angus, nee Alan, had gone to Oxford and, overnight, morphed into an upper-crust Brit. Fact was, though, he had grown up on the wrong side of the tracks in a little town outside of Buffalo, New York.

The one time Angus had shown up at Philomena's apartment when Jackie was there, he'd been wearing a bowler hat and carrying a black cane with an ornate gold knob. Philomena thought it was cute; Jackie thought it was ridiculous.

Jackie was pretty sure that Philomena hadn't told anybody else about breaking her engagement. She and Philomena had become incredibly close, best friends really. Which was why Jackie was going to do everything she could to make sure that Philomena's killer went to jail for the rest of his life, though she would have preferred he get the chair, given the brutality of the murder.

Philomena had told Jackie a number of times about Angus' temper. How he'd go off on people who were driving too slowly when they were in his—what else?—Aston-Martin. Or how, one time, he reamed out a waiter who brought him a lime instead of a lemon. But mainly, it was his insane jealousy. Another time, a young guy recognized Philomena when she and Angus were walking down the street. The guy wanted to do a selfie of himself and Philomena.

Angus grabbed the guy's cell phone and stomped it into a hundred pieces.

Jackie had actually been part of the reason Philomena had called off her marriage to Angus. One day after hearing Philomena's latest story about her boyfriend's temper, Jackie had asked simply: "Are you sure this is the guy you want to spend the rest of your life with?"

Philomena didn't answer, but the next day she broke it off.

Then, three days later, Angus called Jackie and asked where Philomena was. Jackie knew but she didn't tell him.

Philomena was having dinner with Dylan Kidd at that very moment.

Another thing: The talk about Dylan having sado-masochistic sex toys... well, the fact was that Philomena had initiated *him* into the wonderful world of S&M.

Call it S&M lite, but S&M, nevertheless.

So, while Dylan was getting raked over the coals in the press for his twisted proclivities, the fact was that Philomena had pulled out the whips and handcuffs first.

*****

All Jackie had was a hunch. That the cops had the wrong guy. But it was a strong hunch. So, she went and talked to the detectives who had arrested Kidd. She told them all about the broken engagement and everything that Philomena had told her about Angus Benedict. His volatile temper and his violent tendencies. In fairness, the detectives didn't completely blow her off; they brought Angus back down to the station where they re-interviewed him. Once more, he snowed them with his pseudo-English charm. He downplayed everything, admitting that everyone who ever came in contact with Philomena hit on her and how that got old but, hey, that's the price you pay for falling in love with a movie actress. As for Philomena calling off the engagement, he flat-out denied it. He said that Jackie had never liked him and had just made it all up and even implied that Jackie liked Philomena in a way that was more than friend-to-friend.

When the detective told Jackie that, she showed them she had a temper of her own, and as the detectives wrote in his report he had to "calm her down," while assuring her that Dylan Kidd was indeed their man.

So, what ended up happening was Jackie took the law into her own hands.

She called up Angus and said she had just read Philomena's journal.

"Her what?" Angus said, in an agitated voice she had heard a few times before.

"Her journal," Jackie said, "everything you always wanted to know about the life of Philomena Ashburn Soames."

"She didn't have any journal," Angus said, anger creeping into his voice.

"Oh, really?" Jackie bluffed. "Would you like me to read you a few spicy excerpts? *Alan?*"

Angus was silent but, she guessed, seething. "What's your point? What are you after?" he asked at last.

She didn't hesitate. "I bet the newspapers would pay me a lot of money for this journal. But I'm giving you first crack. Three hundred thousand dollars."

"You're fucking mad," Angus said in his upper-crust English accent and hung up.

***

Exactly as Jackie expected, he called back a half hour later.

"A check will be fine," she answered when she saw his name on her cell. "I know you're good for it."

"I want to come there and see this journal you claim to have."

"Sure," she said, "come on over."

"Tonight," he said. "Eight o'clock."

"Make sure you bring your checkbook," she said.

Then she called the detectives.

She told them all about her conversation with Angus. It took some convincing, but she persuaded them to come to her apartment at 7:30.

One of them hid in her coat closet, the other around the corner in the small butler's pantry off her kitchen.

At eight o'clock sharp her buzzer rang.

Jackie buzzed Angus up, then went and got the journal she had bought four hours before at a neighborhood stationery shop. She left the door open and positioned herself on the far side of the living room.

Angus walked in. He got right to business. "Let me see the damn thing."

"Let me see your checkbook first," she said.

He pulled out a pistol with a silencer instead and aimed it at her.

"Jesus!" she cried, genuinely terrified.

The two detectives, guns drawn, stepped out into the open, got Angus to drop his gun, cuffed him, and read him his rights.

Five months later, a jury convicted him of first-degree murder.

Jackie, who was still making a little more than minimum wage at Montana Pictures, decided she was ready for a career change.

2

Diana Milton's mouth was agape. "That's such an incredible story," she said as she hurriedly took notes. "You get a medal from the mayor, or something?"

Jackie laughed. "Yeah, a key to the city... made of plastic."

"So, after Philomena Soames, was that when you decided you wanted to become a detective?"

"No, it was furthest thing from my mind, actually," Jackie said. "Something happened six months later: My college roommate's son, actually my godson, went missing. My friend lived in Savannah, out on Wilmington Island, to be exact. Anyway, I flew down to comfort her more than anything else. She didn't know if it was a kidnapping or what. Never got a note or anything. She was really distraught, as you can imagine. At the time she was separated from her husband and needed someone."

Diana leaned closer. "So, what happened?"

"Well, there wasn't much to it. It was the obvious."

"The husband?"

"Exactly. So, I found out where he was staying," Jackie said, "went there, nosed around a little, and found out the boy was there. Then I waited in my car, just like in the movies, on a stakeout. Finally, the husband came out of the house, got in his car, and drove off. Turned out, he was just going to get some groceries. I thought it was pretty bad that he had left the boy there alone. Anyway, I just went in, told the boy his mother missed him, and he needed to come with me. That was pretty much it. Needless to say, my friend was relieved."

Diana shook her head. "I can't imagine a child of mine missing for two minutes, let alone two days," she said. "So, you ended up moving down here."

Jackie nodded. "I liked Savannah, couldn't afford New York anymore, so I just packed my bags and moved down." She shrugged. "Solving crimes seemed to be kind of, I don't know, stimulating, I guess. So, I figured—what the hell—might as well make it my profession. Plus, I naively thought it would be easy."

"Catching bad guys?"

"Yeah," Jackie said. "So, to get my license I worked for a PI for a year. He had me do fun stuff like follow around cheating spouses to no-tell motels."

"Eww," Diana said, rolling her eyes as she scribbled notes on a pad.

Jackie nodded. "I hated it," she said. "One time the guy I worked for actually broke down the door at a Motel 6 and I took—what they call —'the money shot.'"

"Of a couple—"

"Yup."

"How creepy was that?"

"Big time."

Diana looked up from her pad. "Then you started your own agency?"

Jackie nodded.

"And then you solved that murder of that funeral director?"

Jackie smiled. "Yeah, the press dubbed him the, 'Philandering Funeral Director' or something lame like that. But that was after two years of really boring stuff. Paying my dues, learning the ropes, I guess."

"But didn't you have a few more high-profile cases?"

Jackie nodded. "A couple. And a few I never solved, which is frustrating."

Diana nodded. "At what point do you give up?"

"Oh, I never give up," Jackie said. "They're in my 'cold case file.' When it gets slow, which nowadays is rare, I go back to them, kick 'em around a little more."

"And how long have you been at it now?"

"Almost four years." Jackie looked at her watch. "Oh, I hate to be rude, but I've got a potential client coming here in five minutes, so I'm gonna need to wrap it up."

Diana nodded, stood. "I really appreciate your time," she said. "This has been one of my best interviews in a long time. Should be in the paper in two or three days."

"Thank you," Jackie said shaking Diana's hand. "Probably get a few calls from it, I'd imagine."

"Yeah, I should get a finder's fee if you get a nice juicy murder," Diana said with a laugh.

"Actually," said Jackie, "that's exactly what my next meeting is about."

3

A year earlier...

The four men walked off the 15th green and headed for their golf carts.

"Nice putt," Ted said to his partner Rick.

"Yeah, but we're still three down," Rick said as they got in the cart.

"In ten minutes, you won't give a damn." Ted hit the gas and followed the other twosome in the cart ahead of them.

"Why's that?" Rick asked, then, confused, pointed to the cart path disappearing to their right. "Hey, isn't the tee the other way?"

"Yeah, it is," Ted said, "but we're going to take a little break before we play the last three holes."

"O-kay," Rick said with a puzzled shrug.

Rick, from nearby Palmetto Dunes, was playing as Ted's guest. Ted and the men in the cart ahead had been members of the Mercer Island club for a total of seventy-one years between them.

The man driving the golf cart leading the way looked back at Ted and gave him a big smile and thumbs-up. Up in front of them loomed a large, two-story brick house, which was hidden by majestic live oak trees from the rest of the houses in the upscale development outside of Savannah. The house looked like a knockoff of Tara, with balconies on the first and second floors and a huge Canary Island date palm centered in front of it. Plump pink and lavender azaleas were in full bloom on either side; a boundless marsh and the Intracoastal Waterway stretched out beyond it.

Ted parked his golf cart next to the other cart which had just pulled up in front of the house.

"Okay," Rick said with the same puzzled look. "I've got absolutely no clue what we're doing at this place."

Ted turned to him. "Have I ever led you astray?"

Rick thought for a second. "Well yeah, a couple of times."

The four clattered down the path to the house in their golf shoes. Ted walked up to the front door and knocked four times, paused, then three more times. Like it was code.

A few moments later, a large-breasted woman in her late fifties with perfectly coiffed hair and a flowery caftan answered the door.

"Hello, gentlemen, welcome to Casa Romantica," she said in a whispery voice. Then to Rick. "I don't believe we've met before. I'm Miranda."

"And I'm—"

Miranda's hand shot up and she shook her head. "No names, please."

Rick looked puzzled.

"You are what you drink," Ted explained.

Rick was still puzzled.

"We go by what we drink," Ted explained. "Which means I'm Johnnie."

Rick nodded. His friend drank Johnnie Walker Black. "I guess that would make me Chivas."

"Pleased to meet you, Chivas," Miranda said. "Well, come on in," she said, then stopped them by holding up her hand again. "Hold on. You boys know there are only two rules here."

"Don't worry," Ted said, sitting down in an expensive-looking strap metal bench to the right of the front door and removing his shoes, "we were about to take 'em off."

Charlie reached down, and standing first on one foot, then the other, took his golf shoes off and put them under the bench.

Rick sat down next to Ted and followed suit, as did the fourth man. "What's the other rule?" Rick asked, looking up at Miranda.

Miranda smiled. "That you never say a word to anyone about this place."

Rick nodded. "I'm a discreet guy."

"You better be," Miranda said with a smile. Then she led the four men through the foyer into the spacious living room. Though the furniture was of superior quality, nothing really matched. It was as though Miranda had gone to dozens of high-end tag sales at Mercer Island houses and picked up a chintz sofa here, a walnut coffee table there, a New England landscape painting somewhere else, until she filled the room.

But her bar was something else altogether. Fully stocked didn't begin to describe it. It was located at the far corner of the living room. She had had the fifteen-foot long mahogany bar built by a local carpenter, a talented craftsman who had built a similar one for Jim Williams, the flamboyant art collector whose murder had been the centerpiece of John Berendt's book, *Midnight in the Garden of Good and Evil*.

Stepping behind the bar, Miranda said: "You boys look as though you've had a long day at the office."

"Oh, yeah, brutal," Ted said with a throaty chuckle. "I've been craving a libation since the sixth hole."

"Crave no more," she said. "One Johnnie Walker Black coming right up."

Ted nodded and smiled as she put ice cubes in a glass and poured four fingers into a glass.

She handed the glass to him.

"Thanks, honey," Ted said.

"And for the new sailor in town?" she asked. "Oh right, Chivas. On the rocks or how do you like it?"

"A little water, please," Rick said. "And a twist."

"Coming right up."

"You're going to have to rename me," Charlie said. "I feel like a beer today."

"No problem, I have four IPAs plus your standard German, Dutch and American beers," Miranda said, opening a cooler below the bar. She recited the names of the twelve brands she had.

"I'll have that Sierra Nevada," Charlie said.

Miranda handed the bottle across the bar. "Okay, so from now on you'll be known as both Stoli *and* Sierra."

The four men laughed.

After she poured a Jack Daniels for Ted, Miranda led the men over to two sofas that faced away from the marsh.

Rick pointed out the window. "Don't we want to take in that beautiful view?" he asked Ted. "Bet there's some amazing wildlife out there."

"Sure is," Miranda said, overhearing. "Wild boar, deer, minks, not to mention dolphins, egrets, you name it. But I think you'll prefer this view." She pointed at the grand staircase up to the second floor.

The other three men nodded eagerly and plopped onto the couch, backs to the spectacular marsh and water vista. Their expressions showed they could barely contain their anticipation as they looked up the wide staircase.

And as if on cue, a woman in a short skirt, a bare midriff and a silver-sequined halter-top appeared. She strutted across the landing from the left and took a step down the staircase. Rick's mouth dropped as Ted's eyes lit up and Charlie rubbed his hands together like someone looking forward to a sumptuous meal.

Moments later, another woman appeared from the other side of the second-floor landing, as if on the runway of a fashion show. She

was tall, blond, elegant and dressed in tight black silk pants and a
white collared shirt with the collar popped. She started down the
staircase with a demure smile and confident walk.

Rick turned to Ted and whispered, "What the hell is this?"

Ted whispered back, "Mercer Island's version of heaven."

Then a third woman came from the other side. She was dressed in
a long beige skirt with a seafoam-green, breast-hugging tee shirt.

"Don't even *think* about picking her," Ted whispered to Rick and
flicking his head. "She's *all mine*."

*****

Rick grinned like a schoolboy as he walked down the staircase
forty-five minutes later, tucking in his golf shirt. He looked down and
saw Ted and Charlie with cocktails in hand on the side-by-side
couches. Sitting in Ted's lap was the woman who had been wearing
the seafoam-green tee shirt. Except now, she was bare-breasted.

Miranda was at the bar making a drink, a quarter-inch stack of
hundreds and twenties at the end of the bar.

"You ready to go finish up the last three holes?" Ted asked Rick.

"Reluctantly," said Rick. "After we finish up, I want to go see a real-
estate broker."

"Sounds just like, ah, Jose Cuervo," Charlie said to Ted.

"Who's he?" Rick asked.

"A buddy of mine used to live in Hilton Head," Charlie said. "Only
took one visit to Casa Romantica. Now he's got a big, ol' house on the
eighteenth fairway."

"Yeah," Ted said, "just a hop, skip, and a jump away."

***

The four had to wait at the fourteenth tee for a twosome to come
through. Then they teed off.

Rick's drive flew long and straight.

"Nice one," Ted said.

"Thanks," Rick said. "Fifteen yards more than usual. I think our
little break might do wonders for my game."

"It does have a relaxing effect," Ted said.

Rick and Ted got into their cart. Rick turned to him. "How long's that place been around anyway?"

"Um, I'd say about three years," Ted said.

"And word hasn't gotten out?" Rick asked.

Ted shook his head. "Look at it this way: If it did, it'd be our loss. So only a small group of us know about it. Someone has one too many, starts blabbering, we shut him up fast."

"And the local cops have no clue?" Rick asked.

Ted shrugged. "My guess is, if anyone ever found out, Miranda'd slip 'em an envelope full of 'keep your trap shut' cash."

4

The bearded man was paddling a kayak. Noiselessly, effortlessly, and without any splashing.

Not one light shone inside the large, two-story house. But why would it? It was three in the morning.

The man ran the kayak aground and got out, his weapon in a sheath. Then he reached into his pants pocket, pulled out milk-colored vinyl gloves and slipped them on.

He knew exactly where the woman's bedroom was located on the second floor. Up the staircase, down a short hallway, last one at the end.

The man had experience at dismantling burglar alarms and knew where this one was located. He walked up onto the porch and went down to the living-room window which had been deliberately left unlocked. He pushed the window up, put first one leg into the living room, then the other. His eyes adjusted to the darkness and he could hear the ticking of the grandfather clock on the other side of the living room. Then he went over and disabled the alarm.

He turned around and saw the long bar and the four rows of shelves above it.

He walked around behind the bar and saw a bottle of Makers Mark, practically full. *Don't mind if I do*, he thought, and reached for the bottle and a nearby rocks glass. He filled it halfway, then took a sip.

Glancing up at the majestic stairway, he killed what was left of the Makers Mark.

Time to go to work.

Stepping slowly and softly, he started up the stairs. At the top, he followed the short hallway, which led to two side-by-side mahogany doors.

When he got to the door, he unsheathed the Busse Battle Mistress. It was fifteen inches long, razor-sharp, and weighed two pounds. One thrust was all he'd need. He had read an article in *Field & Stream* about the knife. The writer had graphically extolled the knife's virtues: "Do you want to behead a hippo? Would you like to chop down a telephone pole? Perhaps you yearn to slice a redwood into sections? If you have the Mistress and a strong arm, you can."

He had no interest in beheading a hippo or chopping down a telephone pole, but he did have a strong arm.

He turned the doorknob of the mahogany door and slowly pushed the door open. He took two steps into the bedroom, then stopped. He could hear faint snoring. He took four more steps. The snoring remained steady. Then he walked up to the side of the bed. She was a large woman and was lying on her back. She snorted suddenly a few times but didn't wake up. He suspected she was having a dream. He raised the Battle Mistress high above his head and plunged it down between her breasts.

Her dream had just become a nightmare.

ACKNOWLEDGMENTS

I would first like to first thank Gordon McCoun, astute chronicler of dubious Palm Beach history, fastest New York Times crossword puzzler in Florida and quite possibly the world. Thanks for delivering me the whole wacky plot, Gordon.

Next, Steve Aberle for all the feedback, praise and nice reviews. You're very kind.

Then, my faithful reader/ critiquers: Maria Gerrity, Ted Manno, Betsy and George Longstreth, Ed Tronolone, "Rude" Rob Shaw, Tim Pitts, Don Scarpa, Tamie Peters, Tim Andrews, and all the ones I've forgotten.

Finally, to my beloved Serena and Georgie, who will always be the most wonderful daughters a man could have.

BOOKS BY TOM TURNER

PALM BEACH NASTY

PALM BEACH POISON

PALM BEACH DEADLY

PALM BEACH BONES

PALM BEACH PRETENDERS

PALM BEACH PREDATORS

PALM BEACH BROKE

PALM BEACH BEDLAM

KILLING TIME IN CHARLESTON

CHARLESTON BUZZ KILL

BROKEN HOUSE

Made in United States
North Haven, CT
27 November 2021

11637672R10186